MW00423846

The Pursuer

a Beatrix Patterson mystery

EVA SHAW

The Pursuer

a Beatrix Patterson mystery

EVA SHAW

Copyright © 2023 Eva Shaw

The Pursuer: a Beatrix Patterson mystery

Eva Shaw
www.evashaw.com
evashaw@att.net

Published 2022, by Torchflame Books
www.torchflamebooks.com

Paperback ISBN: 978-1-61153-572-3
E-book ISBN: 978-1-61153-573-0

ALL RIGHTS RESERVED
No part of this publication may be reproduced, stored in a retrieval system, or transmitted in any form or by any means, electronic, mechanical, photocopying, recording, scanning, or otherwise, except as permitted under Section 107 or 108 of the 1976 International Copyright Act, without the prior written permission except in brief quotations embodied in critical articles and reviews.

This is a work of fiction. All characters, organizations, and events portrayed in this novel are either products of the author's imagination or are used fictitiously.

For Ellen.

Thank you for always listening
and laughing with me.

Like your mom, Janet Cederquist, said:
We do have fun.

CHAPTER 1

September 1947, Santa Barbara, California

BEATRIX PATTERSON INSPECTED HER SCUFFED, sensible brown walking shoes, brushing sand off the heels.

Until recently, whenever she slipped them on, she felt a jolt of anticipation. They foretold an adventure. They were with her hiking the Sierras and through abandoned gold rush towns. She wore them in the Alps, on endless excursions to the Mexican Yucatan, and even crossing the Scottish Highlands. When Beatrix and Thomas took off on their California Central Coast road-trip honeymoon, driving along the exquisite Big Sur highway and stopping hours to meander among the sky-scrapping Redwoods, the shoes went along.

She'd never thought that these "old friends" would let her down. That she would stop being pleased taking long walks and energetic hikes. Yet days passed and like scuffed shoes, she felt the ho-humness of predictability.

Worst yet? She knew she had no right to feel that way. She had a gorgeous husband and a marvelous career with huge possibilities in a field she loved. She was healthy and fit and had a bestie and countless friends and extended family. "Not in that order," she said out loud, feeling even more disheartened.

Now, she re-tied the laces. She smoothed her hands over the knees of her well-worn faded denim jeans that were raveling at the cuffs. Sometimes touching the nubby cotton brought her comfort. Not that day.

She yanked at the sleeves of the cotton cardigan, the bright aqua of the Pacific. It was early when Beatrix left the house for a beach walk and before the desert wind picked up. Then the sweater was needed. Now, at ten, the day turned warm even for September, yet she couldn't muster the effort to remove it.

While she didn't know it nor would she have cared at that moment, the blue sweater made her shoulder-length red-streaked hair and forest-green eyes even more startling. Rather, she only felt the claustrophobic and imagined weight of it, as if it were pulling her shoulders down to the pavement. Tilting her head toward the sun to capture its warmth, she counted her blessings, sighed, and then recounted them. A frown tugged at the corners of her generous lips, devoid of color. She felt shattered. She thought, *What's happened? This month I felt certain it would be it.*

That wasn't the case.

Again.

Never one to primp or admire her reflection in a mirror at least for nothing more than make sure there was no lipstick on her teeth and on Sundays that her church hat was on straight, these days she wore the same jeans and shirt or sweater, reliable shoes, and no make-up, although she hardly needed any. The same outfit each day.

That drabness suited her mood. She pretended it was hormonal, but in truth, she knew depression when it bit her on the butt. Her training in psychology pointed directly at that, and although mild, some days she felt void of the sparks and excitement she'd loved to feel in the past, and now was apprehensive about the future. She thought of the gut-wrenching days of New Orleans in the middle of the worst war ever to destroy everything, when her life was dangerous and chancy, and while she was frightened, kidnapped, and nearly murdered, it was thrilling in hindsight. She'd tried to embrace her tranquil life, and wondered if she'd been an adrenaline addict, solving crimes and apprehending villains. But if, no, when, she became a mom, could she do that? *Definitely not*, she thought. *Then, who am I?*

"I'm feeling as dull as these blasted walking shoes. The worst part is that I should be more alive than ever. But I'm not."

She knew that was dramatic but when one is having a personal pity party, a rollercoaster of exaggerated emotions is the outcome. She was well-read on the problem, learned it in the first term of anatomy class. Heard about it more often in the psychology courses she'd aced. For couples like Beatrix and Thomas, there were options by the plenty; nonetheless, acting on those seemed to take too much strength, which was not at all like her previous self. That made her heart sink a bit deeper. *This is what despair feels like,* her clinical self said to the self that controlled feelings. *You must be gentle with yourself and eventually confront it.*

For a moment she was back in a crowded classroom as a learned professor, fondling his gray pointed beard, spouted theories all through the course work that enabled her to become a licensed psychologist and earn her doctorate. Had one of those bearded men ever felt as she did? Hardly. They send forth the theories that if one was out of sorts, one merely pulled themselves up by the bootstraps, dusted off their backsides, and shook away the black clouds, including the teary moments. "Especially in females," she could hear one professor say, nearly as loud as she'd heard army drill sergeants yell at their platoons. He'd continued for a good half hour about the emotional fragility of the female person.

"Yes, during their menstrual cycle, many females fall to this hysterical indicator. They are ruled by a mental state which can become volatile, fickle, and unreliable, unlike males."

At that second, Beatrix was fearful that if she'd caught the eye of any of the other five women in that packed classroom, they'd become a mob and if not tar him, then throw him in a chicken coop to feather him. She truly wanted to race to the podium and smack that academic on his stogy, bearded face. *He knows as much about a woman's cycle as a mechanic who gives driving advice, but never learned to operate a vehicle,* she'd wanted to scream.

It didn't take that sexist professor to give her advice. She'd diagnosed herself and the result was clear-cut. It was home-grown depression. She was clear on the reason. She knew the repercussions. She'd learned how to supposedly treat it. Nevertheless, when it happened to her, she wanted to find a lovely, dark closet, bring along a hot cup of tea with plenty of cream and sugar, a box of Oreos, and a wad of tissues. She thought how lovely it'd be to sit there until she needed more tea, or the floor got hard. While the fantasy helped, a little, she knew that hiding was never the answer. After the long walk to the beach, she found herself sitting on the top step of a cement stoop, in the back garden of a cozy bungalow. Jo Conrad, her best friend, confidante, and home's owner, lived blocks away from the Victorian-style home Beatrix shared with Thomas. There she sat, not ready to return to their house. She needed a friend, not a sympatric husband at that moment.

Beatrix propped her elbows on her knees and held her head in her hands.

It isn't supposed to be this way, she repeated, as she had for the last year. What about the promise of happily ever after? That was the plan. It's drop-dead easy, the mechanics are clear on how to make a baby. But why? Why us? Now here I am. Sitting on the cold cement stoop trying to come to grips with reality. I have no clue what to do.

Inside the tidy Santa Barbara Craftsman-style house, Jo watched her friend and could see sadness on Beatrix's face. She rinsed breakfast dishes, watched the coffee pot perk through the filters, and gazed through the window as the red gingham curtains fluttered in the breeze. The house was quiet, a rare occurrence with four kids under seven, and that was only thanks to rambunctious little Sammy, most likely bouncing off the walls in his first-grade class at Jefferson Elementary on the hill overlooking the city, along with the twins down for their morning nap. "Thank goodness Mama took Gracie," she breathed and tucked an inky black curl behind her ear. Ah, Gracie, at just two her current favorite and only words were "no" and "banana" used interchangeably and with the volume of an accomplished opera singer.

When Jo and Beatrix met, they immediately became besties. They talked about everything and to Jo, it was obvious what her friend was thinking as she stared at the clothesline full of diapers happily flapping in the sea breeze, and with three kids still in them, that line was never empty. The women had had the "baby" conversation before and wondered if this morning would be another questioning session. Jo had no solutions, but she was a fine listener.

Beatrix was a therapist with a doctorate, brought up in a wealthy environment that was ripped away when her adoptive parents were murdered, so she struggled to find herself, which she eventually did. Jo was one of five children, a homemaker with a high school degree, the mom of four, and the wife of a railroad worker. She was a human rights activist with a heart. Beatrix often told her friend, "You are one of the wisest women I've ever known." Jo acknowledged it was due to her mama, Lillian, and the practical upbringing she'd had.

Now, and again this month, what could she add or do to reassure Beatrix? What more advice to give than to be patient, especially since she imagined that Beatrix felt empty inside, especially after last year's miscarriage?

Balancing two mugs of steaming coffee, Jo juggled them while opening the back door with her knee just as the telephone rang. She sighed. *It might be some woman in a domestic crisis or one of her fellow members of the Women's Christian Temperance Union offering to help with the upcoming fundraiser.* As president, secretary and a bit of everything else, Jo put the mugs on the counter and dashed toward the phone.

Five minutes later Beatrix was still in the same spot, still focused on the clothesline, still tugging the cuffs of her sweater when Jo sat next to her.

"Glad I made a pot because the first cups were cold when I finished that phone call," she handed Beatrix a mug and scooted close to her, nudging her friend's shoulder, and then moved in to share a hug. Beatrix instinctively moved into the hug, feeling comfort as their shoulders continue to touch. Her husband Thomas listened, supported her, loved her, and she knew it. Yet where a future child was concerned, he couldn't seem to communicate the depth of his feelings or how to get through to Beatrix's slowly crumbling heart.

Beatrix turned her face up to the sun and the shockingly blue sky. "Hey, thanks." From someplace deep and a world away, a thought came out. "I remember as a child, just once, that there was snow on the Santa Ynez mountains. I'd never seen snow and Mother and Dad bundled me up and we drove the rickety old truck up the San Marcos Pass. There was just enough snow to build a snowman the size of a watermelon, but it was magical." Beatrix's hands hugged the chunky white mug.

"The newspaper said we're going to have these hot desert Santa Ana winds through Friday. No snow in the forecast for Santa Barbara." Jo waited.

Beatrix sipped the sturdy brew. "Mind if we don't talk about babies?"

"I would find that a rare pleasure," Jo laughed, but then slipped an arm around Beatrix, again. "You know, you and Thomas aren't alone. Lots of couples have to be patient when conceiving. Shake off any pressure. It's not healthy, honey. It'll happen when it happens, or so Mama always told me."

Beatrix loved her friend and neither held back in their conversations or opinions even though they had such dissimilar upbringings and lives. Growing up, her mother had a housemaid and servants. Jo's mother was a nurse, and her late father was a railroad worker, like Jo's husband Sam. Jo didn't own a new-to-her dress until she went to work part-time after high school at Woolworths five and dime store on State Street, and even then, she shopped thrift stores for shoes and sweaters. Now with a family of six, she was a mastermind at pinching pennies and conversely, Beatrix, who had had some grim years, had become an heiress to a much-disputed fortune. Yet, closer comrades couldn't be found, and both felt like they'd won first place if there were ever a best friend contest.

"Not you and Sam," Beatrix worked to brighten her tone and was relieved when the teasing came out light. She teased, "Any time that man shares a meal with you, you end up pregnant."

"Yeah, it seems that way, but we're stopping at four."

"You said that at two." She laughed, her mood lifting.

"Who knew triplets ran in Sam's family, which scares me silly. I think of that as family planning. We got off lucky with twins. Now let's change the subject before naptime is over. I just had the oddest phone call."

"And?" Beatrix turned to listen and once more admired Jo's smooth chocolate-colored skin, glowing even as a harried mom.

"It was about a woman who works with Mama, cleaning at Cottage Hospital, on Pueblo. You know the place, I'm sure."

"My mother always donated to their work, feeling that rural Santa Barbara in the 20s desperately needed a facility. Sorry, off topic."

"The woman's name is Gerta Rosenbaum, a friend of a friend of Mama's, which means they're already close even though they probably met ten minutes ago. Just kidding. Mama called because there was a patient in her ward who underwent surgery a few weeks back when the woman was hired. The lady has been through hell and back and is subdued, like someone who had been tortured, which she had been in the war. When Mama heard this account, she demanded that I relay this info to you. Gerta is too shy to contact you, and not secure speaking English, so of course, Mama took over. You've been around my mother enough to know that it's useless to go against her wishes."

"The plot thickens, Jo. Go on and get to the part as to why this involves me. Does Gerta want counseling?"

"Probably, well, most assuredly she does need it after the horrors she's experienced. That's not why Mama got involved. It seems that as the man was coming out of the heavy sedative, he was mumbling in German, and at one time, shouted."

"Gerta's German. too?"

"A Holocaust survivor, Polish and speaks German as well. Forgot to tell you that. Been in the states now for about a year. It's hard, as you can imagine. Mama invited her to Sunday dinner last week, along with another newcomer to our church family. You've got to meet her, her name is Mitzie and she's from New Orleans, incredibly flamboyant. What a hoot. She was an actress, a dog walker, a nanny, a world traveler, a spy, or so she said, but who knows what's true. Now she's a journalist, just got hired by the *News-Press.* She asked Gerta all sorts of questions, apparently wants to do a story on her and her journey from Poland to Santa Barbara and the role of the Jewish community here in the city. I found her questions fascinating, and they would have been more so if the twins were not teething and screaming," she laughed, and actually smiled.

Beatrix thought for the millionth time, *Could I be so upbeat with crying babies?* That part of motherhood scared her silly.

Jo continued, "Okay, to Gerta; I heard a brief version of her tragic background. She was a doctor before the Nazis made it unlawful for a woman and a Jew to be in the medical profession. Then she found work as a delivery nurse. The stories are shocking."

"How sad. Does she have family here in Santa Barbara?"

"A brother, long separated apparently. He's got a little house and a business on Lower State Street. Otto the tailor, Mama called him. Mama says he's a fine man, but I've not met him. Sam only wears those railroad overalls and then when he needs a new Sunday suit, I head to the resale shop. For a guy as big as Sam, it's crazy, but I always find one that fits like it was made for him.

"Gerta's settled in with him. Otto's a bachelor. The unnerving thing, Beatrix, is what the patient at the hospital had been shouting. Gerta was at the other end of the ward, she's a cleaner mind you. There were no nurses around and Mama was on the night shift, attending to other patients. Gerta rushed to him to help, fearing he was having a seizure or trying to get out of bed. As she stood holding his trembling hand he began talking, as if he were having a conversation with someone. She tried to reassure him that he would be fine, and a doctor was coming. Then he yelled again and this time, according to what Mama says, little Gerta froze."

"Did he threaten her? Say something offensive?"

"She thinks he was pledging his allegiance to Hitler, but it was in *Hoch Deutsch,* a different dialect than she was used to, although she speaks four or five languages. She speaks *Plautdietsch.* It's almost the same as the other one, but more from the old Prussian area. There were tears in her eyes when she said that she fears he said Stutthof. "

"Stutthof concentration camp?"

"Yes, that's where Gerta was imprisoned for most of the war."

"Did Gerta say she'd seen him before? Or at the camp, possibly?"

"She'd been put to work in the maternity section of infirmary there and said she couldn't remember his face. Why would she, unless he was a doctor? There were over 100,000 poor souls stuffed in the camp, all subjected to the Nazi atrocities."

Beatrix took a long, halting breath, with images of the concentration camps from the newspapers and news reels swirling in her head. "I've read and heard the revulsion, the dreadfulness of those places, where babies starved to death, that is if they weren't drowned at birth." She put the mug down next to her and hugged her arms around her middle.

"It was unspeakable, more hideous than any of us Americans who weren't there could even comprehend."

"Thomas rarely speaks of the Blitzkrieg tactics and shelling of London. He saw it all. When he does, his face tightens and I know he's reliving the terrors, the blasts, and the stench of wholesale death when he was there during the worst of it."

"You know, Sam was sent to the Pacific, working with the engineers to try to get supplies to troops. He still has nightmares," Jo said, cocking her head to listen for any whimpers from where the twins were napping.

Jo got up, felt the clothes on the line, and began gathering the diapers. Beatrix joined her, folding them as they went, placing the neat piles into the waiting wicker basket. Both knew their men were scarred for life and prayed that humanity would find other solutions rather than battle.

After a few moments, Jo stopped and stared into space as if gathering the right words. "Even after all the woman has suffered, Gerta seems warm and gracious. If my Sammy is any judge of character, which for a six-year-old he is not, he liked her at once, climbing onto her lap, hugging her goodbye when we left. Even the twins quieted their screaming when she rocked them and sang a lullaby. Think Mama was jealous, which was rather sweet, considering it's Mama."

"Anything more?"

"Gerta is in her fifties now and hopes to go to nursing school, that's her goal. She was a doctor before the camp, but has no chance of becoming a doctor in this country. Takes far too long and she doesn't have the funds."

"What happened to the patient? Did she tell you his name?"

"Schmitt, Noah Schmitt. He was discharged last week, and today something happened. The reason Mama called me just now is that Gerta was contacted by Mr. Schmitt. He left a message for her at the hospital and, apparently, he wants to hire her as an in-home health care worker. At far above the salary of a hospital cleaning woman."

"Would she be safe? Does he know, do you suppose, that Gerta was at Stutthof?"

"Good questions. Mama told Gerta to think about the job, it pays triple what she'd be getting at the hospital. She advised her friend to tell Mr. Schmitt she'd get back to him." Jo tilted her head. "What do you think, Beatrix? If Mr. Schmitt is a former Nazi, a war criminal, she'd be crazy to accept employment. But the money could let her go to nursing school sooner rather than later."

"Would your mama like me to talk with Gerta? Is that why she called, knowing we talk at least once a day?"

Jo smiled. "Mama's cooked up a plan. She wants you to befriend Mr. Schmitt and find out if in fact he was at Stutthof."

Beatrix pulled the last pristine diaper from the line and took her time folding it. "How does she expect me to do that?"

"You're on the hospital board, just one of your charities, I know. Schmitt is a former patient, gall bladder surgery, by the way. You're simply a friend stopping at his house to make sure that the system is working."

"That's a huge and crazy stretch, Jo. Besides, as a board member I'd never be asked to do anything of that sort. It's not fear; it'd be awkward. Maybe a social worker would visit, but not an executive of the hospital's philanthropy division." Beatrix carried the basket to the back porch.

"What can we do then, Beatrix? Anything?" Jo smoothed her wrinkle-free forehead. "I know Gerta needs the money if she's going to get into nursing school, and she's a proud woman, a survivor. I want to help."

Beatrix sat again on the back stoop. "Let me think a moment. Yes, okay. As you know I've been writing a column for the *Free Press* about people and places that are making positive changes in Santa Barbara. Does it sound logical at all if I were to interview him for the article, a new citizen of the town who has recent experience with our healthcare system? Good press for Cottage Hospital if he was satisfied with the care, and if not, I won't write it. I will get to speak to him."

"I knew you'd think of something. Yes, that's it, that's perfect." Jo smiled and patted her friend on the back.

"Years ago, I swore off lying, when I stopped being a fraudulent psychic, when I was living in New Orleans and first met Thomas, and you know all that, about my sordid past. It's so easy to fall into that abyss again. By chance did your mama share Mr. Schmitt's telephone number and address?" For the first time in weeks, Beatrix felt she had a purpose, and her drive to solve mysteries had kicked in.

Jo saw her smile and silently offered thanks. "Of course. Mama could probably tell you what kind of ice cream he prefers and the make and model of his car. Thanks for this, Beatrix. Want to stay for lunch? It's just bean soup and crackers and cheese, and a baby for each of us to hold as we attempt to eat." She turned her head at the sound of babies crying, calling over her shoulder, "Will you bring in the basket and turn on the gas under the soup? It's on the stove."

Beatrix paused, put the basket in a corner of the tidy kitchen. "Thomas and I talked briefly about adoption," she called out toward the babies' room.

"Now that's great news," Jo returned with a twin on each hip.

"What if they don't love us?"

She handed Beatrix baby Jackson, or was it Jefferson. Beatrix couldn't quite tell yet. Then Jo sat at the table, unbuttoned her flowered shirt and discreetly fed the baby. "My kids adore you and Thomas."

"That's because we love them, too."

"So, what's your question? It's hard being a parent, hardest job on the planet according to Mama, and she should know since there were enough for our own basketball team. Seriously, have you talked with an adoption service yet? There are private ones, especially in Los Angeles, and the County of Santa Barbara has a division on adoption, too. It takes time to get babies, but once you've got all the paperwork in and home visits and a boatload of red tape, it's just a matter of patience."

"The thing is, I want to go to China and adopt war orphans." She held Jefferson, or Jackson, close to her and kissed his tiny head. "Thomas often interjects how these children will have experienced too much trauma to ever have a normal life. His arguments are sound. We stopped talking about it weeks back."

Jo burped the baby and traded Beatrix for the other, who eagerly waited his turn. "Okay, here's the deal, and you can tell that husband of yours what I've said. Imagine a little Chinese girl or boy growing up in your huge old house on Anapamu Street, playing with my kids, going to their same schools and outrageously loud birthday parties and playing on soft ball teams and spending all summers at the beach. Now imagine being unwanted in China, perhaps shunned as biracial, never knowing a bedtime story or the warmth of a snuggle on a parent's lap. Never getting a chance for an education, a future, or even basic medical care. That's what's happening in China right now, and that's not about to change without America reaching out." She kissed Jackson and traded Beatrix for the one she'd been cuddling.

Beatrix shoved away a tear. "I know all this, Thomas does, too."

"As for not loving you back? You didn't have a great upbringing, I know, as your parents died while you were young. But you're book-smart, all that psychology you know. So learn, read, talk to others who have accepted ethnically diverse children into their families. And tell that man of yours to put on his big boy pants and support you."

By now, Beatrix was laughing. "How did you become so wise in just thirty years, Jo?"

"Blame Mama for that, and just in case you wondered, I'm betting she's going to demand that your children call her Grammie, just like my kids do. You know, you don't mess with Mama."

"That would be an honor for the entire Ling family to have Lillian as our grammie. I'll call her when I get home to find Mr. Schmitt's contact info."

Jo burped the baby. "No need, she knew you'd say yes, even if it took some convincing, and I've written it all down." She pulled a paper from her pocket. "If what Gerta says is true, and there's a chance he was at Stutthof or any of those death camps, be careful."

"If Schmitt is a harmless displaced German, then he's welcome here in the city. If perchance he was involved in the atrocities in the extermination camp there in Poland, I will find out. If so, this is far bigger than Gerta getting a job." Beatrix wrestled with the idea that there was a German war criminal in their town. Could that be true? Should she believe Gerta?

The kitchen was warm and cozy, bowls of steaming navy bean soup were on the table, and yet Beatrix felt a chill scurry along her neckline.

CHAPTER 2

THOMAS DROVE THROUGH THE STREETS from the research lab at the Santa Barbara College of the University of California in Goleta. The college had once been an active Marine base and still had that austere military feeling. It had been opened in the city in 1944, when the Board of Regents took over the facilities of Santa Barbara State College.

There wasn't a science division, but there was office space, and the Regents courted Thomas until he agreed to become part of their fledgling staff. He had everything he needed to work on the outrageously impossible concept of clean energy, all based on a crazy dream and an even wilder hunch. Scientists of Thomas's level rarely made guesses, but then again, Thomas knew since meeting and marrying Beatrix Patterson that he was far from the poster boy for that career.

He maneuvered their old Ford Woody station wagon through five o'clock traffic on State Street, still never quite comfortable driving on the opposite side of the road. Although Beatrix assured him that she hadn't been terrified of his driving in at least five days.

Making the left turn on to Anapamu, where their once decapitated Victorian home stood stately over the other cottages and mansions on the quiet street, he watched a couple push a pram along the sidewalk. They waved, and the husband looked about to burst with pride at the brand-new son they were now taking for his first walk, or so Thomas imagined. The couple lived in the house once occupied by their serial- killing neighbor, but since the home had been gutted and refurbished by the couple, it didn't feel atrocious at all.

Thomas pulled into the driveway and turned off the engine. He couldn't move. He'd let Beatrix down. It was all his fault. He was certain that was the reason they were unable to conceive.

He'd never forgotten getting mumps when he was a university student, a rising star in academia, and with not a care in the world. Mumps kept him in bed for a few days, and then he forgot about it. Nonetheless, the disease changed his life. Now, after researching the long-term side effects, he knew the cause. "The bedrooms are ready, and it's not that we aren't trying," he said out loud and to no one. He frowned, understanding that the damage the disease caused in sperm viability might change over time according to the latest research, but it had been ten years since he'd had the mumps.

The two had no secrets, yet Beatrix brushed off his concerns with a wave of her hand. "There are limited studies on this, Thomas, so don't get caught up in doubt." Instead, they'd imagined five or maybe six youngsters.

Then he put his head on the steering wheel and thought of what they'd talked about at breakfast and what he couldn't get out of his head all day while in the laboratory. "Adoption," he whispered. Unbeknownst to Beatrix he'd been in contact with a global adoption agency connect with the Chinese government in Hong Kong. He had not told Beatrix, fearing that she might not accept his idea, crazy as it was.

Earlier that day, he'd made a decision. He called the agency in San Francisco and wired the funds. He was going to China. He despised flying, fearful with each bump, which was unscientific. His hands started to sweat just thinking of the takeoff. However, he'd deal with his phobia for the sake of their family. He went over the costs, and the flights alone would have been enough to replace their aging Ford Woody with a brand-new station wagon. Then he telephoned the Chinese Counsel in San Francisco and spoke to a representative who assured him, in precise Mandarin, that adoptions in Hong Kong were ongoing, "From trustworthy and respectable services," the clerk was quick to point out. The official could organize everything, making the adoption smooth.

There would always be unwanted female babies and children available in the countryside and parents would, he knew, feel fortunate to sell their offspring to rich Americans, even if Thomas didn't consider the two of them to be rich. However, compared to the dirt farmers, Americans were living like kings. Another reason to adopt, he thought, was to save lives. Right then, he also added that to a list of what needed to be done: from getting vaccinations to physically managing the travel, taking time away from the university, obtaining visas that were required, to how much it would cost to bring home a baby or babies. Then there was the price to be paid and possible bribes, and would they even accept American currency, or must it be an international bank transfer? Perhaps he could get gold coins? "All for a child. Or children. The Ling family will happen," he wrote at the bottom of the list he had made during his telephone inquiries earlier that day. Then he underlined it twice.

Something stopped him. That something was love.

He sat in the car and pulled this list from the breast pocket of his lab coat, scanning it. "Can I love a child possibly physically and emotionally destroyed from their whole lifetime of the war and deprivation? Will the little ones cope knowing they were abandoned by their biological parents?" he said, pulling out a pen and putting a dot next to each item that still needed to be done, considered, or discussed. Beatrix seemed certain that adoption was the solution, but was this because she didn't want to disappoint him, or was she truly ready to put her psychology career on hold or the back burner while raising babies that possibly had special physical and emotional needs?

His anxiety level went way past a healthy limit.

When the knock came on the car window, Thomas jumped, banging his elbow on the steering wheel as he tried to conceal the list.

Surprised turned to joy. "Henry, you just took five years off my life," Thomas said, getting out of the car, rubbing his forehead and greeting his old friend.

"The boss, Mr. Brockman, tried to telephone you at the university but thinks you must have left for the day. He asked that I bring you and Miss Beatrix to the villa for dinner. Something about needing your help finding a treasure."

"Treasure hunting isn't really my cup of tea, Henry. Come in, let's see what Beatrix has to say. I know she always likes a puzzle." Thomas led the way into the Victorian house's kitchen, calling out his wife's name.

It had been in shambles, but now the cabinets were painted bright white, the old wide-plank flooring shone, and they'd managed to save the somewhat scarred farmhouse sink and original window panes, dimpled with bubbles in the glass. It was airy and inviting, while the rest of the house still needed work and furniture.

"Thomas," she replied. "I'm in the living room. I have good news and bad news. I didn't get to the shops and unless you're okay with cereal, we need to go out to dinner."

She walked into the kitchen and dashed to give Henry a hug. His bulk filled the spacious room. "What a surprise, Henry. Come out with us for dinner?"

Henry was employed by Beatrix and Thomas's longtime friend, wealthy John Brockman, as a driver and bodyguard during their time in New Orleans and then they grew closer as friends when they were renovating the then-crumbling mansion. When Mr. Brockman, wheeler and dealer and general money kingpin of the American South, decided to live parttime in Santa Barbara, of course, Henry came along.

While there were plenty of Latinos and Asians in Santa Barbara, the African American popular was not large. Yet Henry was one of those rare individuals who didn't see anyone as anything but a friend. He was the size of a football lineman and as gentle as a kitten, as Thomas had pointed out when he and Beatrix had asked their friend to be the Godfather of their future children.

"Dinner's the reason the boss sent me, Miss Beatrix. He telephoned you and the Doc, but couldn't reach you, so he sent me."

"Is Mr. Brockman okay, Henry?" A worried look passed over Beatrix's face.

"Grumpy as ever, but you didn't hear me say that. Likes the new digs, the cook and gardener you sent over have been swell, and I think he doesn't have enough to do. Some days he just paces like a lion cooped up in a zoo. May be planning world domination for all I know. Something is definitely up."

"What is this about a treasure hunt, my good man?" Thomas asked.

"You'll need to talk with him. I'm just the major domo, remember? I think, Doc, that he's troubled by the Nazi's looting from Paris museums and what happened to the treasures. I saw on his desk, the other day, some newspaper clippings about a private collector in London being arrested for buying black-market figurines. Heck, I could be all wet. Mr. Brockman might just want your company for the evening." Henry rubbed his hands together. "You all aren't going to make me disappoint Mr. B, are you?"

Thomas wondered how a man of Henry's size, those bulging muscles with all that nervous energy, could be so calm. *Nothing ruffles his feathers,* Thomas thought. Beatrix often said that Thomas's favorite exercise, other than martial arts, was jumping to conclusions.

"Give me ten minutes to change, Henry, and we'll follow you to the villa," Beatrix said, realizing that Thomas had yet again worn his white lab coat home. "Thomas, you might want to hang up that white coat. Grab a sweater or jacket if you think you may be cold when the sun sets."

He looked down at his lab coat with a half dozen pencils in the pocket. "It's a jumper, my dear. We British call those woolen things jumpers." He laughed and shook his head. *Crazy American slang*, he thought. "With this warm wind, I certainly will not need a jumper, nor my lab coat."

She turned at the kitchen door. "Whatever. Henry, help yourself to those cookies on the counter, even if Thomas calls them biscuits. They're for Jo and Sam's kids, but I have plenty." And left laughing.

As Beatrix climbed the now-carpeted grand staircase, feeling the softness under her shoes and enjoying how the wood beneath creaked with each step, she came to the second story landing of their spacious hundred-year-old Victorian-style home built by one of the original Santa Barbara cattle barons. There was still a faint smell of varnish from the shiny banister that was the color of mustard when they'd moved in and was a pain in the backside to remove. She felt joy in the honest labor they'd put into restoring the home, and her hand glided over the finial at the end. Everything was shaping up well now, although at one time the porch was so rotten with termites that a visitor had fallen right through the flooring. At one time the only running water was in the kitchen. The banister to the second floor wobbled, and windows were broken.

There was still much to do, but it was comfortable and quirky, and she made a mental note to seek out a history buff to tell her of the past life of their home on stately Anapamu Street. *Maybe I can find photos of it when it was first built on the next trip to the library.*

The main bedroom, even in the September afternoon, felt light, almost beachy and spacious. Rather than the dark wood furniture that was currently all the rage, Beatrix had chosen to paint the headboard a pale gray and add a large muted, gray patterned Persian rug to cover the hardwood floors that were the color of honey. The drapes and comforter were off-white, and she'd found some original artwork of early 1800 sailing ships in an antique shop in town which now adorned the walls.

The bay window was cushioned in a white and gray striped fabric, and the reading chair in the corner was upholstered in a charcoal color fabric with a matching ottoman. They had found what Beatrix hoped was a Tiffany floor lamp complete with a pristine stained-glass shade in the Mission style, which she cleaned up from inches of attic dust. She turned around and smiled, imagining the padded chair in the corner or the window seat as snuggly places for her and their babies to sit and read books.

She shook that notion out of her head and quickly changed into black linen slacks, a crisp white, long-sleeved shirt, and grabbed a yellow cardigan. She clipped a pin on the lapel of the shirt, a sizeable diamond encrusted *fleur-de-lis* and the symbol of her once-home New Orleans. It was a thank-you from a couple, the Ramseys, whom she had helped through a grueling situation.

She tied back her shoulder-length hair with a scarf with yellow and red flowers and put on lipstick. She glanced in the full-length mirror. "That'll have to do," she told her reflection. "Now on to a treasure hunt," she added. She didn't smile, because if John Brockman was involved, this would not be a simple game of hide and seek. She stepped back and wondered if she'd need to take a gun.

CHAPTER 3

Henry drove John Brockman's black Cadillac, the size of a boat, sedately down Milpas Street and made a left onto Highway 101, turning south to his boss's home in Montecito. The day was clear, and as Thomas and Beatrix followed in their utilitarian Ford, Beatrix took a quick glance away from the road and marveled at the mostly uninhabited Chanel Islands glowing in the sunset.

"Did Henry give you any indication of John's reason for suddenly asking us for dinner, Thomas, other than treasure?"

Always happy to be the passenger, Thomas shook his head. He wasn't actually listening to his wife but working through calculations on his current clean energy research, which had to do with tidal currents, and wondering if and how he should break the news about the agency in San Francisco that would guide them through a foreign adoption. "Um, oh, sorry, no, maybe about art thefts."

Beatrix subscribed not only to the *Santa Barbara Sentinel* and *The News Press*, the local papers, but the *Los Angeles Times* as well. She'd clipped out a few news stories about the sale of art with questionable provenance so she could continue to follow them. Sotheby's spokesperson, Beatrix remembered, because she remembered everything, was vague in describing the Santa Barbara buyer of a significant collection. *Could that buyer be John?*

The reporter, who supposedly was quoting an insider at the auction house, had said that art dealers Hildebrand Gurlitt, Karl Buchholz, Ferdinand Moeller, and Bernhard Boehmer had set up shop in Schloss Niederschonhausen, just outside Berlin, to sell a cache of near-16,000 paintings and sculptures which Hitler and Göring removed from the walls of German museums in 1937 and 1938. They were first put on display in the Haus der Kunst in Munich on July 19, 1937, with the Nazi leaders inviting public mockery by two million visitors who came to view as a way to condemn and ridicule modern art in the Degenerate Art Exhibition. Propagandist Joseph Goebbels in a radio broadcast called Germany's degenerate artists "garbage." Hitler opened the Haus der Kunst exhibition with a speech describing German art as suffering "a great and fatal illness."

Because of Beatrix's gift to recall everything she heard, thought, read, experienced, or observed, called hyperesthesia, she'd be able to "see" the entire article in front of her. She made a left turn from the highway and drove up the long, steep hill and the expansive home with its Spanish-style-revival and Moorish architecture, the home of her friend John Brockman. Beatrix put the memory of the article out of her mind temporarily as Thomas opened the driver's door for her. "I wonder what this evening will hold?" she said as the couple walked into the luxurious foyer.

Henry opened the massive doors and John greeted them in the living room with its 180-degree view of the islands and the Pacific. "Glad you could come," he stretched out his hands to Beatrix and then to Thomas.

Thomas, purely British to the core, was momentarily thankful that their long-time friend agreed with more sedate manners than the man hugs typically the preference of some of their male associates and friends. Those were far too familiar and personal, except from Henry, Thomas believed. Thomas had liked John Brockman from the beginning and when the millionaire hustler decided to winter in Santa Barbara, Thomas was only too glad to count him as a regular visitor.

"You're looking well, John," Beatrix responded, and meant it. He'd had some health scares.

"It's the California sunshine. Now don't tell our mutual friends in New Orleans I said that." He was a small man, shorter than Thomas, who was but five-foot-six. John dressed as if he were on his last dime, yet that couldn't have been further from the truth. His features were sharp, and his eyes seemed to take in and understand everything, even in a crowd. Because of his slimness and stature, only strangers disregarded this powerful man. He liked it like that.

Beatrix and Thomas picked up small glasses of amber-colored sherry from a silver tray that was sitting in the middle of a low glass table, and Henry joined them, as was normal. Everything in the room shouted California: light, bright, and directly opposite of how rooms were decorated in John Brockman's mansion in New Orleans' Garden District. In the Crescent City, it was still in vogue to decorate with dark furnishings and cascading drapery, ready to be pulled against the night. This room, even after six o'clock, glistened and caught the fading sunset. It was bright, inviting and, Beatrix thought, *It's happy. John's happy here.*

Previously her friend had nearly died, yet now he looked ten years younger and content. Beatrix smiled watching John tell Thomas an amusing story, and from just what she could hear across the room, Thomas was attempting to work on his "dad" joke repertoire. The jokes were silly and clean, and Thomas was being his typical obsessive self, trying to learn how to be a father, which inexplicitly included practicing telling jokes.

Right after breakfast that morning, Thomas had pulled out the tiny tablet he always kept in his jacket or pants pocket and grilled her with:

"Why did the orange lose the race? It ran out of juice." Followed by laughter.

"How do you fix a broken pumpkin? With a pumpkin patch."

"Wait, one more. Why are fish so smart? They live in schools!"

He didn't even wait for her to answer, laughing as if he were hearing them for the first time. "Now I must memorize more of these, for our future children who will think I'm wicked brilliant."

"You do know, Thomas, that it'll take a few years for our kids to understand humor, right?"

"Here's one more I just learned..."

"More? Where do you get these?"

"Don't be cheeky, Bea. In that room we foolishly call the library, I discovered a book of jokes. It's *Dr. Miles Nervine Medicine Joke Book* and it was stuffed behind a bookcase. What a find. How about this: What did the two pieces of bread say on their wedding day? It was loaf at first sight." He giggled.

"Thomas Ling, you are going to be an amazing father. I only hope the kids appreciate you," she assured him. There'd been far too many dark times in her life, and she couldn't comprehend how lovely and comfortable it was to have a husband like Thomas.

Henry was settled in a corner of the living room, reading the newspaper and then picking up a days-old New York Times, and Beatrix could see him smile as presumedly Thomas was repeating the same quirky riddles to John that she'd heard at breakfast. Thomas bent close and became serious. Beatrix knew he was telling John about his research project on tidal energy, clean and of value if we humans were not to destroy the planet with burning coal and belches of fossil fuel from cars and industry.

Yuri, John's chef, tiny and immaculate in a black dress with a white lace collar, appeared at the entry to the living room. It was the lady's wholesome cooking and cheerful demeanor that had helped put John in better health. "Mr. Brockman, dinner is ready." She smiled and nodded a greeting to Beatrix.

John and Thomas replaced their sherry glasses and Beatrix slipped her arm into John's. "Oh, my dear, I cannot thank you enough for recommending Yuri and Haru. He's a fine gentleman, and what a gardener. We're planning a natural vegetable garden for the springtime." As they reached the spacious dining room, John pulled out Beatrix's chair and Henry took a seat across the table. "Yuri runs the household like the Brits run their rail system, always on time and everything done well. And the other staff respect and admire her. I am a fortunate man."

'I assumed you are going to return to New Orleans for Mardi Gras, John. Won't your friends expect you at the balls and parties?"

He chuckled, shaking his head as they settled at the end of an elaborate dining set. "Mardi Gras is for the young, and the folks who can tolerate a month-long hangover. I've made a decision just today that I'll settle here at least through the end of next summer. Summers in New Orleans are far too hot and humid for this old man." He slowly unrolled the linen napkin, shook it out, and placed it across his lap.

The dinner was as scrumptious as served in a five-star restaurant, with a spinach and arugula salad dotted with garbanzo beans topped with a light balsamic vinegarette to start, and the entree was a rich quiche with white and green asparagus sliced into slivers and tied with a perfect green bean. Fruit and cheese rounded out the meal with strong chicory coffee, the only nod to New Orleans.

John has not just embraced the California lifestyle, but apparently a vegetarian one as well, Beatrix thought. She was patient and knew from her friendship that John would never discuss business over the dinner table. It wasn't done in the part of the South that he'd called home for forty years. Once they retired to the massive deck adjacent to the living room, lighted with flickering candles, they sipped port, and he came to the reason he'd invited them to share dinner.

"I need your help Beatrix, and perhaps yours as well, Thomas."

"Anything, John. Ask," Beatrix pulled her sweater over her shoulders. She wasn't cold, but the sobering tone of her friend's voice mirrored the chill in his eyes.

"I mentioned to you a few weeks back that I've been attending the synagogue, the oldest here in the city, on State Street. The congregation is small but has been pivotal in the community, you know. Since the 1850s, after gold was discovered in the Sierras. Sutter's Mill, I believe."

In some ways, like Thomas, John needed to give background history so that when discussing the issues, Beatrix would have the context with which to assist him in whatever it was.

He continued, "Santa Barbara had an uncommon record of acceptance for Jews because those who had previously settled the city were equal-opportunity racists. Seems they disliked everyone so what was one more outcast, apparently. That continued to be the case until the 1920s, when immigrants from Eastern Europe grew to be important merchants, something the city needed to grow. Hence, they were accepted on their own merits and contributions to the community. We Jews are but a small part of this multi-race community, however."

"Yes, of course. Like the first settlers, Hitler was not alone to instill hatred in people who were different. I pray that he may be the last."

"End of hatred? That is too much to fathom, Beatrix, too much to hope for. Hatred has never really disappeared, which is no surprise to you and in your study of psychology," John concluded. "Now, enough background. The current rabbi for the last few years is Hiram Krause. He and I have met socially a number of times, the latest was about a week ago when I donated a few paintings, the Monet and a Cezanne you may remember from my house in the French Quarter, to our art museum. He's on the board there, a twitchy man. Definitely not a *schmuck*."

Thomas looked at Beatrix and then at John. "*Schmuck*?"

John spoke first. "A fool, an idiot, it's Yiddish, my friend."

"Twitchy? John, what do you mean?" she asked.

CHAPTER 4

"His accent is Polish, and his Yiddish is fluent. I inquired about when he'd immigrated to the States as we were viewing the paintings prior to the event. He told me how he and his first wife and elderly parents left Poland, escaped to France, and went to Brazil in 1939. He told me a fascinating story about the crossing and how they settled in Rio before arriving in New York, a long and dangerous journey. Yet when he told the story, it seemed like he had memorized it. There was no emotion in his words, but perhaps he is a damaged soul from his past life. I do not know."

"And?"

"The first time I met Hiram was on my initial visit to Santa Barbara, before I bought this house. I walked into his office by the synagogue and introduced myself. He'd been moving files or furniture or something and had the sleeves of his shirt rolled up to the elbow. I saw the tattooed numbers from one of the death camps on his inner wrist."

"If he immigrated in 1939, how could he have been in a camp?" Beatrix added, "The Polish Jews in the concentration camp, the extermination camp of Auschwitz, for instant, were systematically tattooed starting 1940."

John shook his head. "Krause noticed me staring at his left forearm and immediately rolled down his shirtsleeve and slipped on his blazer. It was odd. I did not ask because that seemed too intrusive. He covered the moment with small talk."

Beatrix felt her forehead wrinkle. "There is no reason at all to be ashamed or to hide the fact he had been in a camp, John. Why fake how he arrived in the States or his background?"

"Why, exactly." John then continued. "I have always found him to be intelligent and careful with his decisions for our congregation, but that one moment continues to bother me. If a person tells one lie, they often tell more to cover up the first. I'm told it gets easier; so it has been my experience."

"Absolutely, John," Beatrix agreed.

He continued, "It's trivial, perhaps, but I know you like a good puzzle. Now, the reason why I've invited you and Thomas tonight is that Hiram and his wife Sarah were here for dinner two nights ago and shared a rumor, and you know, I do love a good rumor. Hiram is quite the talker and Sarah, quiet and reserved. I was surprised as Hiram is a reformed Jew, but Sarah wore a *tichel.*"

Thomas looked to Beatrix for a translation. "A *tichel* is a headscarf worn by married orthodox Jewish women in compliance with the code of modesty known as *tzeniut.*" She turned back to John. "Did the rabbi want to talk about the stolen artifacts from the museums in Paris and Poland, snatched from Jewish aristocrats and everyday people who were fortunate enough to have inherited a treasure?"

"That's a given, unfortunately. Some, I fear, will never be recovered even though the FBI and Interpol have supposedly teamed up on this. I was in Washington weeks back before a House committee on art recovery. Our elected officials seem unaware of the emotional costs of this issue."

"Then what, John?" Again, as earlier in the day, Beatrix felt her curiosity take over, the need to solve whatever puzzle her friend was about to present.

"You are aware of the ingenious nation north of the city?" He watched Beatrix nod before continuing. "This is about the theft of priceless and ceremonial artifacts purchased illegally or stolen from the local indigenous peoples."

"The Chumash, the tribe of Santa Ynez? Is this about their relics?" Thomas asked, leaning forward. "I've not heard or read anything in the newspapers about that, or actually any news lately about what was happening on the Santa Ynez Reservation."

Instantly, Beatrix's stellar memory kicked in. "I recall that while the group was officially established on December 27, 1901, the Santa Ynez Reservation has been a vital part of the Santa Barbara County landscape for well over a century. It was then home to about 400 members of the Santa Ynez Band of Chumash Indians, who lived just a thin line above poverty, without running water, electricity, access to modern conveniences, or even safe medical care."

Suddenly it felt too cool to be outdoors; night closed in. The wind had died, and the temperature dipped. Everyone followed John inside where the fire had been kindled in the flagstone fireplace. "Hiram Krause, the rabbi, told me that he meets with tribal leaders once a month, providing financial and legal guidance. He's a part-time real estate attorney, I've heard, and while it would be so wrong on many levels to try to convert our local people to Judaism, as the padres and colonial Spanish forcefully did in the past, he says he's there to help, not push the Torah down their throats. That's what he'd told me and others in our congregation, asserting that he's doing God's work out there. I haven't talked with any of the Chumash elders, so I don't know their take on the rabbi or what he's offering."

Beatrix listened and then said, "Yes, I met Rabbi Kraus at a hospital fund raiser, oh, it must be two years ago. Met his wife there as well, an unobtrusive woman. He was glad-handing everyone in the room like he was planning to run for election. How well do you know him?"

"Not well, as I've only been attending temple since I arrived, and honestly not that regularly, never have." He shrugged. "The rabbi seems to like the spotlight. He's a large man, overweight, and uses his arms when talking which makes him seem even larger. That's not a sin. Figure he's in sales, sale of religion, so I cut him slack. What's your thoughts on the man, Beatrix? You're far more perceptive about people than I am."

"You flatter me, John. You can read people well or you wouldn't be where you are today. To answer your question, Rabbi Krause seems pleasant enough, well educated, friendly. I did notice that when I first met him, his wife was standing behind him. He never bothered to introduce her. Like he'd forgotten her or didn't want to take himself away from the limelight.

"I thought that was odd, but he was talking about how the improvements in the hospital could help our city, so maybe he was focused, and overlooked her. She did seem to blend into the room's wallpaper. After he'd gone on to chat with others, I introduced myself to her. She was pleasant," Beatrix added, and then said, "Curious how meek she was and married to someone like the extroverted rabbi."

"He's a bit loud and chummy for me," John replied quietly. "I do not think of him as a friend."

"Tell me the truth, would you go to him for spiritual counseling, John?" She knew that was telling.

John laced his fingers. A tactic Beatrix had seen before, and that meant he was choosing his words well. "No." That said it all.

Those who didn't know the power John Brockman could wield would wrongly think that the man was mousy, and Beatrix would have been the first to correct that about her friend.

"Nonetheless, Beatrix. I choose my counselors with care, as I did with you when we met in New Orleans. I've always been rather put off by the flashy types, with their fine suits and shiny shoes, with the exception of you, Thomas. I know you fancy them." John chuckled.

"You have me there, John. Guilty as charged," Thomas said as he looked down at the brown leather, cap-toed oxfords.

"Do you know others who have used the rabbi's services as a real estate attorney? Does he have a good reputation?" Beatrix asked.

"Good questions, and I have no way of answering. I can quietly ask around, Beatrix, but my contacts in Santa Barbara are limited. Is it important? He seems willing to help the people on the reservation when no one else will step up," John replied. "Did he talk about the reservation or the Chumash when you met?"

"Not at all. We talked about bringing together people who wanted to support those in need in the community with clinics and well-baby and mother programs that could be held at the hospital. The evening ended and the rabbi wanted me and Thomas to visit the synagogue when we were available."

She settled on the sofa next to Thomas. "Not to mislead the rabbi, I mentioned that Thomas and I attend the Baptist church with my friends Lillian and all of the Conrad family, so he knew there was no hope to convert us."

"I'd forgotten about meeting the rabbi, never met his wife. Or did I, Bea? I do not, as you know, share her gift of an incredible memory," Thomas squeezed her hand.

John studied the two and envied their bond. "You know, Beatrix, that the situation on the reservation can be tricky. I was there about a month ago. Krause mentioned he was working on developing some property south of the tribe's land, all beach front, and took me on a short drive to see it."

Beatrix thought of the pristine coastline and knew someday the cliffs might be dotted with beach homes, which was progress, she imagined. "The tribe does control prime real estate, minutes from the city. Are there rumors that developers will take over?"

"I fear so. Rabbi Krause is a man with his hands in many pies, it seems, and since the temple's salary is meager and he drives a luxury sedan, he seems to be doing well. Yet, I never judge a man by the type of automobile he uses, but perhaps I should.

"As for the Chumash, we stopped to visit with an elderly woman. Krause dropped off boxes of staples from the trunk of his Cadillac, canned vegetables and flour. That kind of stuff. There had been a food drive at the temple, apparently, and had leftovers." He sipped the coffee, and Henry stood to replenish his employer's cup, offering more to Thomas and Beatrix.

"There's more, far more on my mind and the rabbi talked about it to me as we drove back here to the house," John said. "This is more than buying the tribal property and building homes. I think there's a larger issue here."

"How is that, John? I'm afraid I'm not following," Thomas said.

"It's about the indigenous treasures that Rabbi Krause seems most interested in, no, that's not right, most worried about. Think of the thievery like Hitler's thugs gathering the treasures of the Louvre and selling them to the highest bidder. And museums around the country, including our Smithsonian, are grabbing the treasures for pennies. That is what is happening right here in our backyard, so to speak. Krause said relics disappeared from a closet in the meeting hall and from caves known to the tribal elders, and everyone has denied knowing who is stealing." Color came to John's face, two rosy, pink blotches on his cheeks. He became even more animated about how vital it was to keep treasures with their owners and then, abruptly, he looked across the room and all eyes followed. Inside a glass-front cabinet was a gold Inca knife, studded with turquoise stones, which she'd seen in his office years before and which was part of his antiquities collection.

Beatrix wanted to believe that John had bought the artifact legally, but knew that many of his dealings were not up for discussion. That was a side of John she chose to ignore, which made his next comment a surprise.

"I bought that from the museum in New Orleans, Beatrix. When you have time, and there's no hurry, will you help me return it to the Inca people? I bought it years back as it was to be sold to the highest bidder, and I always wanted to return it, yet I have no idea how to make that happen without my name appearing anywhere." He looked at his hands as if he were guilty of stealing it from the South American indigenous nation.

"Yes, we can find out how to return it, John. As for the local treasures, do you have proof that things are being stolen? Does the rabbi have thoughts or opinions?" Beatrix sat next to Thomas who had been taking notes, always the scholar.

"No, just the whispered questions from a couple of elders when I stopped there with the rabbi. They thought I was a federal agent. Ha, that's a joke." He didn't laugh as both he and Beatrix knew he'd wrestled with the government more than once. "Yes, me, an agent. A couple of people said that things were disappearing. I was surprised because you see they've never trusted Anglos since the ruthless colonial days, and here they were trusting Hiram. Sure, he'd been visiting for a couple of years, and somehow had gained their trust."

"Gained their trust? That says a lot about the rabbi's character, John," Beatrix smoothed her hands down the front of her slacks.

John nodded, understanding Beatrix's gift, and that she would know more about the tribe's history than he could quicky study. "Tell me what you know; this is important, Beatrix. Please enlighten me about their nation."

She did, and the information was as clear in her mind as if she'd been reading a textbook.

> According to lore and early records, Chumash territory at one time encompassed 7,000 square miles that spanned from the beaches of Malibu to Paso Robles, here in central California. They inhabited the Channel Islands as well. The tribe also lived inland to the western edge of the San Joaquin Valley. It was a powerful and peaceful time for the people.
>
> Because they had always worked the land and the sea, they referred to themselves as 'the first people,' and the Pacific Ocean was their first home. These early Chumash ancestors were hunters, gatherers, and fishermen who lived in

large, dome-shaped homes that were made of willow branches.

As the Chumash culture advanced with boat-making, basketry, stone cookware, and the ability to harvest and store food, the villages became more permanent. The Chumash society became tiered and ranged from manual laborers to the skilled crafters, chiefs, and shaman priests who were also accomplished astronomers. Women could serve equally as chiefs and priests.

Chumash ancestors found caves to use for practicing sacred religious ceremonies and keeping the objects safe. The earliest Chumash Indians used charcoal for their drawings, but as the culture evolved, so did the cave markings, using, red, orange, and yellow pigments. These colorful yet simple paintings included human figures and animal life. Many of the caves still exist today, protected by the National Parks system, and illustrate the spiritual bond the Chumash hold with our environment.

As with most Indigenous American tribes, the Chumash history was passed down from generation to generation through stories and legends, and the population became fearful of the invaders, and rightly so, as stories were lost forever.

In 1769, a Spanish land expedition led by Gaspar de Portola left Baja California and reached the Santa Barbara Channel. In short order, five Spanish missions were established in Chumash territory. The Chumash population was all but decimated, due largely to the introduction of European diseases, of which the tribespeople

> had no immunity. Shockingly, by 1831, the number of mission-registered Chumash numbered only 2,788, down from pre-Spanish population estimates of 22,000.
>
> Our current communities including Santa Barbara, Montecito, and Carpinteria were carved out of the old Chumash territory. After mission secularization in 1834, Mexican authorities failed to live up to their promises of distributing the remaining land among the surviving Chumash, causing further decline in the tribal population. By 1870, the region's now dominant Anglo culture had begun to prosper economically. The Santa Barbara area established itself as a mecca for health seekers, and by the turn of the century it became a haven for wealthy tourists and movie stars. Most of the Chumash who remained in the area survived through menial work on area farms and ranches, far removed from their highly regarded ancestors.

"Today, they're rebuilding, but it's terribly slow," she concluded.

"Heartbreaking," Thomas said.

Beatrix nodded, "John, these are our original peoples and they've been cheated."

Henry and Thomas both blinked at the force with which Beatrix said this. She'd grown up in Santa Barbara, at least until she was twelve, and learned even more from her mother, a staunch advocate for human rights. "Mother often visited the reservation, bringing books, toys, art materials, and medical supplies along with bags of flour and beans, clothing and blankets. Once a month, I remember, as I was always with her, our family doctor would go with us. Dr. Betty, a woman of considerable force and a ready smile, gave advice and cared for those who would accept Western medical practices. I wanted to be Betty when I grew up."

Beatrix closed her eyes for a moment, and then softly continued. "One vivid memory is of how Mother attempted to intervene when uniformed authorities and educators and agents from the federal government attempted to take Chumash children from their families to be sent away to Indian schools." Beatrix blinked at the striking memory of her petite mother using their wealth and position in California to stop that action against members of this tribe, knowing some others, without a champion like Jennie Patterson, would lose their children forever or worse, would be informed that the children died while under care by the US government. Not only were children forced to live in these despicable boarding schools. Untold numbers died of neglect and malnutrition. Others were gravely abused and mistreated. There was punishment if, at the school, the children used their native language, stern punishment.

"Mother arranged for teachers to regularly come to the reservation and petitioned the federal government to change their mandate. Unfortunately, when Mother and Dad died in the car crash, her efforts were forgotten or ignored." She looked at Thomas and they shared the same thought: Jennie Patterson's work must continue.

"What can we do, John?" Thomas flipped a page in the small notebook as the previous one was filled with scribbled notes. His brow was lined with worry. He looked at his wife, who waited as well.

John leaned back in the overstuffed chair and rubbed his arthritic knuckles as if they were a rosary. "I'd like you to use those martial arts skills, Thomas, and kick butt and take names, or better yet, don't bother taking names of any government officials who are caught dealing and stealing and forcing families to relinquish their children." His jaw moved and whatever else he wanted to say, it seemed, he decided to keep his own counsel. Even in California, John Brockman was a powerful man, powerful enough that when breaking laws as in the past, most officials looked the other way, as his decisions were sound, if not altogether proper.

"Would you like me to delve into this, John?" Beatrix asked. It was getting late, but her mind was spinning, already planning a trip to Solvang, about two miles north of Santa Barbara and the current reservation headquarters. "A few months ago, while trying to solve Morty Ramsey's nonexistent murder, I met a shaman from of the tribe. I'll speak to him tomorrow if he still works at a pub in town or I'll track him down. Santa Barbara isn't that big and I'm good at finding people and answers even if he has other employment."

"I knew you could help, Beatrix. Could you investigate, too, if they are intrinsically valuable or if being part of the Indigenous American's heritage makes them priceless? See who could be selling them and why. Find out what universities or museums are buying them. We must discover if it's the tribespeople or interlopers or Anglos who have no regard for our heritage as Americans and the heritage of our indigenous people. This is huge, Beatrix, and I know you're busy setting up your new psychology practice. If there were anyone else I could count on to find the truth, to pursue justice, I would ask. I trust you."

"Be assured, John, I feel deeply connected to this issue and honored that you're trusting me. I won't let you down. Do you think that Rabbi Krause will believe he needs to go with me?" she asked. "It has been decades since I've been to the reservation."

"Might you recall any of the elders you met as a child?"

Beatrix closed her eyes and returned to one afternoon's visit to the Chumash reservation with her mother. Pictures of honest, smiling faces came to mind, especially a tiny indigenous woman, black and gray hair parted in the middle with tight braids hanging down over each shoulder. She was barely bigger than Beatrix at that time; her posture was erect, and her goodness radiated from her smile. She was a proud woman, a tribal leader. Beatrix immediately returned to a memory, so vivid it was as if it were happening right now, and she could nearly feel her girlish cheek resting on the lady's shoulder.

Beatrix had been playing soccer with the other children in an open dusty field and tumbled as she kicked the ball. A rock sliced her knee. At the moment she decided that she wouldn't cry in front of the other kids, this older woman came to her side and scooped her up off the dirt. The lady, only known as Grandmother, embraced her as if she were one of her own. "Come here, Little Bea," and she made a buzzing sound, "Do not be afraid."

Little Bea looked toward the group and saw her mother in the middle of the heated conversation with scowling men in black suits and blacker hats. She could hear but not comprehend what they were shouting. The words weren't yet in her vocabulary. Jennie Patterson stood tall, although she was barely over five feet, and faced the men, never shouting, never backing down. There was a shaman standing slightly to the side, his fists clenched. Beatrix knew, right then, that these were the federal officials who were coming to take the tribe's children to the dreaded and dangerous Indian Schools. Her mother had warned her what might happen that day; her mother always talked with Beatrix as if she were far older, explaining honestly things of the world, yet in ways her only child could fathom.

"Mrs. Patterson," yelled a young but balding man. Angry spittle came from his mouth. Beatrix hid her face, sensing fear in others, but not her mother. "You are naïve and do not understand. That's excusable, as such, because you are a woman. A mother. It is time that you must leave these weighty decisions to men who are able to comprehend the complexities of managing the Indigenous tribes and making the children real Americans." He turned to the others, now inching away from his tirade. "The time has come to gather the children now. Do you hear me? Is that clear enough for your female brain?"

His thin moustache looked like a fuzzy black caterpillar Beatrix had often seen in the garden, and yet his face was the color of an overripe tomato. Beatrix shivered more closely into the grandmother's lap as the older woman embraced her with sinewy arms. Even as a child, she could tell her protector was anxious.

"Do not fear, Bea," the woman whispered, pushing the long silky braids back over her shoulders, almost as an act of defiance. "Your mama is a powerful medicine *shamanka.*" The words were said with conviction, and she nodded her head not knowing then that a *shamanka* was a leader in their tribe, although Jennie was not an official member. Jennie had been visiting and helping the tribe a decade before Beatrix was adopted, and she knew it would take time to gain the elders' trust. Beatrix felt a shiver of pride at her mother's strength.

Opening her eyes and returning her thoughts to John's questions, Beatrix leaned back on the sofa and said, "Then my mother pointed her index finger at the intruder, and he stepped back as if she were aiming a pistol."

CHAPTER 5

As Beatrix recounted the memory to John, Thomas, and Henry, it was as if she were once more in the safe arms of the indigenous grandmother. She could even hear her own mother's voice as Jennie Patterson said, "I will not tolerate your taking any of these children."

One of the men could have easily knocked Jennie Patterson over or pushed her aside. However, her posture and persona commanded attention.

The men looked at one another, taking yet another step back from their leader. It was clear that the strength of the woman had turned them into the cowards they were.

Jennie had pulled a piece of paper from the pocket of her brown linen trousers. "I have a letter here, signed by our President, Mr. Calvin Coolidge, who has appointed me as the liaison between our federal government and the Chumash nation. It says that you, gentlemen, should know that I alone am able to make the decision as to which children, if any, will be schooled off the reservation. This letter has been sent to California's Governor Johnson and your supervisors, too."

"Mrs. Patterson," said a chubby man, who tried to smile with a mouth that seemed unable to complete the task. His next sentence reeked with condescension. "You simply do not understand the situation here," he waved a limp hand around, indicating the wooden handcrafted dwellings and the wide-eyed and trembling children peeking out from behind their parents. "It is not your fault, my dear. It's because you are female. Leave these decisions to men. We alone know what's best to understand the complexities and the management of the tribes."

Jennie Patterson seemed to stand even straighter and then nodded toward the bully. If the official perhaps thought he'd gotten through her insubstantial, womanly brain, however, he was wrong. Out of the shadows came three police officers, each holding their hands on the holstered pistols. She said, "It is time, gentlemen, and I use that term loosely, for all of you to leave. This is not US soil. It belongs to the Chumash nation who have asked me to protect their rights, and these officers to uphold those rights."

Sitting in John Brockman's lavish living room, she could see in her mind how the men dashed to their huge, expensive cars, slamming the doors as tires squealed in the gravel as they drove toward the highway. The big, yellow, and empty school bus followed closely behind. No children were taken that day.

Beatrix clearly envisioned Jennie's smiling face and how the older people encircled her, all speaking their native Hokan language, which her mother had quickly picked up. Beatrix was relieved and proud of her mother.

Beatrix had witnessed it all from the safety of the older woman's modest lap, before the lady kissed her forehead, and said something in Hokan that was unrecognizable to little Beatrix. Then she said, "Your mama took care of those disagreeable men."

As if a movie was being played at top speed, she then remembered visiting the reservation dozens more times, and the freedom of racing through paths in the corn fields and playing hide-and-seek in the eucalyptus grove clustered on the property. The other children never mentioned that their playmate's hair was red or that her skin was paler than theirs. They included her in everything, sharing their snacks and helping her climb over the rocks and wade through the creeks, catching tadpoles to release, running after one another. "Yes, I do recall the faces, although I don't know the names of the elders. But if the children, who are now adults, my age, are still here, I'll recognize them." She blinked back tears. Blissful memories of her childhood were always marked by the recognition of how it ended, when the car accident took her parents' lives.

Yuri, the housekeeper and chef, appeared in the doorway. "Sir? There is a telephone call for you and the caller insists I interrupt your meeting."

John nodded and headed to the telephone in his office.

"You're a good person, Miss Beatrix," Henry said tossing another log on the fire. "Mr. Brockman told me he would try to convince you to help, but it didn't take much convincing, did it?"

"You know my wife very well, mate. Now, without a doubt, she's already plotting and planning." Thomas replaced his coffee cup on the tray.

"You make it sound like I'm going undercover as a spy. Oh, darling, I'll just go and ask some questions."

"To figure out why things are being stolen while apprehending the culprits. I'm going to be completely gray before I'm forty," Thomas said. In the pit of his stomach, dinner collided with worry and twisted it into a square knot. "I'll sleep better if you'd allow me to resume my job as your bodyguard."

"You sleep like a rock. How could it be any better? Besides, the answer is no, and you are not to follow me like you've done in the past, Thomas. I'll be perfectly safe on the reservation, and you know it. Besides, isn't the university paying for you to think up enormous ideas in order to make our earth safter?"

"Well, there is that, my pet. I guess they might miss me. Honestly, I go bonkers when thinking you might be in danger, like when you got involved with that dodgy nightclub singer."

After John returned, he told them the call was from Rabbi Krause. "I hope you don't mind, Beatrix. I mentioned that you will want to speak with Krause, and he said he'd be in tomorrow morning at the synagogue on State Street." John fiddled with his coffee cup, running a finger around the rim as if making a decision. "There's something else. Sheer speculation on my part, as I cannot verify it."

"What is it?" Thomas asked and Beatrix was still.

"A mystery about Santa Barbara's Rabbi Krause. I saw the rabbi once, a few years ago at Touro Synagogue." John rubbed his arthritic knuckles.

"On St. Charles in New Orleans?" Beatrix asked.

"Yes, I was just leaving a Friday Sabbat service and he barged through the doors like the devil had his coattails, nearly knocking me over. Shoving people out of his way. His face was ashen, and his mouth contorted in anger. I stood aside and watched."

"Did you see who he talked with?" Beatrix asked.

"He collided with the senior rabbi, Rabbi Emil Leipziger. Shouted at him in Yiddish, which of course I understood. Something about being hunted by a voodoo priestess who wanted to kill him. The senior rabbi was quite fragile and almost took a tumble. Two men who had been talking to the rabbi intervened, grabbing Krause's arms and escorting him out of the cavernous room."

"Did Krause ever mention this chance encounter, John? Remark on seeing you?" she asked. "In the heat of anger or confusions most people do not focus on their surroundings, but he couldn't have forgotten being in New Orleans."

"In his overwrought state? Fear covered his face like a horrible Mardi Gras mask."

She cocked her head, waiting. "Have you mentioned this to him? He knows you live part time in New Orleans, right?"

"I know this is truly not my business, however, Krause briefly commented at some social event where we talked that in the future, he'd like to visit New Orleans, having never traveled through the South. His wife Sarah was by his side, and she started to say something. He snapped, 'That's not relevant, dear' and she flinched."

"Why cover that up, John, along with his tattoo?"

"I was wondering if you might solve that mystery as well, Beatrix," John replied.

They said their goodnights. Reaching their station wagon, Beatrix nudged Thomas with her shoulder. "I need to spend some time thinking about the friend of Jo's who believes there is a Nazi war criminal here in the city and the rabbi who may or may not be whom he says."

"When we get home, do you mind if I leave you to the thinking, Bea? I'm knackered. I've an early morning meeting with the university provost about funding for the wave energy project. He's not keen on it. It could be the solution I'm seeking and unless the earth comes to an abrupt stop, we will not run out of ocean waves."

"He'll come around. Dazzle him with your brilliance, Thomas."

"The provost is rarely dazzled," Thomas laughed.

Next morning Beatrix kissed Thomas goodbye as he headed to the university and she said, "Off to the synagogue."

The breeze from the Pacific felt velvety on her face and she smiled. *I never tired of being close to the ocean, being home again.* As it was less than a mile from the Ling home to the front door to the synagogue, she walked.

She tried the front door but it didn't budge, so she followed the paved path to the side. There was an open door, and she could hear the click-clack of someone typing. "Hello?"

"Oh, hello. Welcome. Are you here collecting for a charity, madam?" A sizeable man, with a riot of gray hair, looked up from the typewriter which took up most of the cluttered desk. He was dressed in a starched white dress shirt, a blue striped tie, and black leather suspenders.

"Rabbi Krause? John Brockman said you were expecting me."

"Of course, so good of you to call, Mrs. Ling. My secretary is out today so I've taken over her desk."

"My last name is Patterson. I've decided to keep my birth surname as a tribute to my late parents. Are you available now to talk?"

"Yes, yes, just finishing some notes on a paper I'm planning to write about relocating displaced Polish Jews in California," he replied.

Beatrix shook his plump hand and recalled that now he seemed even rounder than when Beatrix last saw him at a hospital fundraiser less than six months before. He opened his arms as if he wanted to hug her but stepped back to allow her to pass into a hall. "Come in, come in. It has been far too long since we had a chance to talk. I heard through the *shmuesn*, the Jewish grapevine, that you and your husband were renovating that majestic mansion near the high school."

Beatrix laughed. "It is still a work in progress, Rabbi, and when we finish the dining room, next on the mile-long list, I would love to have you and your wife join us for dinner."

"I'm holding you to that, Miss Patterson. Shall we have coffee in the kitchen? It's more comfortable than my office, which is a converted closet," the rabbi said.

"Please, Beatrix."

"Hiram. Now, come this way." The cozy room was clean and smelled of coffee. "We have a soup kitchen here on Mondays and I haven't gotten to putting everything away. Excuse the mess." Restaurant-sized soup pots and hefty skillets cluttered the counters. Tins of vegetables and cases of canned fruit were neatly stacked on the open shelves.

"Santa Barbara is a mecca for the rich and famous, Rabbi, yet, as we know, just under that veneer there's a layer of poverty. A few of the wealthiest want that ignored." Beatrix accepted a mug of coffee that smelled freshly made.

"We serve all segments of the community and immigrant workers passing through," he said, his Yiddish accent validating that he, too, had been an immigrant. "Many are coming from as far as Central America where times were unforgiving during the Depression and far even more problematic since the war. With our servicemen and women returning home, there are fewer jobs for workers, especially unskilled ones and their families, even in the ubiquitous lima bean and strawberry fields. There's the issue of prejudice, which I admit has been troubling. It's a touchy situation; nevertheless, the Almighty says to feed the hungry. We are called to obey."

"I've recently become aware of how keen a segment of my hometown is discriminatory even now, and after all we've been through," she added.

He sipped the coffee. "Oy, I didn't offer you cream or sugar." He started to get up."

"I would have said no thanks."

"Beatrix, I didn't realize you'd grown up in the city."

She smiled and saw the opening. "My childhood was spent here but my birth mother is in New Orleans." She waited. "I spent a few years there before and then during the war. That's when I met John. We both had businesses in the Quarter."

"The Quarter?"

"The French Quarter. Have you traveled to the American South, Rabbi? If not, you must. It's so welcoming, and especially New Orleans, the music and the people and seeing the Mississippi is a life experience. Oh, and the food? I sometimes think it's against the law to serve a bad meal in that city."

He chuckled. "Sarah and I must visit after that endorsement. Especially if there is food involved." He patted his rounded belly. "As you can tell, I'm devoted to good food and my Sarah, she is a good cook."

Beatrix was an expert on reading people and saw the micro fluctuation in his eyes. She noted the pupil dilation which signaled deception, as the autonomic nervous system regulates pupil size. One of the "tricks" of her former life as a psychic was to watch for this tell, as they say in poker, because pupil dilation normally indicates an increase in cognitive demand. Liars usually experience a surge in cognitive demand. The rabbi was hiding a truth. But why?

"After dinner last evening, John explained you were worried about possible thefts of antiquities happening at the Santa Ynez reservation and from the Chumash people."

"Oy, again my manners." He stood and reached into a cabinet pulling out a plate brimming with *hamantaschen* cookies, a Jewish tradition, shaped like a tri-cornered hat representative of Haman's hat. Beatrix recalled how Haman was the antagonist in the story of Queen Esther who saved her people, the Jews, from being killed by the edict of the evil Haman. The cookies were still slightly warm and flaky, and the smell of butter and sugar made her mouth water.

"My wife baked these this morning, her specialty, and when she heard I was having a visitor, she insisted that I bring them to the office. It didn't take much persuasion. Please have some, as otherwise I'll eat the entire plateful by lunch." He took two chipped saucers from the counter, along with napkins. "I hope you don't mind how casual this is. I don't often have guests for morning coffee."

Beatrix nibbled the corner of the apricot treat. "Delicious as they smell, thank you."

"I never met a sugary treat that I didn't love, although Sarah warns me to be careful." He whispered, "That disease called diabetes runs in the family and even with insulin injections my *sheyn*, oh, that is Yiddish for beautiful, my *sheyn* Sarah kindly administers, I need to be cautious. Sometimes I cannot help myself, and Sarah loves to bake and cook." Then he popped another cookie into his mouth before he said, "Now, my dear, I do not want to blow my own trumpet ..."

Beatrix knew when someone said they didn't want to brag, they were always about to. She was there to listen and smiled calmly although truth be told, she was anxious to learn about the rabbi and his role with the indigenous people. Then there was the issue of a chance meeting with John Brockman in New Orleans and the concentration camp tattoo on his forearm.

The rabbi took a deep breath, drained the coffee cup, and said, "In our Book of Proverbs it says, 'Let another praise you, and not your own mouth; A stranger, and not your own lips.' Many have told me I should not be so humble, and I really must write my complete autobiography, all the details of my life and the immigration with my mama and dear papa, all rolled into a tale of this," he pointed to himself, seemingly unable to talk without moving his hands. "Yes, Beatrix, I am nothing, just an unassuming rabbi." He chuckled and smiled.

Beatrix wondered if he believed his words as he continued to boast. Her fascination with people and what and how they said things never disappointed her. "Words are cheap," her late adoptive father would say. "Make them count or don't say them." The rabbi had never heard that adage and seemed to get more animated with each accolade he heaped on himself.

"The congregation in New York City and the rabbis there begged me not to move here to California. They cried when I told them my plans and still long to have me leave Santa Barbara and move back to the city. At that temple, I took what was a small gathering in the beginning to hundreds. Oh, it was sweet. Every week more Jews returned to the fold to hear me and be counseled. Oh, the couples for premarital counseling were the best."

"Just curious, Rabbi, then why did you leave?" Beatrix knew the answer would be insightful. She felt assured it would be another pat on his own back, at least that was what she expected.

"My good wife Sarah and I have been called here by Yahweh, by God. He spoke to me, telling me that I was needed in the West. I am bringing the reformed Judaism here to the Golden State, which is much more relaxed and less rigid than the orthodox branches. My dear papa was a rabbi in one of the most traditional areas in Europe and I often wonder if he would be offended by what I do and how I mix with the community, Jews and gentiles and sinners and heathens."

The word 'heathens' sent yet one more unfathomable thought into Beatrix's mind. *Who might these heathens be?* She didn't get a chance to ask as Krause continued, louder, as if he were speaking to a grand audience.

"I was a lawyer in Warsaw, as a young man. We were a fortunate family even as things got horrible in Europe, we wanted for nothing. My father, a notable rabbi, and I realized early in my career that it was not to be in law. Even as a young man, I felt the pull. God was calling me. As the storm clouds darkened through the old country, we sold almost everything and escaped, only by the Almighty's hand," he took a deep breath, "before…" He let the words hang and Beatrix knew he was thinking, as she was, of Hitler's wholesale extermination of Jews, intellects, people of color, midwives, gypsies, those with special needs, and anyone the regime thought to be anti-Nazi.

He looked down at his hands and wiped cookie crumbs that had fallen on the table back onto the plate. He took a long moment and Beatrix wondered if he'd ever stop singing his own praises. "I'd just joined with my father at his temple when… when it was time to leave." He folded his puffy hands over his stomach and closed his eyes.

She waited to be polite; however, after a few extra moments, more than he deserved, she asked, "Did you ever get a chance to use that training? How long before the war did you practice law here in the States, sir? Or did you not practice?"

"Oh," he now smiled. "In New York I first worked in a small law firm because we had to be careful. Before we left the Old Country, my dear mama sewed our accumulation of old German Empire money, called *Deutsches Kaiserreich,* which I'd bought on the black market, into our clothes The gold coins and her jewelry were hidden in our clothing and winter jackets. With my meager salary and selling the gold, it was enough to keep us in food and lodging and then Papa was asked to join the temple in the city."

Could he have passed the New York bar exam that quickly, right after he arrived in the States? Beatrix took a breath but didn't react to the stories. She was an avid student of human nature and, of course, a psychologist, and these tales simply didn't add up.

He squeezed his eyes shut, and when he opened them, tears dotted the corners. "When my first wife and newborn son died in a tenement fire, I saw it meaning I should return to my calling as a rabbi. Years later, Sarah and I met, and we both had enough snow to last a lifetime, which was one of the reasons for the move. A small one, but she was tired of being cold. There was a spot available for a senior rabbi here in Santa Barbara and on a whim, I sent a letter asking to be considered. I included my references. By that time, Mama and Papa were gone. Within a month, the selection board hounded me to join this group and we packed up and headed to California."

Beatrix declined another cookie, and mentally noted how his continued lies about his past slipped off his tongue with ease, apparently having been told countless times.

She'd had enough about his gold-plated accomplishments and asked the questions that instigated the visit. "John said that there were legal issues at the reservation. He said that you'd tell me everything."

He waved his hand as if to sweep away a compliment he seemed to expect from Beatrix. When it didn't come, he said, "I visit there about once a month." He shook his head. "No, Miss Patt...Beatrix, I am not trying to convert them. Love our neighbors is the cornerstone of the Torah and the key to that is to love them as they are, not turn them into some replication of what we think they should be. These people are grievously underrepresented, as you know. Now it seems that their religious objects and antiquities are disappearing, probably sold off to the highest bidder, and they are once more being cheated. Or so is my guess."

"That's wrong, and why I'm here."

"These people, the Indians, granted me inclusion at once; however, that may not be the case for you, Beatrix," he said. "I was fortunate. You may not know this. The group rarely accept an outsider at once as they did with me."

She sat still, yet it ruffled her when groups were referred to as "these people." *They trusted Mother, but will they trust me when I visit?* she thought.

CHAPTER 6

"Rabbi, I am aware of the plight of our Indigenous Americans. I can relate, as my heritage is quite diverse. My late parents, active here in the city, were often vocal and keenly at the center of several civil debates on the welfare of the tribe."

"Ah, yes." He looked longingly at the few remaining cookies, licked his mouth, touched one, put it halfway down, then in seconds popped it into his mouth. When he finished chewing, his voice came out as if he were presenting a message to a crowd. Beatrix scooted her chair back.

He pointed an index finger into the air, punctuating his comments. "This issue has plagued the area since the beginning of the colonial period, although then the Conquistadores were stealing gold. It has come to my attention that on the reservation, near the coastline, there are ceremonial caves and while it is against the Chumash laws to enter the caves without the presence of a shaman, a religious advisor of sorts, there have been trespassers. Of course, there are hikers and picnickers who come to the area, but these seem to disregard that they are walking on sacred ground."

"What are your thoughts on this? Are the thefts funded by private citizens, or even universities and museums or foreign governments?" She finished the coffee and waved her hand, passing on more cookies.

"That has been my thought and I've discussed with John, who is keenly interested in the ramifications the loss of antiquities would have on the tribe."

"Is there anyone who might be suspected of the theft?"

"I could not get them to tell me and the elders, many who are shy or do not speak English, do not seem to know."

Score another lie, she thought. The elders were all instructed by the padres in the missions or at the vile Indian Schools. They simply might not have wanted to talk with Krause. Storing this twaddle away, she said, "Could the intruders be somehow associated with the tribe?"

He nodded. His double chin agreed. "That is the fear. Money has always been an issue for the group, and it is a pox on how this American government mangled, since the beginning of colonization, the relationships with Indigenous Americans."

"I can certainly agree with that, sir. The artifacts could be deemed valuable, even priceless, to collectors who feel the American west is exotic. All of Europe is facing the gargantuan task of rebuilding after the war, however, there are still the extraordinarily rich who could buy these pieces for private collections," she said.

The rabbi lifted his eyes toward heaven or the ceiling, looking even more like a pious religious figure; Beatrix did not know which or why. Then he said, "These people seem not to be aware of the value in their midst. They routinely ignore the idea of keeping the treasures under lock and key. It is outrageous, but this is their naïve practice. No one really knows how many caves there are."

"Yes, I've heard that, and I believe the treasures in the known caves have never been catalogued or documented," she began before he could take a breath and disparage the sovereign nation. "You have heard the argument that the tribes have no way to conserve the treasure. Some believe, as you've said, they cannot ensure the preservation of things that are part of history as they are deemed unintelligent and often untrustworthy, which is farcical. These same experts snatch the objects away 'for safekeeping.'" She hesitated and then added, "It's dreadful. The same holds true on human remains."

Beatrix knew it was essential to hear the tribe's elders' version of Krause's comments. She'd visit the reservation and talk directly to the elders. "Are you aware or have the leaders told you that any of the antiquities have shown up on the market or at the auction houses that deal in buried treasures?"

He frowned. "I have no connections with the marketplace, I'm afraid, but I fear that has happened. It is so troubling. There are powerful people in our town, and I worry someone here in the city might be part of the evil supply chain and selling the historical treasures. Our friend John seems well connected, and perhaps he could ask the board at the Natural History Museum." The rabbi dusted cookie crumbs off his substantial belly and put on a hopeful face.

Beatrix did not explain that she was on that museum board as she had a feeling that Krause might think all women should stay home and bake, not be psychologists, influential donors, and board members of civic organization. She'd found in the past it was better to let others underestimate her.

As the rabbi gathered the cups and plates to carry to the sink, she thought of the discrepancies in his personal story, and she didn't want to share her own. She said, "This feels somewhat like the corruption and greed that spurred on those who looted for the Nazis, and even now when heirlooms could have been returned, the greedy have kept them."

"My thoughts exactly, Beatrix." The rabbi rubbed his chubby hands together. "I'm in the religion 'business,' yet sometimes it feels that civilization only finds more deadly ways of hurting one another."

"It's not entirely hopeless, sir. I have a few friends here in the city and a number in New York and Washington, D.C. from the time when I lived in New Orleans. Perhaps they'll know more." She immediately thought of John and how his less-than-entirely legal contacts throughout the south and along the Eastern Seaboard might know if the relics were being sold on the black market. She would ask John to introduce her to those people or ask the questions himself. Declining to share this, she continued, "The reputable auction house called Sotheby's might have information as well if the artifacts have already been resold to reputable buyers."

The rabbi patted her hand. "John assured me that you'd know what to do. I'm an old man, past my time to hunt down the truth."

It was accurate, the rabbi did look tired, and beads of sweat dotted his forehead, which he wiped away with the linen napkin, all the result of just clearing the dishes from the table. Or was it a response to his fabrications and misrepresentations?

She could tell quickly when people lied; they tended to get nervous and uncomfortable, some broke a sweat over their upper lip or on their forehead, just as Krause did. She knew it was a person's autonomic nervous system working overtime and it seemed to her that Krause's reaction was the only tell that he was caught lying. Why did this lie make him more nervous than the falsehoods he'd told about his personal history?

"Perhaps I can pursue it, be a pursuer of truth because the truth is really freedom," she smiled and thought, *That's what psychologists try to do, help others find their truths.* She reflected back to her time in New Orleans when she tried to find out who she really was and assisted the U.S. Army in finding Nazi terrorist cells in the city. Then quite recently she helped the police solve the mysterious cult-like deaths of young women at the hands of a serial killer, who just happened to live next door to Thomas and her. "I've taken enough of your time, sir. Thank you."

Opening the kitchen door, Krause watched as Beatrix got up to leave. He said, "I was planning to visit the reservation this afternoon. However, I must get these notes ready for my secretary to type up correctly tomorrow. I will telephone an elder in charge of their council and explain that you'll be visiting. I will ask them, as they trust me thoroughly for all the work and help I've given, to extend that same trust to you." The rabbi blinked as if he had trouble keeping his eyes open.

"I can go out there in the morning." She stopped at the end of walkway that connected to the sidewalk on State Street and looked back. The rabbi stood, watched her leave, and then waved.

Beatrix started to walk home, reviewing the details of the conversation. The rabbi seemed to have knowledge about the thefts on the reservation, yet was lying about his this past. "What else is he covering up and why?" The question would not leave her until a sporty green car zipped by and she jumped back onto the curb. It wasn't the near miss but the car itself that got her attention. *That's something I have needed to do for months and now it's a must.* She turned around and headed south on State Street, made a right turn, and within a half hour had completed her business.

The afternoon sun made the Pacific sparkle like a million dots of silver dancing to music only they could hear. Beatrix, slightly breathless after climbing the steep hillside above the house, turned and drank in the view. She spread an old army blanket on the hillside and settled among the eucalyptus trees surrounding their five-acre parcel that rose up in back of the home. They lovingly called this part of the property 'the grove,' and Thomas talked about building a gazabo in the trees so that they could picnic here and see the ocean and Channel Islands while never leaving their address on Anapamu Street.

She crumbled a pungent eucalyptus leaf in her hand and replayed the conversation with the rabbi, her own childhood visits to the reservation, and then the chance meeting of a bartender she'd met just months back when investigating the cult that was killing young women.

"He said he was a shaman, a tribal medicine man, a leader. It's Tuesday so the bar won't be too busy later, if he's still working there," she said out loud, planning her evening, then glancing at her watch. It was nearly five thirty. Santa Barbara was a small city, yet it was the city hub and county headquarters. Workers were leaving their desks, right then, perhaps stopping for a drink before heading home.

Beatrix was deep in thought and startled at hearing the crunch of leaves and a bit of tumbling gravel. The noise pulled her away from pondering the approach she'd take with the elders and the barkeep. "Thomas, you're early." She smiled.

His years of martial arts training somehow allowed him to walk as if his feet barely touched the ground. She knew he purposely made a racket when approaching her, calling out, to give her time to compose her thoughts. "Bea? Yes, I got off early for good behavior, and I'm afraid my superpower to dazzle the provost never got tested. He was in meetings all day. I'm now on the schedule for tomorrow so I'll need to improve the concept of dazzling tonight."

"Then we'll work on it later and you can see if your dazzle will do anything for me," she winked.

"Any chance you brought tea along with you when you scaled Mount Everest, um, our hillside? I would murder for a cup."

"No need to kill, darling. The tea is strong and hot, and right in the thermos." She pulled it out of the basket by her side.

They shared the red plastic cup that came with the thermos. "That was close. You'd be as disgusted as I am with the tea they offer in the university cafeteria, like brown water. Worse, it's lukewarm tan water."

Beatrix scooted over and left room for Thomas to sit on the blanket next to her, brushing off some leaves. "With all your Bunsen burners and heating equipment in the lab for experiments, Thomas, why not brew your own? I've seen you make tea thousands of times here at home."

"Yes. That would be a rational solution."

"But why aren't you logical about tea?"

"I have considered your suggestion, nevertheless, then I'd have no excuse throughout the day to leave the lab, feel the breeze, look at the sun, smell the Pacific. Why, I'd turn into one of those balmy nutters who only manages to concentrate on one topic at a time. I'd probably have to grow a mousy little moustache and I'd frown all the time for lack of exposure to the sunshine. Oh, perish the thought of what it would do to me. Could you love me even if I started to look like a lab rat?"

"Oh, my, let me get back to you on that. If walking to the cafeteria for tea keeps you from becoming a rodent, I understand your quasi logic. To change the subject, what did you think of today, other than creating clean energy from the waves in the ocean?" She nudged him with her shoulder and smiled.

"I thought of you. Also, about a million other thoughts, one of which we need to discuss."

"I have a few things on my personal agenda too, but you go first."

Thomas refilled the plastic cup. "Any joy finding out if Jo's friend Gerta is right? Is the hospitalized man who was vowing allegiance to Hitler an evil Nazi war criminal, or just a deranged oldster? I worked on formulae all day that turned out to be useless and I need some exciting news."

CHAPTER 7

"I'M TRYING TO LOCATE BOTH. Gerta and this man, Noah Schmidt, are on my 'must- hunt-down' list for my next free day. I was caught up with Rabbi Krause today and then wrote up my advisory notes from the last Natural History Museum's board meeting and consulted with a new client, a returning Marine who was in the worst of it." Thomas offered the half empty cup, and she finished the tea. "You know, John was right. The rabbi's stories simply don't match and the tattoo on his forearm means he isn't who he says he is. I did find out, up close and personal, that the man seems not to have a humble bone in his large body, which got old quickly. Who really is the rabbi?"

"You agree with John? Krause is twitchy?"

"Doubly so after our conversation today. Is there any way John could have been wrong about seeing Krause in New Orleans?"

Thomas spilled the now-cold remaining tea on the ground and replaced the cap on the thermos bottle. "You've known him for years, Bea. Is John ever mistaken? The man's sharp as a tack, always has been."

"That is what also troubles me. While I can remember the most obscure detail, John is also great with events and faces. If he said he bumped, literately, into Krause, then he did. I am going to quietly ask around about the rabbi's time here in the city. Gerta has a brother, a tailor with a shop on State Street, and I'll stop in there first thing tomorrow and catch Gerta too, so we can talk. I don't want to make a silly assumption, so I'll ask if they know the rabbi, not presuming they attend temple. Krause told me that the Jewish grapevine thrives. Maybe the brother and sister will feel okay to share any tidbits with me."

"Anything else?"

"No, that's my plan for tomorrow. How about yours? What are you trying to convince the provost to do? Is this about money, Thomas, because you know we could fund, privately, your projects if it comes to that."

"No, no. It seems the provost wants to get more publicity for the university. He's got this idea that someday in the far future it'll be big deal and the man is ace at convincing us underlings to do things out of our comfort zones. I heard mention from one of my colleagues that the provost is pressuring him to write a book. That is too comical for me to even ponder."

"At least listen with an open mind, Thomas."

"Speaking of my mind, was I imagining something different, something new I have not seen before? Or do we have visitors?"

"No, no one else here. Although I asked Jo and Sam, Jo's mama Lillian, and the kids to come for Sunday dinner. Those twins are growing like weeds and Sammy has to be the smartest kid in first grade. Besides, Lillian and I need to chat a bit. She's a wise lady and often knows more about the backstories of our community than the mayor, the police, and even the newspaper editor combined. She's probably got the goods on the Jewish grapevine as well. Wouldn't surprise me a tad."

"Beatrix Patterson. Stop talking. What about the MGB? What about the car? Why is it blocking the entire carport? Who in the world does it belong to?" He was leaning closer and his eyes wide with curiosity.

Beatrix flicked a leaf off her slacks and dusted dirt from her fingers, enjoying and avoiding telling everything about the mysterious car in the carport and Thomas's barrage of questions. "There's a new seafood restaurant by Stearns Wharf, I thought we'd try it tonight. Scallops sound divine, don't you think?"

"Darling Bea, please halt your banter at once. Oh, my days, how long are you going to string me on? Who is visiting? Not your father, the famous Charles de Gaulle? Is it our late president's wife Eleanor Roosevelt? No, she doesn't look like the sports car type. Wait, it's the King, George VI? I could see him zipping around in that car." He laughed and gently shook her shoulders. "Tell me quickly. Wait, was the tea drugged and there's no car in the carport? I'll have you know that the US Constitution forbids cruel and unusual punishment."

She laughed. "Oh, you're asking about that car? So, you'd really like to know who that sweet little MGB sports car, green and comely, belongs to?"

"Have you not been listening?"

"Did you examine it?"

"How could I miss it, Bea, since it's smack dab in the middle of our carport and I had to park the Woody on the street. That is a rhetorical question, you realize."

She laughed, "You are sexy when you're rhetorical." She fished in the pocket of her trousers and pulled out two keys, dangling them in front of Thomas.

"I don't understand."

"Understand what? The meaning of life? You once tried to explain Einstein's theory of relativity to me, so that can't be it."

He grabbed the keys. "These?"

"They're yours."

"I have a car, Bea. We have a car. It's currently parked on Anapamu Street and so big, it's probably blocking traffic."

"You're right. You have a car and you're gone with it for eight or ten hours a day. I'm good biking and walking around the city, lovely exercise, even now that I'm setting my practice here in the room we foolishly call the library because it has shelves and some ancient, musty books. Yet, darling, I also need a car."

"So that metal thing of pure exquisiteness and automotive happiness is yours?" His face fell just slightly, and he blinked, attempting to hide his disappointment. That made Beatrix chuckle again.

"Darling, however did you get a doctorate from Oxford? And that is not a rhetorical question," she teased. "I bought the car this afternoon for you. It's your birthday present. You practically drooled over one we saw when we took that road trip to Pismo Beach a few weeks back and I saw one in town today."

"Number 1, I do not drool. Number 2, I lust. Number 3, it's not my birthday for six more months."

"Surprise. You can get your gift now and I get our Woody station wagon, which will have plenty of room when the babies come along." And she thought, *Perfect for transporting books and medical supplies out to the Chumash reservation as well to carry on Mother's legacy.*

"Well, Bob's your uncle. I am buzzing," he pulled her up off the blanket, wrapped his arms around her and kissed her soundly. "That's brilliant, especially after my long, dreary day in the lab. Let's test her out. Let's go for a drive and see how that baby runs."

"There's one more thing, Thomas."

He stopped and cocked his head. "Yes, I saw, the steering is on the right, the correct side for us British drivers. You are the best wife in the galaxy."

"No, well, yes, I am, but wait." Her face was in the shadows and yet Thomas knew that troubled frown.

"Tell me, what is it, Bea?" He didn't budge from the hillside. "Whatever is it, we'll work it out together, as always."

"I don't know this time because I don't know how I feel." No tears dotted her eyes, but she stared out toward the Pacific trying to get her thoughts into some emotional alignment. "It's a coincidence that you mentioned Charles. I got a letter today from him."

"Ah, your biological father, the famous war hero and now president of France, Charles de Gaulle. But that can't be a concern as he writes often. Is he unwell? What's wrong?"

"Thomas, he told his family about me."

"That's marvelous, darling, and it's about time. This is 1947, not the dark ages when things like babies being conceived prior to marriage or even without the paperwork and promises of the marriage contract are history and for good reason. Your biological parents had their own motives and they loved one another. Your bio mother loved you so much that she made the ultimate sacrifice to allow another couple to adopt you, to raise you as their own. What could be wrong?"

"The confession, his acknowledgement of me, an adult woman, a married adult American woman, nearly caused World War III at the de Gaulle home." She brushed some leaves off her backside. "Now they'll never speak to me, now they won't let him. I had dreams that even though we're thousands and thousands of miles apart, we could visit and let him know his grandkids, when we have kids."

'Come on, Beatrix. We're talking Charles de Gaulle who fought and won against the horrendous Nazi war machine, rallied the ragtag resistance into a viable army, and ousted the Reich's puppet Vichy government. He's turning the country straight around. I find it hard to believe that he's going to let his wife and adult children tell him what he can and cannot do, especially about you. He loves you, Bea. Let's be realistic. They may be as dysfunctional as the next family, yet Charles remained faithful to you as a father, even when you didn't know the truth, even when you thought he was simply a kind quasi uncle."

They walked down the path to the house. In the kitchen Beatrix rinsed the thermos and said, "You're right, Thomas. I'll write him back tomorrow and ask if we can visit next year, maybe early spring or even fall. Paris is lovely in the fall."

"Now come on, grab a scarf and a jumper, um, I mean sweater, because we're going joy riding in my new birthday present."

"After dinner, there's a bar I want to stop at," she said turning and smiling.

"Why, darling, this is going to be the best non-birthday yet with a new, flashy car, dinner on Stearns Wharf with my gorgeous lady love, and drinks afterward."

Within five minutes Thomas was behind the wheel on the right side of the British car, and Beatrix was holding on for dear life. They were whizzing around the streets of Santa Barbara at a cautionary twenty miles an hour. "Just until I get the hang of driving on the wrong side of the road with the steering wheel on the correct side, I need to take it slow," he called out.

Beatrix had always adored Thomas's enthusiasm for life. Sure, he'd find himself embroiled in tricky situations and managed somehow to escape unhurt, plus he was intelligent and made her laugh. However, driving was not one of his gifts. When he turned left on Pacific Coast Highway and momentarily swung into the right side of the road, she screamed, "We are not in England. Get over, Thomas."

He did, and they lived through the first outing. "Now for dinner? You mentioned scallops in that new fancy restaurant. That said, would you mind if we don't? It must be the car. This car put me in the mood for good old fish and chips from that shop on the wharf," he said, pulling sedately into a parking lot across the street from the historical pier.

Later, walking back to the roadster, Beatrix said, "Now let's go to Garcia's."

"Is that the dive bar near the newspaper building?"

"When I was chasing down the cult, I stopped into that bar, trying to meet the coroner, who supposedly spent every afternoon in one tavern or another. That didn't happen, but I made the casual acquaintance of a member of the Chumash nation, a shaman."

"That was months back, darling. Think the barman will still be there?"

"This might be a wild goose chase, but if he's not working there, perhaps the current bartender might know his name."

"Let's go. You know I always enjoy a good wild goose chase with you, my little gosling." He pulled her to his side and opened the driver's side door of the MGB for her.

"Thomas, I'm honored. I was wondering if you'd ever let me take this gem even around the block." She looked quickly at

Thomas's face and saw him relax. Maybe the car wasn't a great idea after all.

Ten minutes later, Thomas and Beatrix pulled the car to the curb and walked into Garcia's tavern. "A quiet Tuesday," she said. There was a couple in the corner, whispering in each other's ears, and a lone customer, nursing a beer, staring at the dart board against the back wall. The place smelled of beer and cigarette smoke mixed with faded dreams from those who spent too much time huddled in the dark.

"Is that your man?" Thomas nodded toward the barkeep.

Her eyes adjusted to the dim pub as she headed to the bar. She caught the man's eye.

"Welcome, guys, what can I get you?" he smiled, looking exactly as Beatrix remembered. Even his white dress shirt's sleeves were rolled to the elbow, revealing the Chumash turtle tattoo on his muscular forearm.

"A few minutes of your time, actually," she said. "I don't know if you remember me. We met late last year when I was trying to solve a mystery of several young women falling to their deaths on the reservation property."

He stuck out his hand. "Read all about it in the newspaper. You were the talk of the tribe. Miss Patterson, right? Gordon, Gordon Blackfoot."

Beatrix shook it, turned and nodded to Thomas. "This is my husband, Thomas Ling. I am so glad you're tending the bar tonight, Gordon, because I have another mystery to solve, and I believe you can help me."

They settled on stools and Gordon asked, "What can I get you?"

"Two of whatever is on tap," Thomas replied.

"We won't take up much of your time," Beatrix answered. "You mentioned that you were a shaman. Would it be possible to talk with you privately soon on the reservation? Perhaps with some of the other elders, too?"

"Not more cults? Please don't tell me that. Right now, I'm working with a local man, an attorney. He's here in town and offered, pro bono, to figure out what to do concerning a heated tribal matter. It's complicated and shocking."

"Hiram Krause? The rabbi. That the man?"

"Yes, Mr. Krause. How did you know? Housing developers want to buy our ceremonial land for a pittance, they're putting pressure on us with visits from the government about fake laws we're breaking. Krause noticed some unsavory situations that might be connected, too."

She whispered, "That's why we need to talk. I've met with Rabbi Krause, and he told me about the missing art and antiquities."

Gordon lowered his voice. "This is a crime, but I do not know who the criminals are, Beatrix. I will be at home, on the property, throughout the day tomorrow. Can you come in the afternoon? We can talk in private then," he added as a couple came in and called out to place an order. Gordon turned the couple, "What can I get you folks?"

Beatrix let Gordon do his job and watched Thomas throwing darts in a match with a customer. They'd been together for two years, committed to their relationship since the beginning of the war, and she'd never known he was a darts champion.

"Another game, mister?" his opponent asked, "I've got two bits here saying I'll win this time."

"Wish I could take your quarter, old man, however, my wife awaits, and I never keep a lady waiting. Perhaps again sometime?" Thomas finished the beer and left a five-dollar bill on the bar for their drinks.

Beatrix called out, "Thanks, Gordon, I'll see you tomorrow. Appreciate your time."

Back on the sidewalk, Thomas rubbed his hands together. "Now you know the dangerously dark side of my personality. Thought of going into the game professionally, well for about a month, because I was addicted to it. Dad, however, wasn't as keen on that career choice. Blimey, he said I was demented." Thomas laughed, "Dad was right, what was I thinking. Then, the mysteries of the sciences pulled me back. It did help that luscious Loretta McDonald, a Scottish beauty, signed up for Advanced Calculus and hired me as a tutor."

"Thanks to this Loretta, you became a noted authority on clean energy rather than a pool-playing wastrel? How can I find that woman to thank her? If you hadn't switched back to the real world of Bunsen burners and outrageous mathematics, you would have never been asked to be a secret document courier and we couldn't have met in New Orleans, when you were running away from the law."

"Next time we're in London you can meet her and thank her in person. Loretta married my best chum Binky Wilks-Hamermesh right after graduation. They now live in Brighton, both barristers, criminal law I think, with a pack of little Wilks-Hamermesh's. Yes, two sets of twins. That mate always was an overachiever and Loretta would have run me ragged. Full disclosure: I wasn't that serious about Loretta, and she was besotted by Binky from the moment I introduced them."

"Cheers, then, to all of the Wilks-Hamermesh clan," and Beatrix slipped her hand into his. "I'm buying a dart board and darts at my earliest convenience, my dearest. I think you might be surprised, as I'm not half bad at it. Uncle Charles, I mean my father, taught me the game one summer, while my parents and I stayed at his villa. Same year I learned poker and chess."

"What other secrets lurk within you? I think you must confess it all, and this could be serious pillow talk if you're ready for pillows."

"Thomas, pillows, darts, cars, oh my. It has been a busy day. We certainly do need some serious pillow time."

Moments after Thomas left for lab at the university early the next day, Beatrix was maneuvering the woody station wagon out of the carport she was happy to share with the smart little British racing green MGB.

It would have been just as easy to walk to Otto Rosenbaum's tailor shop on lower State Street, but she planned to go right from her interview with Gerta's brother to talking with Gerta, and then to the Chumash reservation. Gordon said to come in the afternoon, which meant there would be plenty of time to stop in Buellton for a luscious bowl of soup. "Ah, Pea Soup Anderson's, here I come," she said out loud, thinking about the eclectic restaurant and the Disney-inspired cartoons, mascots of chubby cooks making soup.

As she reached the main street of town, which would be bustling in another hour, it seemed too quiet, as if there had been a tragedy, with the wide thoroughfare in mourning. Beatrix felt a shiver and thought of her biological mother who truly did have a sixth sense, could see into the future, and make sense of the past. *Is it in me as well?* she thought and rather dreaded to know, trying to push the notion out of her mind, knowing full well that she couldn't. Later she'd have to examine her feelings on clairvoyance, or "spirit gifts" as her mother called. The idea would haunt her until it was thoroughly dissected and clarified. It has been a huge weight on her mother, forcing authorities to commit her to a mental hospital when anyone who seemed different was thought of as insane.

It was just 8:30 and on the street a few were buying the newspaper from the corner shop. Beatrix parked the car and sat there for a few minutes. There had been moments, out of the blue, when she recalled thinking of someone or something and then it happened. Perhaps it all had to do with her superior ability to recall even details of things that occurred to her. "Not now," she said out loud, "I need to meet Mr. Rosenbaum and see if Gerta is home to talk. If her accusation is correct and Schmitt is a war criminal, the sooner I turn that information over to authorities the better." She gathered a tablet, which was merely a prop and thought, *People expect those who ask questions to make notes and while I pretend to jot down their answers, it gives them time to reveal more.* This was exactly what she'd told Thomas when he asked why she bothered carrying the spiral notebook.

She walked to the tailor shop, with its window display of bolts of bright green and white silk fabric artistically draped over an ornately carved walnut chair, which looked to be an antique. A bell above the door jingled when she started to push it open at the same moment a burly man was about to exit. Seeing Beatrix, he quickly stepped back, greeted her with a nod, and held the door. His extra-large t-shirt, that stretched mightily over a barrel chest and muscular shoulders, read SMITH'S HARDWARE. On the front was a drawing of a hammer dancing with chorus line of nails.

Smith's was an institution in the city and Thomas and their house's carpenters, she felt certain, would know the worker as they frequented that establishment daily, sometimes hourly, getting materials to renovate their once-dodgy house.

"Good morning," she said to the rail-thin middle-aged man standing behind a waist-high counter, his hand resting on the top of an old-fashioned treadle sewing machine. Beatrix could tell he was fashioning a suit jacket of fine navy wool and she briefly realized that the suit-in-progress might have been for the previous customer, as it was as oversized as he was.

"Good morning, madam. How may I be of assistance this fine day? I am the owner and the tailor, Otto Rosenbaum. At your service, madame." His English was smooth but there was a pleasing hint of an accent that lingered on his tongue. His face was drawn, and deep wrinkles formed parentheses around his mouth, but his cocoa-brown eyes, although forlorn, seemed kind.

"Good morning, Mr. Rosenbaum. I am Beatrix Patterson," she extended a hand and he took it, but without energy, his eyes downcast, almost defeated from the ability to make close contact with her.

She continued, "I've come for two reasons. My husband and I will be traveling to Paris, France, and London next year, on a family matter, and I would like to get the details such as cost and then commission you to make four or five suits for him." She smiled and realized traveling to France was the truth. She'd go and meet her half siblings on their own ground. They'd become a family or at least be able to acknowledge one another. Or not. *Then I can disappear before they murder me if that's what they're planning,* she thought.

"Ah, yes, I would be happy to show you some fabrics, perhaps wool flannel, that would be desirable for a gentleman to wear in Europe." He indicated that Beatrix should examine the fabrics lining one wall. The shop smelled of sewing machine oil, a hint of tobacco, and peppermint. The herbal smell was coming from the steaming mug on the corner of a cutting table.

Beatrix touched the bolts of wool, silk, and linen on the shelves in the shop. A rainbow display of crisp cotton, for shirts and women's dresses, was held on another wall. "Do you know the month you'll be traveling? September can still be warm in Paris, so perhaps a light wool? London can be cool in the fall, however. If you have a better idea of the season when you'll be traveling, that will help. Three-piece suits are also an option so that should you stay when London is chilly, your husband will have the option of the vest."

She smoothed a hand over the fabric, thinking how stunning Thomas would look in a charcoal gray suit. Then she imagined them, arm in arm, strolling down the Champs-Élysées, passing the Arc de Triomphe with the Place de la Concorde. She knew there would still be damage from the war, yet she longed to see Paris once more and walk on the world's most famous commercial street. In her mind it was always fall in the French capitol, her favorite season. There would be a brisk breeze blowing from the Seine and making the trees seemingly shiver, allowing the falling leaves to dance and flutter on the sidewalks to music only Nature could hear. Or she imagined.

"If you do not see what you like, I can arrange to provide other fabrics from my suppliers. I have smaller samples. Would you care to see them? What work does your husband do? A doctor? No, a banker? Wait," he smiled and displayed yellowed, crooked teeth. "I have it. He's an attorney." The tailor ran his fingers over the bolts as if he were caressing a favorite pet or perhaps a lover.

"He is a scientist. He really does like a dapper wardrobe, but we've been so busy with a renovation of our home that his clothing is now hopelessly out of date. I do like this brown one and a dark gray would be good as well."

"Your budget, madam, if I may ask?"

"Would it be possible to have a well-tailored suit about $50 each?"

"Oh, my manners," he swallowed and smiled.

The smile to someone like Beatrix who could interpret micro facial changes meant that $50 was far greater than he had planned to ask, however fair that price would have been in New Orleans or on the East Coast.

"Beatrix Patterson and my husband is Thomas Ling."

The name differences, including the fact that the woman's husband had to be Asian, made his forehead wrinkle, but he did not miss a beat. "May I offer you some appointment times for Mr. Ling to come in to be measured and discuss the style and materials?"

"Might we return on Saturday?" she asked, still fingering the brown wool.

He squinted and quickly said, "My apologies, Madam Patterson. I am closed on the Sab..um, I am closed on Saturdays."

"Now I must apologize, of course, you're closed on the Sabbat. How rude of me to assume otherwise. I'll talk with Thomas tonight to find out a weekday when he can take a long lunch break from the university, and we can come back to the shop then."

"You are too kind. You said you had two things?"

"Yes, Mr. Rosenbaum. I have been trying to contact your sister, Gerta, and I've been unable to reach her. Might you know where she is? How to find her?"

He had been picking up tiny silver pins from a small cardboard box, sticking them into a pincushion in the shape of a bracelet attached to his wrist, but Beatrix could tell he was choosing his response, buying time to figure out what to say.

"Ouch." He'd missed the pincushion and jabbed his wrist. They both stared at the drop of blood before he wiped it on a handkerchief. "My sister? You know her or perhaps know of her?" His frown was deep and his eyes wide. Those eyes showed fear.

"Just helping a friend. Why? What is there to know?"

He shook his head vigorously. "Nothing. She is my only living relative. I left Poland as a boy when a distant cousin paid my father to have me come to California as his apprentice. He has since passed, and I inherited this." He waved a limp hand indicating the shop. "Gerta chose to stay. Was imprisoned in a horrible place. End of story. No, I do not know how to locate her. What is wrong? Why do you ask?"

"I often assist people to find things and through a mutual friend, I was asked to locate your sister. Gerta gave this person the telephone number here in the shop and it was on her employment application at the hospital. She's not living with you?"

He didn't look at Beatrix, but shook his head and resumed gathering the pins. "If she comes back here, I will let her know you're seeking her. She may have moved away. She may have left the city. I am not her keeper." That last sentence was emitted in a huff and Otto picked up a pair of long, sharp silver scissors, bouncing them from hand to hand. His face was grayer than moments before.

"Thank you." She turned to go and then stopped. "Do you attend synagogue here?"

"You ask because I have an accent?" The question was gruff as if Beatrix were accusing him of some crime or that she was a racist.

"Not at all, but I know your sister is Jewish. I thought perhaps you practiced the same faith."

"I do," he ground out the words and then studied his shoes, avoiding eye contact.

"Do you know Rabbi Krause well?" She'd watch his face and that would tell her more than his words. The expression stopped her.

He suddenly shook, as if someone were shaking his shoulders. Then he gulped. "Krause? The Rabbi? Did you not hear?" Now he focused on her and started to nod his head. Forcefully. His face puckered, resembling a pale prune. A second later, he stared out the window at the passing traffic and seemed too stunned by her question to respond.

After a long pause waiting for the tailor to explain, Beatrix quietly asked, "What? What's happened? Please tell me."

"*Gott im Himmel.*" He scrubbed his small hands over his mouth and then rubbed them together as if he were washing something horrible off them. "It was so sudden. His Sarah, his wife, found him collapsed in his office, on his desk, earlier this morning. He always went into his office before dawn and when he didn't return to their house on Garden Street for breakfast, she went to get him. He hadn't answered the telephone in the synagogue's office."

"He's dead? The rabbi?"

"*Oy vey*, it is horrible. Sarah unlocked the office, called out, no answer and then she discovered him. She ran screaming down the street screeching something about evil spirits. It was like the sound of a wounded animal, and I thought perhaps it came from a dog fight. I was sweeping the front sidewalk when I looked up. She ran straight at me, hysterical, and collapsed. At last, I managed to get her to her feet. She is a large woman, and I am not as strong as I once was. I had her sit right here," he patted the visitor's chair. "I called the police."

"Were you close to the rabbi? Are you close to Sarah?"

"Sarah and I exchange pleasantries from time to time. She walks past the shop when heading to the market." He clasped his hands, and they still shook. "She's a bit of a *yenta*, a gossip, but harmless and has a kind heart. Never heard her say one troubling thing about anyone, never complained about Hiram."

He picked at his index fingernail. "Suppose I am, as well, a bigmouth."

"There's always a bit of truth in gossip, don't you think?"

It was as if Rosenbaum hadn't heard her. "She'd told me before a police detective whisked her away that Hiram's eyes were wide open when she found him. She tried to shut them, but he was stiff and cold. They wouldn't close, which had to be horrible. She took a hankie from her pocket and placed it over his face. It was too frightening to have him stare at her even after he was dead, with his eyes wide open. She screamed it was murder."

"Did she mention that the rabbi was afraid of anyone or had enemies?"

"She said he'd been agitated lately, moody, and on edge. '*Oy gevault*,' she kept crying, wailing actually."

"She was saying, 'oh God'? It had to be ghastly for her." Beatrix's mind flashed to a scene she'd experienced in New Orleans where voodoo was considered real and countless swore by its powers. In New Orleans, she'd once been hired, when she was a fake psychic, by a distraught man who came to her to get rid of a voodoo curse. She had visited the voodoo priest who had sent the threatening message and a doll with pins stuck in its heart. "The wife hired me, Madam Patterson," he told her. "He is a serial cheat, and the lady is tired of his dishonesties." The priest had been known throughout the French Quarter for powerful curses, although from what Beatrix could gather, it seemed that his reputation exceeded his abilities. However, she would never have told him that or crossed the flamboyant character.

According to the priest, the unfaithful husband needed to be punished, but the punishment didn't take into consideration an unknown and preexisting heart condition. After the menacing visit from the voodoo practitioner, the husband had had a heart attack, was hospitalized, and subsequently died, possibly after another doll was left at the end of his sick bed, or so Beatrix was told through the rumor mill.

The priest was not charged; he'd not done anything criminal except tell the husband he was cursed and wave an effigy in front of him. The priest had visited the unfortunate gentleman and stuck pins into an effigy. Right in front of the man, confined to his hospital bed. The wife of the philandering husband? Cashed in his hefty life insurance policy. While the client died without paying Beatrix, the wife was so happy to rid herself of the two-timing lout that she paid Beatrix handsomely.

Could that be the case here? But who would have a grudge against a rabbi, for goodness's sakes? Although, he was a narcissist and seemed to be a compulsive liar. Is that enough to kill the man? If it was murder. She could see that, she realized and then thought, "Voodoo in Santa Barbara, land of perpetual spring, orange groves and wide sandy beaches? Come on? Impossible. If there was one important lesson that Beatrix learned as a pretend psychic was that if someone believed something strong enough, it became their truth. Was this all connected to that time John bumped into Krause in New Orleans?

Beatrix had been only half listening, lost in theories as the tailor continued. "It was early, not even seven. She trembled and sobbed. I pulled out a bottle of schnapps. A thimbleful to calm her."

"Have you talked to the police about what you've observed? About the rabbi's mental state? Did you see anything or anyone suspicious near or around the synagogue this morning when you came to work or even in the last few days?"

The tailor motioned toward a curtained door. "I live in the back of the shop so the first I saw anything was when I discovered Sarah on the street."

"Did the police talk with you? Or any of the other shopkeepers?"

"The detective came back about a half hour after she took Sarah to the synagogue for more interrogation." He gulped. "You don't think Sarah could have murdered her husband?"

"Mr. Rosenbaum, no one has said it was murder except the rabbi's widow. Did the detective?"

"Ah, no." He lowered his voice, "I have heard the rabbi was not a nice person." And then waved a hand. "Oh, just gossip. A detective asked how I knew the Krauses. You know the officer? She is a tall woman in the most ill-fitting suit a lady could ever wear, I might add. The style and size were inappropriate for a person of her proportions and authority. *Ja,* she asked me questions, but I know nothing, really."

"My condolences, sir. Was that detective Stella Rodriguez?"

He started to fumble and pick up papers, looking underneath. "Wait, she gave me a card." He dug into the wastepaper basket in the corner. "Detective Rodriguez, Santa Barbara Police Department. Are you a detective, too?"

"No, not at all," she responded, but perhaps that wasn't true. She'd never be an investigator, but if there was a puzzle, a mystery, and help was needed, she was there. "Thank you again and I will telephone you for an appointment, once I confirm Thomas's schedule, for you to make some suits for my husband."

On the street the desert breeze was picking up again and the sky was a shocking blue. Beatrix looked north toward the synagogue. There was a black and white patrol car at the curb, and she spied Detective Rodriguez talking with a uniformed officer.

Beatrix looked both ways and crossed in the middle of the street. "Stella?"

The detective turned from her colleague and beckoned her closer. She reached out and shook Beatrix's hand. "If you solve this case even before the coroner arrives to pronounce the rabbi deceased, it's going to reflect really badly on the department."

"Is it murder?" Beatrix asked.

CHAPTER 8

THE DETECTIVE STROLLED AWAY from the synagogue's door, taking Beatrix by the arm. In a whisper, she inquired, "Won't have any exact time of death until that coroner decides to grace us with his presence, but rigor mortis has set in, so he's been dead more than two hours. How did you hear already?" She sighed and looked more world weary than usual.

"By chance, Stella."

"I swear in this city if one sneezes on Upper State, there's somebody at Stearns Wharf to say, 'Bless you.'"

Since helping the police solve a previous case of cult killings, Detective Rodriguez and Beatrix had stayed in touch. When a bank was robbed in Goleta, Beatrix had been hired to interview the employees, and to detect and translate microfacial expressions as they talked about the crime to ascertain if anyone was complicit. Two were.

Because of their association and as head detective, Stella knew whatever she shared with Beatrix would be confidential. "The rabbi was older, seriously overweight, and it looks like natural causes. Understand he'd been through terrible times. Death camp. The Holocaust. Saw the tattoo on his arm as his shirtsleeves were rolled up when I arrived on the scene. Terror takes a toll on a body."

"Were his eyes open?"

"Yeah, why?"

Beatrix thought through her conclusions before asking the detective. "Have you ever seen someone so frightened they died?"

"Nah. There's always a reason, natural or not. Most of the time, when I'm called in, it's the not. Somebody's decided a person has to die and they're the one to do it."

Beatrix explained during her time in New Orleans she knew the quasi-religious leaders who practiced voodoo supposedly could kill someone who truly believed in their evil powers. She mentioned the priest who frightened the adulterous husband and the man died of a heart attack. She tried to shake off the premonition or suggestion or whatever was starting to connect the random thoughts and memories in her brain.

"If you hear there's been foul play, Stella, and it's appropriate, could you let me know? I knew of the rabbi from various social and civic events, and we had met just yesterday. He was helping on a delicate matter concerning the Chumash on the reservation, informally, and asked me to gather some information."

"I never met the man, don't travel in his lofty circles. Heard a few rumors he was a know-it-all, but that's not grounds to kill, if in fact he was murdered."

They both watched a black sedan pull to the curb. "Ah, look who's arrived," she nodded to the coroner. "The show must go on."

Beatrix looked at her watch. It was nearly 10. She'd not found Gerta nor gotten any information from her brother on the sibling's whereabouts or any information on the rabbi, other than he was dead with a hysterical widow.

She could drive home and stew over how or if any of these things were connected, as it seemed the rabbi was somehow in the middle of it. The now deceased rabbi.

Or she could stop and visit her friend Jo, hold the twins, and watch Gracie dash around the garden as if she were on some magic energizing formula rather than the pure mojo of a two-year-old. She got in the car and turned the key; the engine purred, but she sat there. "Or I could talk with Schmitt."

Again, out loud, she said, "Noah Schmitt lives near the mission. It's time I check in on that loose end, if there is anything unseeingly happening. Could Greta have started working for Schmitt and be hiding out there? Or could she have left town?" Beatrix drove the station wagon north, heading to the address that Jo had given her.

It was a modest house, two-story but not ornate like the one on Anapamu Street that Beatrix and Thomas were restoring. There was a car in the driveway. Gerta's? *I don't even know if Gerta drives, I don't know anything about her,* Beatrix thought as she knocked on the ornate carved front door that reflected the Moorish style of the bungalow.

A small, dark-haired boy appeared, peeking out a crack.

"Hello there. I'm Beatrix. Who are you?" She smiled and bent down.

"Hans." His brown eyes flickered toward his shoes and the door started to close as the child pushed a curl from his forehead. Then he opened it again, as if checking that Beatrix was gone.

"Hi, Hans. Does Mr. Schmitt live here?" She smiled one more and this time the door opened five inches.

"Which one? My daddy or *Opa*?"

"Yes, your *opa*, Mr. Noah Schmitt, your grandfather."

"I'll get mama," he turned and as the door nearly shut, a slim blond woman pulled it back.

"I'm sorry, I was with my father-in-law and didn't hear the door. I'm Elsa Schmitt." She ruffled the boy's hair and he scampered away. She had a soft accent. Thomas would have called it "posh." Probably from boarding school on the East Coast. There was a sweetness about her that made Beatrix refuse to believe that her father-in-law could be a Nazi war criminal. *Looks are deceiving,* her thoughts shouted, *Don't be a fool.* In New Orleans she deceived for a living.

"Yes, I hope so. My name is Beatrix Patterson and Gerta Rosenbaum, who works at the hospital and met Mr. Schmitt when he was recovering from surgery at the hospital, asked me to check on him. Once patients leave, often the staff never hears about their recovery." Beatrix phrased her query without lying. Gerta did want to know about Schmitt, and Gerta had asked Beatrix to check on him. She did infer she might be connected with the medical staff or the hospital. "I was in the neighborhood and thought I'd stop for a moment. I don't mean to intrude." Then she explained how she wrote human interest columns for the newspaper and hoped, when he was well enough, to interview him at some future time.

Elsa smiled and her face glowed, skin peachy and soft. She smoothed down the bib apron and only then did Beatrix notice the baby bump. "Not at all. How kind of you to inquire about his recovery. *Opa* and I were just having coffee on the patio. Please come through."

Beatrix entered the foyer and then the living room expecting heavy brown furniture and dreary paintings on the walls. She was wrong. Inside everything was bright, fresh, and clean, and decorated tones of light taupe and white. A Picasso, or a very good reproduction, hung over the fireplace and Beatrix recognized a small statue of a woman, clearly the modern work of Alberto Giacometti, the Swiss sculptor, painter, draftsman, and printmaker, prominently displayed on a bookcase.

The house smelled of lilies and good coffee. She glanced toward the dining room. An ocean-blue vase that had to be by the glass artist Pierre Gire held fragrant, bubblegum-pink Asiatic lilies and graced the middle of the pine table.

They walked toward the open doors and the patio. Noah Schmitt sat in the shade. The day was bright and sunny, and the air felt dry, announcing the forthcoming, erratic, and forceful Santa Ana desert wind. The small man made a slight motion to get up and then exhaled as he flopped back into the blue-cushioned wicker chair. "Please excuse me, madam, I have not been well." He did look fatigued, but when he smiled, there was joy.

She extended her hand, introduced herself, and briefly explained her visit. She settled in a comfortable patio chair next to him. "Is your condition improving, sir?"

"Phooey, it is nothing, zilch, and I am an old man who has lived a long life. This body is wearing out." His accent was thick as rich German vanilla pudding a cook used to make when Beatrix was small.

"You've experienced a lot of things in your life?" She smiled and tilted her head, making eye contact.

"Oh, so much. Love, death, war, peace, and now I am a refugee without a home."

Beatrix asked, "This is not your home?"

The boy, Hans, dashed from the house straight into his grandfather's open arms. "No, not my home. My home will always be Munich or even Berlin and when I think of those cities in the 1920s so alive with prosperity and happiness, I can get lost in memories. Germany of old is where my heart wants to dwell." Schmitt moved slightly to the side and the boy, with a practiced squeeze, snuggled next to his *opa.*

"This is your home now, Papa," Elsa said, sitting up straighter on the bench across from them. She reached to her father-in-law and patted his wrinkled hand. "My husband, Walter, teaches at the university, in the medical research and sciences, looking for tiny molecules that cause cancers, especially in women." She had whispered the word "cancer" as did most people, knowing that it was a death sentence so feared even saying the word could be deemed dangerous. "I'm originally from Boston, where Walter and I met. The university lured us here and we couldn't pass up the adventure. Now Papa is with us, so we are a family again, a California family."

Beatrix turned to Elsa. "The university? My husband is there as well. Dr. Thomas Ling? Perhaps they know one another? Although Thomas works in the research sciences department."

"It is a small world," Noah interjected. "Smaller now that the horrors of war have ripped apart our communities, separating us from our loved ones, and changed our futures forever. Ah, now, growing up in Bavaria, it was heaven. Back then, I only knew about California from books." He chuckled. "Never saw the ocean until I was an adult."

The boy whispered, "When you get better, *Opa*, Mama will make us a picnic. Like we did before, we'll go to the beach, play in the waves, or build sandcastles. Right, Mama?"

"I think that would be a splendid idea, Hans," she replied.

Could this man, a beloved grandfather, be a feared Nazi murderer? If he was as innocent as he seemed, why had Gerta heard him swearing allegiance to Hitler? There was no way Beatrix could weave those questions into this cheerful discussion. However, she was there for information. Something had to be discussed. "A friend, Gerta, was with the nursing staff at the hospital during your time here. She asked me to stop by and see how your recovery was proceeding." Not a lie, Gerta was a cleaner and that role was essential to the hospital, to the staff, Beatrix justified. As for a friend, perhaps that was stretching it.

"A tiny woman, dark hair, cut like a boy?"

Not having met Gerta or even thinking to ask about her appearance, Beatrix simply nodded.

"I liked her. She was always busy; she sang when she mopped the floors. We talked about medical specialties as she'd been a doctor. All before...before the war when she became a midwife, of sorts." He frowned. "I was a physician, as well. She seemed hungry for conversation, and we chatted in German. She was a comfort to me."

"How generous of you to talk with her. Had, perchance, your paths crossed in Germany, before the war or during it?"

"*Nein*, no, although I taught for a short time at the University of Berlin, but she never mentioned having been educated here. Said she was born in Poland, of course. I did not ask personal questions, madam. The pain of those years still cuts like a carving knife." He was quiet and watched as the little boy "drove" a small red toy truck over the arms of the chair. "These were the old days. There were riots," he huffed. "Authorities called them 'disturbances' in 1929 and '30. A precursor to greater unrest, but we were blind to that. No. I chose not to see. There were severe clashes between left-and right-wing students. Politicization of the student body increased and when a protestor hit me with a brick and kicked me to the ground, I left academia."

"I didn't know."

"I returned to my original love as a country doctor in private practice outside of Munich."

She smiled. "During the war, sir?" Beatrix held her breath waiting for him to growl, lash out or ask her to leave.

"Papa, you don't have to answer this lady," Elsa scowled and stood up, glowering at Beatrix.

"Elsa, no, it is fine. We must talk of these things, so we remember. It is good for Hans to know the truth and why we must work to keep our peaceful life in America." He turned his attention back to Beatrix and Elsa sipped her coffee.

"*Nein*, it is nothing. Yes, in the early 1930s incidents started to happen. I could no longer avoid seeing what was transpiring in my beloved country. At one point, I either had to agree to be a doctor to the loosely organized, at that time, Third Reich or die. The military had men come to my practice. They threatened to murder my wife and child, in front of me, if I did not agree. I choose to obey and privately disagree and a month later sent my late wife and teenage son Walter to France, then they immigrated to Massachusetts."

"My biological father fought in the war, often in North Africa, and is now working to regain stability in France. It is an immense undertaking. So much ruin everywhere. I understand those horrendous times far too clearly and my condolences, sir. I'm so glad you're here in Santa Barbara now with people who love you." She didn't mention that her father was the newly elected leader, General Charles de Gaulle.

"One more question, Dr. Schmitt, if I may," she began. "Gerta told a mutual friend that you'd talked of needing a private nurse."

"It's all been settled," Elsa interrupted. "I am Papa's nurse now." She smiled.

"By chance, did Gerta stop by to ask about the position?" Beatrix looked to Elsa and the doctor.

Dr. Schmitt shook his head. 'No, I am sorry, I cannot help. I would have enjoyed talking with the lady once more."

Beatrix thanked the family, apologized for the impromptu visit, and asked if she could return again when Dr. Schmitt was stronger. "Or we can meet at the beach for a picnic." She turned to the child. "I have a friend, Sammy Conrad, who is just about your age."

The boy looked up and he giggled as he turned to his mother. "Mama, is that my friend Sammy?"

Elsa squinted, "You are a friend of Josephine Conrad? And her little ones?" She laughed now. "What a household. I don't know how Jo does it, especially with Sam working such odd hours for the Santa Fe railroad. I met Jo when we first moved here and now we volunteer together with the Women's Christian Temperance Union, attempting to help women in need of safe housing."

Beatrix felt her shoulders relax. At least now she knew that the family were not racists, which had been a niggling fear because of Dr. Schmitt's forced conscription into the Nazi government. "We must all get together, then, for a day at the beach. We will still have this summertime weather for another few months. Please, Elsa, let's do it."

On the way to the door, she stopped and admired the family photos, including one with Hans and Sammy, which made her smile. Then she touched the frame of an older one, turning brown around the edges. "Is that Dr. Schmitt and your late mother-in-law?"

The woman fingered the framed, slightly tattered photo. "She was stunning, creamy skin, golden hair. My father-in-law, when he did have hair, I understand, it was nearly white. It was that blond. Good times. She died at the beginning of the war. I only got to know her when the cancer had nearly consumed her body. It was breast cancer and there's nothing to fight it except a mastectomy. By the time she'd found courage to visit a doctor, the cancer had already spread."

Beatrix thanked Elsa again, then getting into the car, she sat for a long time, trying to enjoy the dry desert wind, yet, fearful as well. A small spark and the world would be ablaze. The breezes had caused ruthless and uncontrollable wildfires in the past. Now the faintest smell of burning eucalyptus during a Santa Ana set her nerves on red alert and she searched the mountain view behind the home for billows of smoke. *Probably someone burning trash,* she thought, relieved.

She rolled down the window and changed her mind about a singular lunch. She wanted to talk over the meeting with the elderly man, and Thomas was always her sounding board. He asked the right questions to help her clarify all the information she'd retain forever.

Could Noah Schmitt, a loving grandfather, turn in a second and become the vicious Nazi killer Gerta Rosembaum suspected? Where in the world was Gerta? Then there was Krause's mysterious death. When she returned home, Beatrix would call Jo and ask if her mother, Lillian, knew Gerta's whereabouts or even if Lillian knew any more about Dr. Schmitt. *There is sadness in his expressions and voice but no evil,* she thought.

It was a slow, thirty-minute drive from the Mission area of the city to the university because overloaded trucks of fresh hay seemed to crowd the two-lane highway. The campus had started out in the late 1800s as a school for women to learn home arts, then it became a normal school, a teacher's training academy. Eventually, it morphed into a state college and recently it became part of the University of California system. Beatrix was not in a hurry and planned to surprise Thomas and join him for lunch, so the crowded road let her gaze out the windows to the fields and the Santa Ynez mountains, nearly purple-blue in color during mid-day. After lunch, she'd head to the Chumash reservation and her meeting with Gordon Blackfoot. She glanced at the verdant vegetable fields that seemed to stretch forever, guessing what was growing in long rows. There were lima beans, green beans, broccoli, and even tomatoes thriving in the warm early fall day.

Turning into the school, she recalled how her late parents' philanthropy helped fund new buildings and turn a rural college into the university. She drove through the campus buzzing with students and tried to picture it fifty or a hundred years in the future, unable to even conceive what that might be like. She parked next to the flashy green MGB, grabbed her purse, and headed across the lush grass to Thomas's lab. The door was closed. She twisted the handle. "Locked?" She glanced at her watch. "Oh, I didn't realize the time. He's teaching in the science department's large classroom."

Just inside the three-story structure was a bank of telephone booths. Entering and then closing the bi-folding glass door into the small enclosure, she fished a nickel from her purse, picked up the chunky black receiver, inserted the nickel into the coin slot. No need to wait to talk with her friend until late afternoon. Jo answered on the second ring.

"Hi Jo, it's Beatrix."

"Come for lunch? Gracie is riding the tricycle up and down the sidewalk so she should be ready for a nap soon, as will the twins. We might even be able to have an adult conversation," offered her best friend. "Although I don't know if I'm up to that."

"Love to, but need a rain check. I'm surprising Thomas and will have lunch here at the university. Then I'm driving to the Chumash reservation near Solvang."

"Oh, another mystery. I demand that you come over soon so I can hear all about your adventures."

"It's an adventure, of drastic sorts, that I'm calling about. Has Lillian heard from Gerta?"

In the background, Beatrix could hear the little girl singing "Happy Birthday" at the top of her lungs and one of the twins was crying. "Excuse me. Gracie, use your indoor voice, please. The girl's going to be a Marine drill sergeant. Gerta? No. I haven't seen the lady since Sunday dinner, and Mama usually keeps me up to date about anything happening at the hospital. She did mention that Gerta missed her shift the last few days, but a nasty cold has been going around."

Beatrix gave her friend the abbreviated version of her visit to the tailor shop and Gerta's brother being suspicious when asked about his sister. Then told Jo about the death of the rabbi.

"They can't be connected. This doesn't make sense, Beatrix. Do you think something horrible has also happened to Gerta, or that she could be involved?"

"When you do have a bit of quiet time, if you do, Jo, could you call Lillian and see if Gerta showed up today? I'm worried about her, especially after the incident across the street from where she and Otto live."

"Absolutely, as soon as everyone goes down for a nap, I'll call Mama. Her hospital shift ended at one today."

"It's been a crazy, busy morning. I visited Dr. Noah Schmitt, whom Gerta inferred might have Nazi connections. He did."

Silence. Then Jo said, "Oh, no. Beatrix, I do not like this. You're frightening me. A Nazi here in the city? Gerta was right? Oh, that poor lady. What are we going to do? Is this a police or FBI matter?"

"Please don't worry, it's horrible, but not in the way we both were thinking, Jo. He was honest and kind. I liked him. He told me the whole story. He'd been forced to join the Reich's medical staff."

"Forced?"

"The option not to agree to their ungodly conscription was to watch as the Gestapo murdered his wife and young son. I'll share the details when we meet up. He's living with his son, daughter-in-law, and grandson, about a block from the mission. I'll tell you more when we meet. Want to come for dinner?"

Jo laughed. "I know you're inviting the entire, wild Conrad bunch. We'd love it. I'm baking French bread. I'll bring two loaves?"

"Lovely. It'll be shrimp étouffée."

"Shrimp étouffée? Honey, I'm a California girl now. Is that a scald-my-tongue recipe from New Orleans? I'm a lightweight when it comes to spicy foods."

"Not hot and yes, it's a classic Louisiana stew made with shrimp, the Holy Trinity of onion, celery, and green pepper, and a simple roux to thicken it up. I serve it over rice for a true Cajun meal, but Thomas thinks that is sacrilege and puts the rice on the side. Men. Now, my friend, just to throw a bit of wonder into your day, Elsa, part of your WCTU team, is the doctor's daughter-in-law."

"What?" She laughed. "Sometimes I think the world is the size of Sammy's favorite basketball. Sweet and funny Hans is Sam's bestie in school and out. I didn't know, didn't connect the name."

"Off to find Thomas, Jo. Dinner at six? Will you see if your mom might want to come too? When I make shrimp étouffée I make enough for a small European nation."

"Phew, that's good because after working on the railroad tracks all day, my husband eats like he *is* a small European nation."

She'd visited the campus countless times, but never once had seen Thomas in front of his students in his role as a professor. She had always wanted to, especially since he talked enthusiastically about the give and take, the theater of teaching. He loved research, Beatrix knew and felt this was where he needed to be; however, he'd share the wittiest anecdotes about his students and the occasional teaching assistant. He didn't ask for a regular assistant in order to take over the lecture duties because he said, "Being in a lab all day makes me long for youthful energy."

"Since you're ancient, darling, this is a riot."

"Okay, I like being the center of attention for two hours a week."

That day, she quietly opened the door to the theater-style room and made sure that her entrance was as soundless as possible. In the center was Thomas, leaning against a lectern, looking movie star handsome, she thought, although her husband would never believe that. Once more, for the millionth time, she reflected on when they first met and how dark and dangerous her life had been when she pretended to be a seer, a psychic to the rich and well-heeled of New Orleans. Because of her connection as a clairvoyant to the then First Lady of the United States and since New Orleans, a mega transportation hub, was fearful of Nazi invasion up the Mississippi, she'd been hired to flush out homegrown terrorists in the Crescent City.

Thomas, admittedly addicted to Hollywood spy and gangster movies, unwittingly and on a lark, agreed to leave Cambridge and war-torn England to transport a supposedly vital, but honestly useless, treaty into New Orleans. At that time, Beatrix was making money to help support the French Resistance and in order to locate her birth mother. In a moment that changed their destinies, their paths crossed. Thomas believed at one time he was mesmerized, thinking Beatrix was a *wu,* a Chinese witch, who had power over him. Through dangerous situations they realized their attraction could last a lifetime and it was only the final three years of the war that had kept them apart, as he had to return to England.

She'd expected the classroom to smell stuffy, but all the windows were open and the ocean, a half mile away, provided the salty breeze as it fought with the one coming from the desert. The blackboard was covered with countless equations, all scribbles to Beatrix. She took a seat and marveled at his interactions with the young people, answering questions and asking them, too. His style was engaging, and the students laughed at his corny dad jokes that he somehow turned into part of the curriculum. He had just finished addressing a comment from one of students, when he looked up and saw his wife. A smile stretched on his face. "Well, blimey. Who have we got here in our midst?" He blew her a kiss and every head turned. Mouths opened. The room was shockingly stunned. Then a riot of whispers broke out.

So much for sneaking in unobserved. Now the famous scientist and professor was gone and her playful and fetching husband winked. "Ladies and gentlemen, please welcome my wife, Dr. Beatrix Patterson," he said.

All eyes turned to him and then flipped back to Beatrix. "Good day, everyone," she said. How like Thomas to introduce her to his students.

"I must warn you, ladies and gentlemen. My wife is gifted with an incredible memory. Do not tell her anything about how I'm ruining your lives by making you write paper after paper on the possibilities of clean energy as she'd grill me about what you've said for months on end." He clapped, "Righty oh, that's enough learning for the day. Please review chapter 12 in your textbook and be ready for an examination on Friday. Cheers and thank you."

The students stood and clapped. What university professor gets applause, except her husband?

A handful of eager men and women gathered around him and one by one he answered their questions or gave them information. Beatrix remained in the background, once more marveling at his patience. What a good father he'd be and then she reflected on Dr. Schmitt's daughter-in-law, and the love she'd shown patting the baby that would soon add to their family. *This is not the time to dwell on babies,* she scolded herself, shoving the thought aside. She stood taller and walked down the steps toward the front of the room as Thomas stuffed notebooks into a black, scruffy leather satchel.

"Bea," he said and kissed her cheek. "You've come to buy me lunch? Let's see, it's Wednesday, and that means there's macaroni cheese on the menu. Wait, Americans called it mac and cheese, right? You do know that American English is not an easy language, too much slang for a Brit like me to grasp. Back to lunch, there's always salad, fruit, cakes, and horrible pots of tea."

"Sounds delish."

"Wait. I must warn you. You'll also see heaps of mystery meat covered is a thick, congealed brown sauce that could be used to repave the faculty parking lot." He looked to make sure they were alone. They were, and he kissed her soundly.

"Yum. Now that was worth the drive up here," she laughed and held tight to the lapels of his white lab coat. "Any chance we could sit outside for a bit, much has happened and it's not quite twelve." He replaced the lab coat with his suit jacket and folded the coat into his satchel as well.

She took his hand and they walked outside. They found a bench under a small California oak that provided some shade and Beatrix told him of her morning. The demise of Rabbi Krause, meeting Detective Rodriguez, wondering if it were true that the rabbi had been frightened to death. If voodoo could have been the cause? "I haven't telephoned John yet with the news of the rabbi's passing and the conversation with Otto Rosenbaum. Knowing John, he probably already has heard since he's been attending the synagogue."

Then she told him about visiting Dr. Schmitt on behalf of Gerta Rosenbaum to ascertain whether the elderly man could be a war criminal hiding out in Santa Barbara. She skipped the part of the lovely daughter-in-law's glowing pregnancy. Once again as she inwardly vowed not to allow it, the niggling, uninvited thought surfaced. She squished it back out of her mind.

"I liked him, Thomas, liked Noah Schmitt. I didn't ask what the Nazi government demanded that he do, or whom he treated during the war, but I do get the sense he'd be above board with me. He told me how he was forced to leave his practice for the Third Reich and subsequently sent his late wife and their child away. I cannot imagine having to do that, but the war made heroes out of the least of us and martyrs out of too many. Do you know his son, Walter, who researches in the medical labs and teaches here on campus?"

"Clever of you to ask. There he is, reading and walking as usual. I'm always amazed that he doesn't collide with a tree or students," Thomas nodded to a tall, trim man with a mop of curly jet-black hair. He balanced a book while juggling a bulging briefcase. "He must have some kind of sixth sense or radar to avoid collisions."

Walter glanced up just in time to jog a step away, avoiding a trash can. Then saw Thomas and Beatrix and abruptly stopped. "Um, hello. There you are, old man, wondering if I'd find you. Headed for lunch? You'd promised a joyride in that new sports car," he said and stuffed the book he was reading into his jacket pocket. "Oh, I beg your pardon, how rude of me," he stepped back nearly knocking into a student. He was staring at Thomas's hand on Beatrix's thigh. Seeing that apparently for the first time.

Thomas looked at his friend and then followed Walter's eyes to Beatrix's leg. His eyes widened. His face became serious. Beatrix chuckled. She whispered, "He thinks I'm one of your devoted students possibly trying to seduce you."

"You've already done that, repeatedly, thank you very much."

"You could kiss me passionately and spread rumors across the campus, except you introduced me to your students."

Thomas relaxed. "This is so not what you're imagining, Walt." He and Beatrix stood and exchanged glances. He took her hand and gestured. "May I present my wife, Dr. Beatrix Patterson."

Walt blinked rapidly as if processing the information. "Oh, now there's certainly mustard on my face. I clearly took you for a co-ed. Mrs. Patterson? Not Ling? I am habitually confused, just ask my wife, Elsa, and I often forget I can filter questions and comment before they escape my mouth. Please forgive my rude behavior. Elsa once told me, even before we married, that I have the common sense of a doorknob." His face was a rosy pink and he continued to spout apologies until he seemed to run out of them. Then he waved his long, artistic-looking fingers in dismay.

"It's a common mistake, mate. Most people meet me and cannot but wonder why a smart and sassy woman like this would even look twice at me. I question the same thing every day. Now, come on, let's get lunch before all the tasty things are gobbled by the student body."

The three walked to the cafeteria chatting about the weather and the newest buildings on the campus. They managed to avoid the mystery meat with congealed brown sauce, if sauce it was, instead feasting on salad, mac and cheese, and Dutch apple pie for dessert. "New chef behind the scenes?" Beatrix asked. "No wonder you no longer pack a lunch, darling, this was excellent except that the idea of consuming that horrible gravy thing."

Walt nodded. "I may take some of that sauce back to my lab and see if it could fight cancer cells. It certainly looks dangerous enough."

Beatrix finished her tea, which contrary to Thomas's opinion was not bad, simply too weak for his British sensibilities. She folded her hands on her lap and as the conversation between scientists slowed, she asked, "Walter, your father seems to be adjusting to America. Is that true?" She'd previously explained how that very morning she visited his home to inquire after his health and surgery and possibly to interview him for a human interest feature she'd write for the newspaper.

"Dad is amazing. He's been through hell at the hands of the Nazis, risking his life time and again to somehow smuggle people out of homes where Good Samaritans had hidden them. He managed to send Mother and me away before the terrors touched us. It's tragic, and he never got to be with her as she died, in Boston, in the early years of the war. I do not know the details of what he did. He won't say. He continues to tell people that he was just a country doctor and yet, I sometimes hear him crying in the middle of the night."

"Walt, as Thomas may have mentioned, I'm a psychologist and have a few patients who are trying to come to terms with their war experiences. There's much to be done to help with this ailment, often called shell shock, soldier's heart, combat fatigue or war neurosis. It has roots stretching back centuries and was widely known during ancient times. Talk therapy can help."

"I've tried to chat with him, but he changes the subject or leaves the room. As you can attest, I'm not insightful about situations other than medicine and I'm often unable to translate facial clues or body language into what someone is trying to tell me."

"Would you like me to visit Dr. Schmitt again and offer, as a professional, to talk about my experiences with those suffering horribly with combat fatigue? It never goes away, but there have been breakthroughs with therapy."

"How kind of you, Beatrix. I will talk with Elsa. She's far more attuned to what is happening with my father." He turned to Thomas. "You did say your wife was a peach, old boy. Now I must agree." He tried to smile, but it disappeared. "If Elsa agrees, and I believe she will, we'll discuss it with him this night, perhaps after his evening cocktail and before he and Hans, my child, begin their daily ritual and ruthless checkers games.

Walter cocked his head. He said, "Something did happen in Germany in the 1930s to Dad. It was about then that Mother and I left the country. It was horrible. I remember his clutching me to his ample belly and telling me something like, 'We will always want you, son.' But we were leaving Germany, so why would I need protection? It felt as if someone or something might snatch me away. I was their child and always a bit confused about how people acted and then said things that didn't jive.

"Ah, just one of the mysteries with my father. I am thankful that Dad agreed to leave Germany after the Reich crumbled to become part of our little family. Didn't know how he'd adapt to the California lifestyle, but Hans has been the catalyst. They can't seem to get enough of being together and that makes Elsa and me so happy."

"Thomas, I'm going to have to run. I have that appointment shortly, the one we talked about with Gordon?"

Walter nodded. "It's been good to meet you and thank you, Beatrix, for your offer. May I telephone you and if Dad agrees, we can set up a meeting time?"

"Please, Walter. I'm seeing patients in our home so it's comfortable and he won't feel like he's in a clinical surrounding."

Thomas kissed Beatrix's cheek and said, "Be careful on your next stop, darling. As your former bodyguard, I'm extremely ill at ease sending you off to a reservation filled with people who just might know how to produce evil spells."

"Thomas, this is 1947, and Indigenous Americans do not practice voodoo or cast evil curses. I'm just wondering if I'll remember any of the people I met there when I was a child, visiting with Mother."

"My money's on that," he replied as they stood in the faculty parking lot ready for a joy ride in Thomas's new sports car. "Mind if we leave you here?"

"Off you go. Oh, one more thing. Will an appointment for Monday at noon for you to visit Otto Rosenbaum, the tailor, and get measured for some new suits work for you?" she said.

"Monday? Yes, I'm in the lab all day. Wait? Am I that out of fashion?" he asked getting into the MGB.

"Yes, most definitely you are. I want you to look dapper whenever we travel to France, and to spend time with your parents and family in London."

Thomas clicked off the ignition. "France? September? Are we braving the lion's den of the de Gaulle family? I have a black belt in Jujitsu in case my father-in-law, the general and president of the country, doesn't take kindly to me or to you. Even though he'll tower over me, fear not, my dear, I am courageous."

"You are the silliest husband around. I love you and he will, too. His adult children? You may have to teach me a few moves to protect myself when we knock on their front door and we come face to face." She tried to keep her voice light and make the future meeting with her half siblings an adventure, yet in her heart she wondered how they'd all take to their father, the premiere guardian of France's future, and his 32-year-old illegitimate daughter.

She got into the station wagon and watched as the two careful and studious scientists careened out of the parking lot, laughing like schoolboys. Beatrix checked her watch and drove toward the Santa Ynez Chumash Reservation.

CHAPTER 9

TRAFFIC CHUGGED ALONG ON HIGHWAY 101 as Beatrix headed north to the reservation.

She never tired of the scenery, with the breezes kicking up waves that looked like silver confetti on the Pacific. The gusty Santa Ana had calmed somewhat, and Beatrix sighed, knowing that meant the danger of a wildfire had lessened. However, the winds were unpredictable and could flare up at any time. She watched in horror as a truck driver flicked a smoldering cigarette out of the window. "That's all it'll take," she said out loud. "A spark and the chaparral will be toast. As will neighboring towns."

The flatbed truck pulled onto a dirt road toward fields of lima beans and Beatrix fought the urge to follow the reckless driver, to give him an earful. Yet, she was on a quest and a scolding from a strange woman would probably not have been accepted by the farmer.

She replayed in her mind what she had learned over her life concerning the history of the indigenous people.

Beatrix recalled how the children had been forcibly taken from their homes to the Indian schools, often beaten for speaking their native tongues. Poverty gripped the trive, and any of the Chumash who remained physically able were forced into manual, menial work on the farms and ranches. *Not a lot has changed, and it is shameful,* Beatrix thought, *how poverty plagues this once-proud nation.*

Beatrix drove down the dusty road and through the open gates. She pulled the bulky station wagon to a level area shaded by a massive and spindly eucalyptus tree, then changed her mind knowing how brittle the trees could be and parked in the open. She didn't need to end her meeting only to find a huge limb atop her car. She grabbed her purse and headed for the first wooden dwelling. There were no signs indicating a tribal office or even where she might get information.

"*Haku*?" she called out, having learned the Chumash word for hello as a child. Nothing stirred except the Santa Ana wind, stronger here in the north of the county. "*Haku*?"

A creaky door from a wood structure opened and six tall, muscular Chumash people walked toward Beatrix. "*Haku*, Madam Patterson." Gordon Blackfoot came closer, smiling, greeting her with a warm handshake. Today he was dressed in a white t-shirt and jeans, and his pointed-toe boots were dusty from honest work. The others were dressed similarly, and each introduced themselves. Slowly leaving the porch was a woman the size of a dime and not much taller. She was wearing black slacks and a long pale blue denim shirt with geometric embroidery up and down the sleeves. Her shockingly white hair was in two long braids.

Recognizing the woman, Beatrix pushed tears from her eyes and off her cheeks, rushing forward, kneeling, taking the lady's her hands and kissing them. "Oh, Grandmother," she gulped back emotions that overtook her. "I never hoped, never thought we'd meet again."

"I am ancient. You remember me, but I do not recall you," she said, still allowing Beatrix to grasp her withered and wrinkled hands.

"Forgive me, Grandmother." She tried to release the lady's hands, but at once the grandmother clung to her fingers. "I knew you at once when you walked from the meeting house. I'm Bea. Little Bea. You'd teased me about my name and made buzzing noises. On days when I visited with my mother and needed reassurance, you cradled me. When I skinned my knees or tumbled from trees, as would always happen, you patched me up. My mother was Jennie Patterson and I remember how she stood up to government officials, on one of our countless visits here, when the men were going to take your children, your babies, to the terrible Indian schools. You said for me not to be afraid. You told me, 'Your mama is a powerful medicine *shamanka*.' I believed you, and she was. Those men left the reservation."

The elderly woman eyes opened wide, and a smile transformed her. Her face was filled with deep wrinkles and deeper compassion. Her calloused fingers smoothed over Beatrix's soft cheek. She dried the tears with the sleeve of her shirt. "Look at you." She then laughed and her face was now rewritten with joy. "No more skinned knees, I would imagine." And she made a silly buzzing sound, just the same as she had twenty-five or more years before.

"No, not recently. Oh, Grandmother, it has been so long, much has happened. May I hug you?"

The group was still, observing the matriarch and the visitor. "Now," Grandmother said, "We must hear why you have come for a visit. Stand tall, little Bea. Gordon is my grandson and our shaman. He told me we were to be blessed with a kind visitor today. Gordon," she called to him, "Please take Miss Bea to the meeting room. Is there coffee?"

"Yes, Grandmother. You will join us?" The others nodded, already aware of why Beatrix had scheduled a trip to the Santa Ynez reservation.

"In time, child, in time." She allowed Beatrix to hold her hand as she got down the stairs from the porch. "Bea, as it is my custom, I do not say goodbye. Instead like your writer and my good friend John Steinbeck once told me, 'Farewell.' He said that farewell has a sweet sound of reluctance. Goodbye is short and final, a word with teeth sharp to bite through the string that ties past to the future. I promise to see you before you leave."

The wind rustled the eucalyptus leaves, the smell of sage and sunshine permeated the air, and the cloudless sky was the color of the azure ocean. Beatrix remembered the love this gentle woman had freely offered when she could have turned her back on a light-skinned mixed-race child.

Gordon motioned toward a rough-built home. "Come inside, Beatrix. The wind is kicking dirt everywhere."

The group, along with Beatrix, sat at a well-worn table, Chumash art hung on the walls, and everything felt orderly, scrubbed. "What news do you have from Rabbi Krause? He didn't want to come with you today? I'm sure he's far too busy to help at a moment's notice, and we appreciate how he's begun to investigate the robbery of our ceremonial caves, the religious objects that have disappeared, and how the California government ignores our pleads for investigation by the Bureau of Indian Affairs."

"It's always been this way," snarled a man twice the size of Gordon. He squinted and the corners of his mouth turned down.

"Heathens don't count for nothing," another spat the words. "The authorities always have considered us second-class citizens."

"Listen, brothers and sisters. We are here to talk with Mrs. Patterson. She's known to Grandmother and supported our nation since she first came here as a child with her mother, the late Jennie Patterson."

Eyes shifted away from Beatrix and as if reliving memories, the group nodded. Quiet was reinstated, heads nodded, and Gordon continued, "Now please give me any information you've come to share or ask us anything. Nothing is to be withheld from you, my friend."

Beatrix squared her shoulders. Rabbi Krause had been their only hope with any legal proceedings to regain their lost treasures, and she had to tell them he'd died earlier that day. After she explained his death, there was shock and disappointment clouding their faces. Hopelessness settled on the group's shoulders.

Then from the doorway, the grandmother spoke. "This is a blessing, my daughters and sons. Look who God has sent to us in place of the boastful man." She smiled at Beatrix. "You are here to help, is that right, little Bea?" she said, ending with a buzz.

"Yes, Grandmother." Beatrix turned back to the men circling the table. "I want to help, in memory of my mother, and more so, because it is the right thing to do. Do you have a list of objects that have disappeared? Have you seen anyone in the caves who is not authorized? May I have a list of all your names and the people who live here on the reservation?"

Gordon pushed back his chair, his rugged face clouded with worry. "Do you think someone from our own tribe might be stealing our valuables?"

"I don't know what to think yet," she responded. "I do know that there is a great market and lots of money to be made in selling Indigenous religious objects and even human remains to universities and museums, including the British Museum in London."

"Why?" one of the men barked. "This is wrong."

"The people who steal or even buy the objects at a ridiculously low price know that organizations falsely believe and tell themselves the original owners, such as your tribe, do not know how to care for the treasures. They insist that groups like the Chumash and other indigenous bands do not have the ability, money, or wisdom to keep the relics safe for the future."

Gordon laughed, but there was no warmth in the sound. "We've kept our inheritance safe since before recorded history. What idiots would think we couldn't do that for another thousand years?" The groups mumbled agreement.

"My condolences on the great losses. You asked for the truth and that's what I am sharing. As for who is stealing from the tribe, I cannot promise I'll find the answers," she gestured to the men, women, and to the grandmother, "But I will do my best."

"Listen to my little Bea, children. She is honest and powerful."

Gordon was on his feet. "Do we all agree to allow Beatrix access to our ceremonial artifacts?"

Heads nodded. "I'll get you the lists. We keep a ledger, but I'll have to write it all out," said one of the brothers.

"Is there anyone here in the tribe or perhaps even a regular visitor who seems to have more money than previously or acts in any odd way?" Beatrix asked. "Do you keep a record of visitors, even delivery people, who come through the gates??"

The group looked at one another as if she were speaking Martian rather than English.

"A log? Of visitors?" asked one of the younger women. "I suppose we should, if nothing else but to keep our elders and children safe."

"Perhaps add some signage as to where visitors need to check in," Beatrix added. "When I arrived, everything was so quiet. I didn't know where to find anyone to help me locate Gordon; no one seemed to notice that I'd entered the reservation until I called out."

Only because Beatrix was an expert at reading micro emotions did she detect the smallest nod between Gordon and Grandmother. The elder was clearly making the decisions although Gordon was second in command as the group looked to him for approval.

He said, "I don't know, Beatrix, if this is somehow connected. As the tribe has been historically mistreated and misinformed, I'm skeptical of any offers from the authorities."

"Rightly so," she responded.

"About six months ago, the California government sent us letters offering to update our entire electrical power grid. It was always patchy out here in the wilds and most of the electrical lines were installed by our tribe. We all keep kerosene lamps in our homes for backup. The agency said they'd just completed a better substation in Solvang. All this was for free. We're a democratic organization, we voted and agreed. There have been workers coming and going for months and it's still not completed. I've written to the electrical company and asked the workers for updates and as typical of dealing with our government, the tribe never gets a straight answer."

"Did the trucks, Gordon, say Pacific Gas and Electric on the sides? Any markings?" Beatrix looked to the group and some nodded yes, while others said, "No."

"The first trucks did, as I remember," Gordon said. "Later, the crews seem hired for the day and arrived in beat-up pick-up trucks, whole groups of them. They looked like they're doing the right things, but I'm not an electrician."

"Another thing, Beatrix. The tribal elders asked me to tell you, we've gotten some hate mail, the usual racial slurs saying that it's time for us to get our backsides out of California. But in a much cruder way."

"Are you wondering if the thefts could be connected to the letters? Have there been any personal threats?"

"Nothing we can't handle."

One of the women spoke up. "About a week ago some of the kids were playing in the field across the highway from our entrance. A group of teenage boys, the kids said, stopped and yelled terrible things at them."

"Do you still have the letters? I might be able to have the police department check for fingerprints," she said. "Do the children remember what the ruffians looked like?"

Gordon replied, "No, we burned the letters with sage to cleanse us. We prayed over the children and asked that the incident be forgotten."

"Okay, well, should that happen again, promise me you'll call me and not burn evidence of hate mail.

"Can one of you, if you're comfortable sharing the location, take me to where the caves are, where the treasures were buried or stored? I cannot help you unless you trust me, but I do understand any hesitancy you may have."

"I'll go with her, Grandmother," Gordon said. He looked down at Beatrix, dressed in smart black trousers and a light-weight pale yellow linen shirt, sleeves rolled to the elbows. Her feet were in ballet flats.

She smiled. "I brought a change of clothes," she responded to the raised eyebrows.

"My home is there," Grandmother pointed to a modest building. "You will have privacy, child."

After grabbing the olive drab, heavy cotton backpack from the car, Beatrix changed into a cotton long-sleeved red plaid shirt, sturdy denim jeans, and tall, tan cowboy boots.

When she walked out of the lodging, Gordon was just filling two canteens with water. "I'm relieved you know how to dress for a hike in the back country, Beatrix," Gordon said, reaching down to tuck his pants' legs into his boots. "Snakes share our land and hide this time of day. However, it wouldn't do to have one crawl into your boot, so you'll want to do the same." She bent and shoved the cuffs of her jeans inside the boots.

Just as the two headed toward a trail head with a glimpse of the Pacific in the distance, a white truck pulled into the compound. There was no insignia on the side. One of the women stood in the middle of the road, her hand held up with the symbol to stop. Apparently, the woman didn't recognize the driver and Beatrix overheard her say, "We now require all visitors to sign our logbook, sir. Park the truck and follow me, if you would. What is your business today?" Beatrix nodded. They'd at once accepted her advice, and she smiled following the medicine man over a narrow twisting trail deep into the chaparral.

The wind whipped Beatrix's shoulder length hair and she tied it back with a red bandana. Then asked Gordon, "Did the shaman or Chumash priests create the paintings in the caves?"

"The elders have always said so, Beatrix. There's no way of knowing why or for what purpose. Like much primitive art, it was probably to record their history or leave a footprint that they'd done something of significance. One theory, which I like, is that our spiritual leaders made these paintings to influence supernatural beings and forces to intervene in human affairs. Rather like praying.

"While the mysterious symbols are, well, mysterious, they are highly valued. I've always regarded them as representing mythic figures, natural phenomena, or abstract concepts. They show graphically who we were, from the beginning, or the beginning of when ancestors wanted to leave us, the future, a message."

"How old are the cave paintings?" She stopped briefly when Gordon loosened the cap on one canteen that had hung from a loop on his leather belt, handed it to her, and then opened the second one. The day was in the high 80s and the gusts there from the coastline were getting fierce, stirring the loose dust, throwing leaves heavenward and making the essential oils in the native sage even more pungent as the scent was caught up in the wind.

"When I attended Santa Barbara Teachers' College as an art major, I heard an expert on the topic. She said that anthropologists estimate that the paintings date to the 1600's and most likely earlier; these look pre-colonial to me." Gordon took another long drink and continued. "The artists didn't confine themselves only to the caves here or the caves on the Channel Islands. There are numerous ones throughout the ancestral territory, high into the mountains, cliffs, or other rock surfaces. Often when hiking in the back country or out on the islands, I've seen small drawings on the rocks, unusual designs I have never seen before. I'm trying to photograph it all, but it's a huge undertaking."

"The pictographs and petroglyphs are common throughout interior California, I know," Beatrix responded and walked on. "What did the Chumash use to paint?"

"The paints used to create the images were made from charcoal or manganese which created the black color, then hematite for red, limonite for the yellow tones, and for white, diatomaceous earth was used. They used serpentine for blue or green."

They came to a small opening, a low cave concealed in a boulder outcrop. Inside it would be inky and cool. Beatrix knew she'd only get inside by crawling. She waited for him to take the lead. "Are you still practicing the ancient arts of cave painting, Gordon? You know so much."

He was quiet standing before the cave, as if he were entering a church, then turned back and said, "This is my heritage and if I don't learn it and share it with the children, it will disappear. The meanings of the human figures, the animal and spiritual entities are now guesswork. They belong to the Chumash, not some rich Anglo in a stuffy museum in Britain."

"You are so right. Those who truly respect your culture would never steal."

Gordon knelt and crawled through the opening first on his hands and knees, then shined a flashlight so Beatrix could see where to crawl in. "Don't try to stand at once. Let your eyes adjust to the darkness. Inside it's about five feet; you'll be able to stand but will have to keep your head low. Our ancestors were shorter than we are, I believe." He rubbed something off the sleeve of his shirt. "I hope you're not terrified of spiders or bats."

It took a minute for her eyes to adapt after the nearly blinding daylight outside. "Terrified? I'm good unless a bat lands on me and then all bets are off. Now, if my husband Thomas were here, just the word spider would have him hightailing it back to be comforted by Grandmother," she sensed she was entering an ancient temple. What rites had been performed there. Gordon would tell her in his own good time.

As her eyes adjusted to the semidarkness, she began seeing the figures and abstracts of animals painted on the walls. "They're magical. And the mandala, like the turtle tattoo on your forearm that I noticed when we first met. Is it still part of the tribe's ceremonies?"

"Yes, it appears more often than not in all of the cave art, and it remains essential to our traditions," Gordon said. He shined the flashlight on the walls, then turned to display more art hidden slightly deeper into the cave.

Beatrix felt the presence of ancestors and longed to understand the how and why of cave art. She said, "I learned about the cosmic significance of the mandala recently, taking a workshop on cross-cultural spiritual studies. In the ancient Sanskrit language of Hinduism and Buddhism, mandala means 'circle.' Traditionally, a mandala is a geometric design or pattern that represents the cosmos or deities in various heavenly worlds. It's about finding peace in the symmetry of the design and of the universe."

"Our traditional life, pre-colonization, was all about balance, living with the creatures and flowing through the seasons. We referred to it then and do know about how nature governs our lives. Most of us are Christians, Beatrix, but still, we follow the early traditions, proud of our heritage and the deeply rooted ways of the long-gone elders."

"I know our world would be better if others adopted this philosophy."

He shined the flashlight into the dark and it too came alive. "This is one of the caves that has been disturbed. As a shaman, I am allowed full access to the caves, but my family of brothers and sisters must be accompanied by me to enter. Primitive and prehistoric baskets once lined the walls. There were bowls and baskets filled with the tribe's early money, shells made into beads. Now they're gone."

"I assumed the site wasn't guarded and you kept watch here after the first items were missed, or had someone do that."

"It was the first thing I did months ago. I spent two weeks hidden in that outcrop of rocks on the hillside. No one came, nothing was taken. I went back to work at Garcia's Bar and that night, two more baskets disappeared."

"Gordon, so someone on the reservation must be involved, otherwise how would they know you weren't here?"

"Yes, in our tribe everyone was told about the desecration of the caves and why I was camping up here. You're right, Beatrix. Honestly, I didn't want to think about that knowing that someone I trusted, trusted with my life as blood related, could be involved in this."

"They may not have wanted to. There are always underlying reasons why people are corrupt or deceitful. Please try not to say anything on this topic until I've done a bit of digging."

He nodded.

"Gordon, you don't have to answer if you don't want, but why are you working as a bartender?" She couldn't see his features in the limited light, but with a teaching degree in art, it seemed like a waste of this talent and education to be serving beer and cocktails.

"Easy answer. No one hires us except to work with the migrants in the fields. That'll change, but for now a Chumash teacher working with Anglo kids is impossible. Some time I'd like to show you my work. Most is based on these traditional drawing with the same color pallet."

"Where do you sell your work?"

"Sell?" he chuckled briefly. "Who wants to buy this stuff?" he motioned to the wall. "Stuff that looks like this."

"Don't be so certain. If your art looks anything like what these masters did before recorded history and what is being stolen, people do want to buy it. You deserve to have your paintings noticed." Beatrix knew just who to talk with about exploring the art and if the shaman needed a patron, John Brockman just might be the right man or have the right connection. Yet, that had to wait.

She reached out, longing to touch the masterpieces but would not have dreamed of putting her fingers to the paintings. Then her mind took over, calculating all that she still had to accomplish. There was a missing hospital worker to find, a rabbi who may or may not have been scared to death, the concern about the incident in New Orleans that John had seen, the mysterious reason behind the Auschwitz tattoo on the rabbi's forearm. Then there was Dr. Schmitt and she wondered, *Could he actually be the kindly old man he portrayed? Is he a Nazi war criminal because he had to follow the Third Reich's orders or die? What determines a war criminal?* She knew her biological father Charles de Gaulle would know the answer, but since all hell broke loose when he admitted her existence, she knew contacting him would be a grave mistake.

Without warning, Beatrix's internal debate of raising children crept into her head. Would she be willing to give up helping to pursue truth and investigate mysteries to be a mother? The choice seemed intolerable. *I'm a psychologist and I cannot even help myself. Some psychologist,* she thought.

Beatrix squared her shoulders and pursed her lips. Then looked to her companion, focusing on the theft of antiquities and not the babble that was clouding her thoughts. *Babies have to wait*, she scolded herself, and that damn biological clock needs to stop pounding in her heart.

"What is or was further into the cave? How much deeper does it go, Gordon?" she asked.

"Our elders say this is the place where the shaman's bodies were left. I hope when my time comes that this ritual will continue. However, Beatrix, the remains I have visited and paid tribute to over the years are gone. They have been stolen as well. The crypt is empty."

CHAPTER 10

The Patterson-Ling house and garden rang with children's voices, laughter, and squeals of delight and Thomas ran around like one of the Conrad's kids. Jo shook her head. "It all started as hide and seek and somehow turned into a game that only the kids and Thomas seem to know the rules of, if there are rules."

"Thomas wants children so badly and I do, too," Beatrix sighed, watching Sammy, now growing like a weed and in first grade, grabbing Thomas's hand and yelling, "You're it."

The women sat in the shade and sipped iced tea, as the day remained warm and dry from the Santa Ana winds. Sam Conrad was reading the newspaper and cradling one of the twins. He always seemed content and smiled at the other twin asleep in the baby carriage. Beatrix told Jo of the events of the day, and how Gordon Blackfoot would need to think hard about who might, among the tribe, be stealing their precious treasures.

"I'll visit with Sarah, the rabbi's widow, in the morning. Then stop and talk with Detective Rodriguez. I don't know when the autopsy was or is scheduled, but she'll have that information."

"Do you think foul play was involved?" Jo asked and then whispered, "You don't think this could be some anti-Semitic perverted cause, do you? A hate crime?"

"There are bizarre truths that seem to be coming out and I cannot say for sure that hate isn't a possibility. As an African

American, Jo, have you experienced prejudice here in Santa Barbara?"

She looked at her children and then the babies, as a softness came over her face. "Yes, I know of it, and the Hispanic population gets the brunt of it as well. I have never felt looked down upon or afraid because of my skin color. Now Mama often whispers another story and has some tales from when she and Dad first came here, in the twenties. The war, the first one, was just over and there was a boatload of repercussions from the Jim Crow laws. You know my parents came from Alabama, right? Dad served in the trenches of that war and thought, foolishly, that when he returned from France, things would be more equal."

"Got worse, didn't it?"

"Sadly. I was adopted just before they drove out, which you must ask Mama about. She's got wild and hilarious stories of my brothers and Dad who joined them in crazy pranks."

"Here? You're okay?"

"Yes, Beatrix, we're okay. There'll always be people who care more about the color of another's skin than what's in their hearts and heads. I'm a simple person and know the only way I can change that is by changing my attitude."

"I must disagree with you, Jo. You are one of the most intelligent women I've ever met." Beatrix nudged her friend's shoulder. "Thanks for always being honest with me and allowing me to ask tough, personal questions."

"You let me do that to you, too."

"Now back to the rabbi? The concentration camp tattoo on his forearm is disturbing and then there's the disappearance of our friend Gerta Rosenbaum. Could she be a victim rather than a missing person? Could someone be targeting members of the synagogue? Or is she hiding because she was involved in the rabbi's death? I need to know more about the Krauses' background." Beatrix had explained previously to Jo about the chance meeting between John Brockman and the rabbi.

"How are you going to do that?"

"The rabbi at the temple in New Orleans spoke with Krause the day John saw him; perhaps he remembers something. John is the person to ask him. I doubt the rabbi would tell me. Add that to my list of things that must be asked."

"There's also Dr. Schmitt. Will you see him again, in your role as a mental health professional? Or possibly to write about him for the newspaper?"

"Not for the paper, unless the editor is interested, and especially if there's even a hint of the doctor having been a war criminal. Now as a therapist, I know you understand, though, he must want it. We can't force people to accept help. Whether he was complicit in war crimes or not, the man is suffering grave mental anguish, from what his son told me. If he can talk it through a bit or perhaps write what is breaking his heart, it might alleviate some of the pain."

"Even if he took part in some of the Nazis' horrible human medical experiments that have come out since the Nuremberg criminal trials?"

Beatrix thought for a moment. "He never mentioned anything about being involved in experiments; you're right, Jo, I'll need to ask."

"I could not do what you do, Beatrix. Can't even imagine how I could pose such a question."

"I start with simple questions and then move to the harder ones. Then I will, like with other clients and the felons I've interviewed at the jail and in court hearings, read facial movements and see if his pupils dilate, which would or could indicate he's lying. Often a tiny bead of sweat will show up, and that's a tell that someone is lying."

Lillian, Jo's mother and one of the finest women Beatrix knew, took a patio chair across from them. She had refused to let Jo or Beatrix clean up after dinner. "You two are whispering like schoolgirls and I want to know what it's about."

Beatrix chuckled. "Oh, we're gossiping about cute boys, lipstick, and favorite movie stars."

"Baloney. I know better than that." She took Beatrix's hand and squeezed it. "Now I know it's none of my business," she began.

"Then, Mama, maybe you'd better not offer your opinion," Jo said, knowing full well her mother wouldn't take that advice.

"Don't listen to my little girl. I'm older and wiser. It's just that as I was washing dishes, I thought about how you and Thomas, Beatrix, will be perfect parents. I can see that. Okay, well colicky babies and teenage angst come with the package, but honey, that's why you've got me. I'm taking over officially for all future babies, and I'll be their grammy."

Beatrix kissed Lillian's hand. "I'd be honored for you to be their grandmother, when we have little ones."

"Have you signed up with the county to get on the foster parents' list? Or started any adoption process? Want me to go to city hall with you?" Lillian took a glass of iced tea from the table, smiled, and waited.

"Would a foster child or an adopted one tell my loud and annoying biological clock to shut up? Yes, it's crossed my mind. I do wonder if Thomas could love a child not of our own making."

"Honey, look at your mister." She pointed a finger across the grassy play area. The kids had Thomas down on his back in the grass and a unique game that seemed to be tickle Uncle Thomas was in the works. "He loves those kids and kids know when grown-ups do or don't."

Sam put the now-sleeping Jackson into the second baby carriage and called out, "Beatrix, your telephone's ringing."

"Thanks, Sam." She hadn't heard it over the giggles and the thoughts of adoption. She put the glass down and dashed into the house and to the front room, which had been a parlor in the original construction. There on an antique table was a large black telephone, and yes, it was ringing.

As the children ran off, Thomas joined his friend and Sam once more attempted to explain the strategies of baseball to Thomas. "They play right at the field on Cota Street, just a good walk from here. We should go. You haven't lived until you've had a hot dog and a beer at a baseball game, Tom." Sam was the only person to call Thomas that nickname, and Thomas liked it, feeling like he'd been accepted, even with his posh accent, as Beatrix teased.

Thomas had stopped listening to his mate when Lillian had said the word "foster." When Beatrix left to answer the telephone, Thomas said, "Sam, hold that thought. I need to talk with Lillian."

"Sure, Tom. There are five more games for the Santa Barbara Dodgers, just minor league, you know, but man, they're fun to watch. And the popcorn? Lordy, that's good, too."

Thomas took the seat that Beatrix had just vacated next to Sam's mother-in-law. In a voice far lower than he'd normally use, he asked, "Are there needs in the city for foster parents, Lillian?"

She patted his knee, "Honey, lots of kids don't have safe homes, and that's criminal in my book. Just look at my Jo over there," she waved to her daughter, who was modestly nursing one of the twins. Thomas could never tell the babies apart, although supposedly the parents were able to, so that was all that really mattered.

"Jo? You're not saying..."

"You bet that's what I'm saying. Got Jo when she was five and before you ask, of course, she knows. Her parents came from Alabama like me and my late hubby. They got swindled, I was told, caught up in a land scheme in Florida. Tried working as crop pickers but a little one out in the fields all day was too much and 'sides they had another baby on the way, which is my daughter Louisa. You remember her? Sure, you do, because your pal Henry and she are still close friends, pen pals, I understand.

"A group from my church was bringing food to the workers. They saw Jo playing on the side of the road. Talked with her parents, and they made the courageous decision to put her in foster care. After five boys, I longed for a baby girl, and just look at what God brought me. Yep, they were both fostered and then my husband and I adopted them months before we moved here to Santa Barbara. By then their parents had left for only

God knows where and the girls accepted us as their mama and pappy."

Thomas looked again at Jo, who had traded one twin for the other and now Sam was rocking the plump and gorgeous little boy who'd just finished nursing. He swallowed hard. "Is it difficult to love someone else's child? I am afraid, Lillian, that I could not do it."

She laughed and heads turned to the two of them, close and whispering. "You chose Beatrix, right? Did it take you awhile to understand her?"

He looked down at his hands and smiled. "Still not sure if I do."

"Okay then, but you love her, right? Silly man, of course, you can love another's child. It's always about learning their quirks, helping them grow, nurturing them through the rough patches. Much like a good marriage."

"Do you think Beatrix would be open to fostering?"

"I'm no mind reader, Thomas, but the way she looks at you and then to Jo and Sam's brood, I'd say you need to do all this talking with your lady, not me." She patted his knee once more and gave him a one-armed hug. "Beatrix and you will be marvelous parents, but you gotta' lighten up a bit."

Thomas thanked his friend and began making a list in his mind of the plusses and minuses of fostering. *Maybe I won't need to go to China to find little ones.* He thought it through and then realized that he'd just that morning bought airfare to Hong Kong, at the price of a king's ransom. He had to continue with the original plan, telling Beatrix he needed to go to San Francisco for a conference. However, he'd fly to Asia, gather the war orphans, and bring them home as an anniversary surprise. It all sounded marvelous. He imagined Beatrix surrounded by children, giggling little ones, all inching in for hugs and kisses. He closed his eyes and pictured how he'd snuggle into that circle and spread his arms, showering everyone with love, respect, joy, and a witty sense of humor that he'd been cultivating with the dad jokes. *Ah, to have the house filled with laughter, the greatest gift ever to my darling Bea.*

He felt a finger tapping on his cheek. "Uncle Thomas, Mama says you need to tell me a story," Gracie dimpled, and Thomas truly doubted that Jo had asked, which tickled him even more. Of all the Conrad kids, for Thomas, she was the most enchanting. "Tell me again about Cinderfellow."

"Cinderella? The story of the girl who became a princess?"

"No, silly. Not that one. Tell the one where Cinderfellow meets the bonnie *wu,"* she stopped and whispered, "tell me again how a *wu* makes magic...and tell me again how Cinderfellow is kinda' afraid of that power and the beautiful lady. You haven't forgotten this story, have you, Uncle Thomas?"

"Is this the one where Cinderfellow goes to a tea party and eats too many sweeties and gets a sick tummy?"

"No, silly," she put a tiny, pudgy hands on his face to cover his mouth. "This is the one where the enchanter-ness, um, enchantress persuades him to do whatever she wants, like the time he was installing a water heater even though he doesn't know a wrench from a bicycle, like you said. Remember the story now? Remember how he gets the water heater to work but only because in secret he calls his best friend, Sam the Magician, and then takes all the credit when they have hot water to do the dishes? Cinderfellow is so clever. Do you know that Sam the Magician has the same name as my daddy?"

Sam looked over at his daughter and raised his bushy eyebrows just as his oldest son, Sammy, snuggled under Thomas's right arm, and he said, "Cinderfellow? He wouldn't be the same guy who might just be my baseball buddy?"

"Absolutely not, my good sir," Thomas replied to the children's father. "Cinderfellow is unstoppable and one day he might even understand America's favorite sport."

"Oh, okay, then not the guy I'm thinking of."

They both laughed and Thomas hugged Sammy and popped them both on his knees as he resumed making up exploits of

Cinderfellow and fell more deeply in love with this friend's little ones.

He knew, at that second, that no matter the make or model, as they said in radio advertisements for automobiles, the children they'd adopt would be theirs, lock, stock, and Cinderfellow.

While this was happening on the patio, Beatrix answered the telephone. It was Detective Stella Rodriquez, from the Santa Barbara Police Department. "Beatrix, thought you'd want to know. Rabbi Krause was, according to the new, capable assistant coroner, who became chief coroner today, Dr. Rayne, there's a possibly he could have been frightened to death, but there have been a few oddities as well."

She blinked. Scared to death? "What? I thought that was only theoretical. That it only happened in B movies from Hollywood with Lon Chaney and Bela Lugosi. Not real life. Sure of this?"

"She is one smart cookie. Still hasn't made a final decision."

"She?"

"Thought you heard. The Head Coroner has officially taken leave. The boozy buffoon slammed his car into a tree last month."

"It wasn't in the paper, Stella. I would have seen it."

She huffed. "The mayor managed to keep it out. Don't know what favors he had to call in, but the city council thought if the reasons came out, all the previous autopsies would have been considered suspicious, their rulings possibly overturned. Attorneys would have a field day and criminals, even the ones caught with the murder weapons in their hands, would be upended. That would have been a catastrophe."

"Alcohol? Yes, I knew he had a problem with it, but thought he was in rehab."

"Naw, that was just for the newspaper. The city's marketing team pulled off a good spin on that one. The truth was, he was so blotto that he didn't even see the sycamore. Too drunk. Mind you, Beatrix, this tree was in his front lawn. Seems the mayor and Chief of Police had enough, or that's the rumor that filtered down the food chain to us detectives and the cops on the beat."

"This must be a good thing. I know when I tried, a few months back, to corner him when investigating those cult killings, he was not to be found except in one tavern or another come two in the afternoon."

"You'll like Dr. Rayne. She dishes no poppycock, six-year Navy veteran just out last month. Spent her time as a doc on the destroyers in the South Pacific, seen a lot worse than our local deaths throw at any of us. Can you come and meet with her in the morning? We could use your help with this. Unofficially. As a consultant?

"Ten tomorrow?"

Early next morning, Beatrix opened the upstairs bedroom window that overlooked the garden, felt moisture on her face, and said, "Ah, finally." The mid-September morning promised to be more tolerable. The hot winds from the desert were over for now. The Channel Islands off the coastline were shrouded in a layer of fog, soon to burn off. Wildfire danger was gone, until the next Santa Ana, and the community released its collective frightened breath.

Kissing Thomas goodbye as he left for the day, Beatrix checked her appointment book, tidied the house a bit, and walked toward the police station by way of the city library. It was too nice a day to drive, she'd decided, enjoying the exercise and the simple pleasure of being back in her childhood hometown. Walking gave her time to review and evaluate Lillian's comment on fostering children. *But with all that's on my plate, slopping over on my shoes and running over on the carpet right now, do I have time for children?* The word "selfish" shouted at her from inside her head. *Why am I being this cautious?* She knew that oftentimes fear masquerades as caution. *Does that mean I'm afraid? Why am I putting other things over my own maternal dreams and needs and the hopes of Thomas? What kind of mother will that make me? What if I'm horrible at it?* From her training as a psychologist, she often noticed even the most astute in the field often couldn't see what was in front of them. That hurt, she realized, because it was true. She didn't want to wrestle this demon at the moment and increased her pace toward the Santa Barbara City Library.

She was on a mission to find medical material about the prospect of being scared to death, and the library didn't disappoint. It still felt like a mausoleum inside, quiet as a mortuary, and she knew that she'd need to whisper her request to a frowning librarian. Then she thought, *Will our children even want to come here if they're scolded for being kids at the library? Again, that's a wrong to right for another day.*

She walked up to the information desk and the librarian, remembering Beatrix and her wealthy and generous parental connection, grudgingly allowed her to peruse the medical reference material that they kept under lock and key. She gathered a few fat books and carried them to a table. Her meeting with the coroner wasn't for an hour and that would give her time to learn as much as she could.

Reading the medical textbooks and reference materials, she knew there had to be newer research. She returned to the reference desk. "Does the library have an index of the American Medical Association's Journal, called JAMA?

The librarian gave it to her and provided the appropriate issue when asked. *Far more up to date,* she thought.

Scanning the material, she would recall it all, and forty-five minutes later as she walked to the police station, she was satisfied that she could share what she'd learned and reviewed in her mind.

As if she were rereading the article, she reviewed it in her mind. When it comes to being scared to death, she'd read, there are basically two ways you can go. If you have an underlying heart condition, or hardened arteries due to high blood pressure, and/or you smoke, then the chances of dying of a sudden shock increase, either from a heart attack or a stroke.

In those cases, the cause of death is a huge surge of adrenaline to the brain, which pushes the body into immediate fight-or-flight mode. The heart beats faster, pupils dilate, and blood flows to muscles, all in a prehistoric attempt to escape danger. However, a sudden influx of adrenaline into the heart can cause a dangerous condition called ventricular fibrillation, where the heart quivers or "fibrillates" rather than beating properly, and blood is not pumped through the body. That's fatal on its own, but it's especially dangerous when combined with another effect of the hormone surge: the release of calcium into the heart.

Calcium rushes into the heart cells, which causes the heart muscle to contract strongly. Basically, in a massive response, the calcium keeps on pouring in, and the heart muscles can't relax. It ultimately leads to a drop in blood pressure, because without blood for the brain, a person loses consciousness. Anyone might be at risk.

"What could frighten the rabbi that much?" she asked out loud, and already knew the answer: The same thing that terrorized him that day John Brockman saw him speed into the synagogue in New Orleans. They must be connected. But how?

Dr. Rayne greeted Beatrix with a firm handshake. She was tall and had the posture of a military officer. She was dressed in a smart, navy blue trouser suit with a sunflower-colored man's style shirt beneath and yet she looked approachable, with a fat gold bangle on her right wrist and an aviator's watch on the left. Gold hoop earrings completed the outfit. Her radiant smile, especially for someone who dove into dead bodies all day, broke any hesitation for Beatrix to work with her. "Detective Rodriguez asked me to let you know she'd like to see you after we meet. I'll tell you whatever you need, answer whatever you ask."

"Glad you're here, here in the city," Beatrix said.

"Grew up in Brooklyn," her accent was thick and warm, "Coming here feels like a vacation location, especially after spending four years in the South Pacific with little or no cultural opportunities. Can't wait to get to the baseball game in town, as I'm a die-hard Brooklyn Dodgers fan. I heard there's live theater at the Santa Barbara Bowl, too.

"I was a surgeon; saw too much in the war. Had enough of that, so retrained and here I am. It's weird, to some, yet I see it as an honor to find out why a person died, so their loved ones know the truth. Sorry, you're not here to learn about my war duty or philosophy. Understand you've got questions about Rabbi Krause?"

They sat at her desk. Beatrix had been in the retired coroner's office before. Then layers of dust even blanketed the skeleton hanging in the corner, dust easily from the previous century. With Dr. Rayne taking over the helm, everything was already tidy, sterile-looking, and organized. It surprised Beatrix that there was a bouquet of yellow roses on the coroner's desk.

"Pretty, or what?" Dr. Rayne smiled and looked toward the flowers. "My husband's on active duty in Pearl Harbor. Guy still remembered my birthday."

"Smart man. They're lovely. Is it possible for me to see your initial observations?"

"If you want. The detective said to give you carte blanche. I trust her and she told me to trust you."

"I realize you have a question on the cause of death, or at least a supposition on one," Beatrix said.

The coroner picked up a manilla folder and opened it, spreading her findings on the tidy desk. "I checked the usual. The rabbi was a smoker. That's never good, no matter what the manipulative and foolish tobacco companies and their ridiculous ads tell us. He'd also been a prisoner in a German death camp, from the look of the tattoo on his forearm. He was obese; studies of others who spent time malnourished such as those held captive by the Nazis often end up that way. I took a blood sample and that's when it got interesting." She pushed back her chair and handed Beatrix the folder. "Look at this."

"He had heroin in his system?"

"I'd say by the needle marks on his arms, he was an addict. For a long time. Surprised the heck out of me. Hey, in New York, okay, that happens. But to a religious man like Krause and in this sleepy little town, I was momentarily puzzled."

"I was told that he had diabetes. Could that be the cause of the needle marks from insulin shots? But you said arm, and I thought that insulin was administered in the thigh?"

"Yes, he did have diabetes, which isn't surprising since he looks like he ate extremely well, his heart was enlarged, and his eyesight was failing. Terrible disease." She ran her finger down the noted results. "Stella, Detective Rodriguez, tells me that there are drug runners in some of the cities just south of here. Heck, everybody who reads between the lines in the gossip columns about movie stars knows that drugs aren't that uncommon. Think he could have had contacts in Hollywood? I'm told heroin is the drug of choice to a few of the stars."

"Oh, what a shame, but he'd been through so much in the war," Beatrix sighed. She pondered, as well, where he could have gotten heroin.

"That's true, however, not only Holocaust survivors resort to substance abuse to survive. Happens with the medical teams coming back from war." She pointed to a number. "The amount determined in his blood wasn't high enough to be an overdose. Not the cause of the death. Contributing factor? I'd stake my peep-toe slingbacks, that I just bought for $20 for my birthday, on that." She rolled her swivel chair around to where Beatrix was sitting to expose the prized patent leather shoes.

"They are delectable." Beatrix tucked her feet under the chair and vowed to stop wearing her old scuffed brown walking shoes and upscale her wardrobe. If a doctor who dealt with dead bodies all day could look glamorous, it was certain a reformed fake psychic and licensed psychologist could do so. "Okay,

Doctor. Could he have been scared enough to have caused his death?"

"Hm, curious, Beatrix, and please call me Gloria." She wrinkled her forehead. "Intriguing theory. Sure, it's possible but, by what? That's to say, he'd already suffered a great deal of trauma which should have weakened his body and a fright might trigger that."

"I think it's some horror from his past. A colleague of mine saw him in another city, terrified of something, quaking with fear."

"I'm not up on the latest on how that could cause death. I did spend some time in Jamacia before the war as a medical missionary. Voodoo was practiced there, you know."

"I, too, have knowledge of the dark arts," Beatrix replied knowing this was not the time to discuss her previous occupation or working with practitioners of clairvoyance when she was in New Orleans.

"If one was told that another person held power over them and the subject was convinced somehow, then yes, being scared to death could conceivably be the result. No way to prove it, no medical test that I know of. I'll leave that to you and the detective. Out of my job description."

"Thanks for the help and the newest wrinkle in this: Drugs. I'll follow it up." Beatrix shook the doctor's hand. "When I was here months back, there was a young man, an assistant? Has he moved on now that you're on board?"

"Ah, yes, bright lad. He works nights right now. On the contrary, he did well to hold it together when the previous coroner, well, wasn't functioning professionally. The department has recommended him for a scholarship at the university, pre-medical school, and a stipend so he can attend school and get a few hours a week here with me. Kid doesn't have the money for school, and with his disability, a childhood farm accident, the military won't take him. Good guy, think he's got what it takes to make in this 'dead end job'." She laughed, "Sorry, coroner humor. The man just needs to be a bit more mature and not read comic books during working hours, especially when staff and visitors might scowl on his choice of literature, even though everything is pretty much dead around here." She laughed at her own, well-worn joke and Beatrix liked her even more.

Beatrix continued to smile as she left the office. One happy ending in a world of miseries, good to hear about that young man and that'll he'd have a future.

Other officers looked up when Beatrix walked into the open-bay bullpen room and Detective Rodriguez raised a hand to motion her over. Beatrix took the chair to the side of her desk. "Did Krause die of a shock, then, Beatrix? Could it have been triggered by the drug in his system?"

"Dr. Rayne says that it's a possibility, although he was an addict. Heroin. But not enough in his system to be an overdose. No heart attack, no stroke, and no unexplainable marks on the body. Marks from daily insulin shots in his thigh. No one touched him, yet he died."

They both were quiet, thinking of the possibilities, but none seemed to fit. Then Beatrix asked, "What of his tattoo, Stella? Is there any way to know how he could have gotten out of that death camp alive and well before the end of the war? There's a witness who says Krause was seen in New Orleans in 1943, which would make it impossible that he was liberated when it was over."

"A witness? Reliable? Quite a coincidence that they should both end up here on the Central Coast in 1947. I do not like coincidences. Do you think that the witness might know more about Krause's death, or even his heroin use?"

Beatrix took her time to speak. Was it just a fluke? Did John Brockman know more than he was saying? He might kill, Beatrix knew, if there were ample motivation, but he didn't speak ill of the rabbi. Yet right then a seed was planted, and it bothered her like a pebble that gets stuck in a shoe. *How can I ask? I've always trusted John. How do I accuse a longtime friend of murder by fright?*

CHAPTER 11

BEATRIX ACCEPTED John Brockman's questionable dealings and hazardous connections with the underbelly in the American south. While John might not be culpable directly to crimes, he had the money and influence to manipulate others to do his bidding.

She rubbed a fist into the palm of her other hand, not at all liking where these dark thoughts were heading. John had saved her life. He had become a close friend to both her and Thomas, and their pal Henry, John's major domo, thoroughly respected him. *Yet, darn it all,* she thought and admitted the truth: Countless in New Orleans and throughout the region had reason to fear the fragile looking but notorious man.

"Beatrix? You've got that faraway look. Anything you want to tell me? You are aware that withholding information from the police is considered a crime, right, my friend? While I'd hate to lock you up, anything you can tell me that might solve this death would be appreciated." The detective was silent after that and waited.

Beatrix shook her head more quickly than necessary and if Stella Rodriguez had Beatrix's insight on micro facial changes, the detective would have known at once that something was not being disclosed.

"Oh, no, not at all. Just a random notion that I'll check out later today. Most likely not even connected to the rabbi's death. If anything comes of it, then we can discuss it." The words came out too quickly and the tone was unconvincing, at least to Beatrix.

A heartbeat later, the detective nodded.

Could John have done this, or hired someone to do it for him? But why? Beatrix needed to talk with Thomas and stopped herself from leaving as she realized the detective was still talking.

"Besides," the detective continued, "Krause has been here in Santa Barbara since 1945, when the previous rabbi retired. The previous rabbi moved to a Jewish settlement in Palestine. You know they're preparing for Israel to become a country, right?"

"I need to meet with Sarah, the rabbi's wife. You've been here in Santa Barbara for a long time. Who else might I talk with that could have been in on the decision to place Krause at the synagogue?"

"There's a fellow who was faithful to the group, a tailor on State Street. But he's recently broken away, according to my sources, and I talked with him after Krause's body was discovered."

Beatrix blinked. "Otto Rosenbaum?"

"You don't read minds, do you?

"No, not at all. I spoke with him yesterday and he didn't seem to be a big fan of the late rabbi. I'll visit as soon as I can."

"I need to solve this quickly, Beatrix, it's making our community of ministers and priests queasy, wondering if other spiritual leaders are going to be targeted. Wondering if there's a greater increase in racism and hate crimes in the county. Don't know where that wild thought came from, but the chief of police wants this done and dusted."

Beatrix nodded. "Now that the autopsy is over, will the rabbi be buried tomorrow, as is the custom? I'm going to visit Mrs. Krause, intrude on the shiva, the period of mourning. Hope she can help, although if drugs and who knows what else are the cause, she won't divulge it in front of those mourners who might be with her."

"Don't say anything about the body being released just yet. Something is niggling me and until this itch is scratched, the family will have to be patient, for now."

Moments later, Beatrix was in the sunlight in front of the police station. Krause's murder, Otto the tailor, and even the sacrilege of the stolen Chumash artifacts would have to wait. Beatrix desperately needed to talk with Thomas.

For two days in a row, Beatrix headed north on Highway 101 toward the university campus. It was once more noon and when she pulled into the parking lot, in a space marked "visitor," Beatrix spied Thomas sitting behind the wheel of the convertible MGB.

Thomas's eyes were closed as she walked the short distance and stood next to the driver's side door. "Oh, Bea. I smelled roses and then realized it was your perfume." He quickly got out of the car and hugged his wife.

"Can we walk and talk, Thomas? Something's come up and I need your input."

They linked arms and set off toward the park on the west side of the campus.

"I want, no need to talk to you, too, Bea. I need to confess."

"That sounds ominous."

"It's..." he began and was going to tell her about heading on China to bring back war orphans, to transport babies and children into their home, to make them a family. Would doing all this in secret, as a grand surprise, destroy their confidence in each other? Would she be angry? Over the moon? Although they'd known each other for six years, he could never quite predict what her reactions would be. A Chinese wife would have submitted to her husband, but Thomas did not want a dishrag for a mate, so he hesitated just long enough that she spoke.

"It's the car, isn't it, Thomas?"

"The car? Oh, my yes, the car." He swallowed back the crazy solution to their childless life.

"You appreciated it, but you don't love it, do you? You're too sweet to tell me so. That's why you were sitting there, am I right? You know I can't read your mind, darling."

"You may as well have been reading my thoughts," he quickly said, thankful that he could figure out a way to tell his wife about his plans for their family, until he conjured up the right words. "Yes, it's the car." Wherever that notion came from, he thanked the heavens. He'd wait until a better moment to tell her.

She stopped him by putting an index finger to his lips. "Let's sell the MGB, you take the Woody and enjoy driving that bulky old tank of a car and I'll stop by the car dealership where I purchased the sporty car, and arrange something, maybe another Woody."

Once again, he started to confess about the forthcoming trip, but before he could say a thing, she kissed him. "Honestly, with the driving you do back and forth to the campus and our narrow roads, I think a station wagon is a better fit for us. I'm forever hauling plants and trees home for the garden; I need room in the car. And you still bring home building supplies. We could buy a pickup truck, I suppose."

"Are we fuddy-duddies for not driving that MGB? You certainly are not. Are you truly okay to sell the car?"

"With the fact that we're going to being having a family soon, two station wagons seems to be the right decision." He wanted to smile but the lie of omission about his forthcoming Asian adventure was tragically front and center in his mind and the confession got stuck in his throat. Again.

She grabbed his forearm. "What's going on, Thomas? Are you pregnant?"

Thomas laughed and regained his confidence. "Pregnant with thoughts of a family, darling. It'll happen. Trust me?"

"With my life. Can we sit for a few minutes before you must get back to the lab?"

"Hey, I'm the boss. Let's take that bench under the shade of the bigger oak."

Beatrix put her head on Thomas's shoulder for a moment, then took a deep breath and told him about how Krause died, the heroin, and her atrocious and unfounded suspicion that John Brockman with his unscrupulous past may not have told them the truth about his connection with the rabbi. "John has been such a stable and good friend, how can I even approach this, Thomas?"

"Well, you could do what I try, putting my head in the sand until everything blows over," which was exactly what he was trying to do about the upcoming adoption plan.

"I cannot believe that; no head in the sand for you. I've seen you go off on a wild goose chase, careering with one wild thought after another." She remembered when he'd been drugged by a cult leader and in a psychotic trance decided he had to return to his lab in Cambridge to find the meaning of life, or something of that sort.

"What would you tell me to do if there was a heavy burden on my heart?"

"You know, Thomas, what I'd say. Spit it out. Rip off the bandage, just spill the truth."

"Okay, then you see, darling..."

"You're right," she interrupted. She kissed him, jumped up and said, "I'll head to John's right now. I'll talk with him. If he had anything to do with Krause's death, he'll tell me. You are a genius. Oh, and give me your keys, so I can sell that car and get a sensible one for our forthcoming family." She put out her hand and he fished the keys from his pocket.

"Here are the ones for the Woody. See you at dinner, and thanks for the advice."

Thomas watched her climb into the MGB and marveled for about the millionth time how a stunning, smart, and sassy creature like Beatrix Patterson could have ever fallen in love with him, a guy with his mind always filled with mathematics and his common sense the size of a pea.

As the breeze ruffled her hair, Beatrix headed toward Montecito, coming unannounced. "Tomorrow, I'll talk with Sarah Krause and Otto Rosembaum. Right now? I need to know why or if John killed the rabbi. Or hired someone to do it."

Beatrix found John in the shade of a sycamore tree that was grudgingly agreeing it would soon be fall, as its broad green leaves were a touch more yellow than its summer color. He was reading the best-selling novel *Gentlemen's Agreement*, a book Thomas had lent him and one that Beatrix recommended.

How apropos, she thought, recalling how the book tells the story of Philip Green, new staff writer for a national magazine. A gentile, he is assigned by his magazine to tell the story of antisemitism. He decides to do so by telling people that he is Jewish. This ruse causes problems with his fiancée, who is a social-climbing suburbanite and divorcée.

"My friend Beatrix," he called out and stood as she entered the manicured garden. He moved a bookmark to hold his place and made room for her on the bench.

Will I still be a friend after I accuse him of murder? She knew the answer to that.

"John, good day. Apologies for barging in."

"You can see I'm ready for company, although I know why this book is a best seller. Compelling reading. I'm no stranger to antisemitism."

Beatrix sat for a moment and marveled at the view. It was one she'd never tire of even if they lived in Santa Barbara for twenty decades. The islands were gems in the middle of glittering ocean.

"John, may I come straight to the point of my visit?" Her face was grim.

"Always liked that you are forthright, Beatrix. What's troubling you? I didn't become the once-most-famous bookmaker in New Orleans by not being able to read a few faces."

"It's the rabbi, John."

"Terrible shame, but to be candid, I never trusted the man. Twitchy, as I said before."

"Because you saw him seemingly running for his safety that Friday evening in New Orleans in '43?"

"No, I never got to the bottom of that, although it was peculiar. Hoped you'd find the answer, but now we won't know. There's more. Do you have a bit of time? I know you came here to talk about an issue, but let's get Rabbi Krause off the table, so to speak. I'm glad you came."

Beatrix relaxed. The stress of possibly accusing her friend of murder slowly dissipated, the knots in her stomach loosened, and her shoulder muscles returned to their pre-anxiety position.

"Krause liked to trapeze out to the Chumash nation's reservation to feel like a bigwig, like is talked about with the arrogant rabbis in your New Testament, and yes, I'm familiar with the Hebrew and the Christian versions of the Bible, just like you are. Krause liked to show off his religiosity, to be called "teacher," and to have others defer to his judgment, including his meek wife, Sarah. While I don't have a wife or partner, it's certain that I would hope to treat that person with respect. Krause, from what I saw, did not.

"I don't like, I didn't like, how honey dripped from his compliments to our richer members and then he discarded opinions of those less fortunate as if they were hopelessly naïve. I heard, yes, even when I was in New Orleans, that Krause had become the rabbi of the temple here in Santa Barbara. Remember, I do have old friends in this city. Asked around, under the radar, as the younger generation says, and found things that didn't add up."

"Like what?" she leaned in.

"You know he escaped from Stutthof? No one, I've never known, did that. What did he have to deliver to the Nazis for his freedom? That's the big question to me. I broached the subject with him once and he covered it with something about God's grace. Twaddle like that. My right foot. He turned someone in as a possible spy or leader or troublemaker to the guards in the Jewish barracks. That's my guess."

"That followed him to New Orleans? It seems a stretch, John."

"I have contemplated that concept for six years, since the day I was told his name after he nearly knocked me to the floor obviously running for his safety and into the arms of the elderly rabbi. When I settled here months back, I was curious. I was. I felt certain he wouldn't recognize me. He didn't. Took him to lunch. We talked about plans for the community, and he was exceptionally keen on how my money could build a Hebrew school for our children. Talked about my legacy to future generations. He'd found out about my financials before we met, which I'm not grudging as I would do the same.

"The odd thing was that habit of yanking on the left cuff of his long-sleeved shirt, because, as I learned, the tattoo was here. If by the grace of God, he'd escaped the death camp, why not share the story, even a terrible and painful abbreviated version. He bragged about everything else, and escaping the Nazi's punishment would have made him a hero. That is what had me questioning his story."

"The coroner says he just may have died of shock or fright," she waited and knew there was more. John liked to drag out a response. Beatrix was in a hurry; she had a fear in her chest that this would not be the only death surrounding the rabbi. More might have already happened.

"Hm, his past caught up with him." It was a statement of fact. John nodded and raised his eyebrows. "Happens to the worst of us."

"John, the honest reason I'm here today is to talk about Krause. To hear what you're thinking of the incident. Any other connections that the rabbi had, close ones, friends or confidants that could provide insight?"

His eyes widened. "Rumor had it that he was working some business on the side and that's why he refused to be paid for his position at the temple. Even heard he was thinking of giving our current mayor a run for his money come November. I do admire an entrepreneur, yet..."

"Yet?"

John moved the book to the patio table in front of him, straightening the dustjacket. "Yet, there was something in the man that put me off. I thought perhaps it was the theft of the Chumash religious objects and he had something to do with it. Goodness, when I questioned him, in a round-about way, he shrugged it off as only giving legal counsel and talking to the elders. I'd thought he'd done more." John realigned the bookmark in the novel and then said, "He seemed keen on land development, around where the university is springing up and along that unusual strip of beach property south of the city. Also heard he was in a deal to sell one of the Channel Islands. Anacapa, I think. Be a sweet spot for a housing development, and even considered nudging him to let me in on the deal.

"Then I thought of his face when he was running away from something horrible those few minutes our paths crossed in '43. I don't mind working with scallywags, because I've been one and still am, but those who are in mortal danger for something they've done? Don't want to be a part of that, Beatrix. Too old for that kind of risk with my money. That said, he seemed sincere about helping get the tribe representation to stop the theft and sales of their relics."

Beatrix released a breath she didn't know she was holding. John's reputation for being part of crime's underbelly in the South had clouded her common sense.

CHAPTER 12

"JOIN ME FOR A LATE LUNCH, BEATRIX?" he offered and when she agreed, John's chef and manager of the house Yuri did not disappoint. There was an appetizer of salmon souffle over spring greens, Greek shrimp and orzo for the main course, and silvers of papaya and pineapple over pound cake for dessert.

"She spoils you," Beatrix said, marveling at the chef's expertise.

"You'll never hear me complain. Taking your suggestion and hiring Yuri and her husband to work the grounds was one of the best decisions I've made in a long time."

After coffee, Beatrix felt she needed to "waddle" home, as she said when thanking John and Yuri. Once she got to the house on Anapamu, she changed into old denim jeans and one of Thomas's T-shirts, baggy and long. She puttered around the house; however, she couldn't settle. She made the bed, rinsed the coffee pot, watered the pots of shocking red geraniums making the front porch look glamourous. Swept the sidewalk, chatted with a neighbor, also out sweeping the piles of leaves scattered by the hurricane-strength Santa Ana winds. Then vented about the price of gasoline. The neighbor stopped mid-sweep and said, "It's horrid, and up to twenty-one cents a gallon. I never expected it to go that high, and wonder what people will pay, say, fifty years from now. My goodness, probably fifty cents a gallon." They both shook their heads in dismay and returned to their own gardens.

Beatrix strolled down the sidewalk to the entrance to the Santa Barbara Bowl, just two blocks east of the house, turned, and continued to review the conversation with John. She returned to the house and with the final watering can emptied, she looked up and down the street. Quiet as usual, and it was not even four. She left the watering can on the porch and changed into tan gabardine slacks, a western-inspired belt with a large silver buckle, and a trim white silk shirt. She brushed her hair and twisted it into a low ponytail, grabbed her purse, and headed downtown. *I'll figure out how to offload the MGB tomorrow. I've got to find out what happened to Krause in Germany and here in Santa Barbara,* she thought crossing the street in front of the huge colonial-style courthouse and the expansive emerald-colored lawns.

The walk to the synagogue took her five minutes and she asked a clerk sitting in the office where she'd first met Krause for the rabbi's home address, "I want to pay my respects," was her reason. The woman never even blinked and scribbled it on a piece of paper.

The rabbi's home was on Chapala Street, a white stucco bungalow with a neat flowerbed brimming with red roses, purple petunias, and white sweet alyssum around the borders, almost giving the garden a patriotic red, white and blue motif. She had made a quick stop at a chocolate shop and still just ten minutes had passed since she'd left the synagogue. The front door was open, but Beatrix stood on the porch and knocked.

"Welcome." A middle-aged man, dressed in a black suit shiny from wear, produced a warm smile as he pulled the door open wide. The cuffs of his white shirt were slightly tattered, and his shoes were beyond shining in order to improve their condition. He bowed slightly, taking the candy from her hands, as this was a traditional offering for the mourning family. "Please have coffee or tea and sit with us."

"You are kind." She didn't enter. It didn't seem right considering why she'd visited. "My name is Beatrix Patterson and I'm working with the police concerning the rabbi's passing."

He stepped back, then shook his head, his voice low as well. "Terrible business." Then joined her on the porch and quietly closed the front door.

"Were you part of the temple or a friend, sir?"

"I'm a distant friend of Sarah, met in New York, I now live in Hollywood, work for the studios. Not an actor. I drive movie stars around, buy things for them, make their lives easier. Guess I'm an errand boy, but it suits me."

"Could we speak for a moment?"

"Of course," and he followed her to the sidewalk as moaning and crying inside continued as a backdrop to their conversation. The shiva would continue for a week and many, Beatrix imagined, from their flock would come to pay respects.

"Do you know when the rabbi escaped from Stuffhof?"

"It was 1942. *HaShem*, that is what we call God, smiled on his horrible experience and tragic future. *HaShem* changed that. Hiram told me this in strict confidence, seemingly needing to get off his chest that he had help from a close friend, someone he came to know in the camp. The friend was an American of German descent, who had returned to Germany to locate his father, only to be swept up into Hitler's nasty laws."

"He was Jewish?"

"That I do not know. Hiram once mentioned that this friend, oy, I cannot remember his name, was not like us. I do not know if that means he was a gentile or could have been a gypsy or a person of color. You know, Hitler hated Blacks as well as us. I do not know why they were in the camp; the Red Cross seemed too busy to help them. At least that's what Hiram said."

"They?" she asked.

"Oh, yes, he had a young sister with him. She too was captured and sent to the death camp."

"This fellow prisoner, he helped Hiram? Why?"

"Only God knows. Hiram had a good heart and he and the prisoner became close friends, confidants. The unfortunate man had worked out a way for all three to escape. It was because he could get money to bribe the guards. Hiram helped him hide the US dollars. They trusted each other.

"Hiram warned him that it would be lunacy to try to escape, but the man was determined. My details are foggy after that and it was too painful for Hiram to tell me or his Sarah, I believe. We never talked about it again. Somehow that unfortunate man was caught, and Hiram used the plan to disappear from the horrors of the extermination camp. He took the young girl with him, and they fled."

"Why? Why take the girl?"

"Because it was the right thing to do, I believe."

"Where did they end up when they came to the States?"

"New York first, where Hiram had distant family, and eventually where he met Sarah."

"The girl?"

"They lost touch, he told me, when I asked that question. That's a shame, because I think she could have used a friend like Hiram after the execution by the Nazis of her brother."

CHAPTER 13

BEATRIX WATCHED as the man buttoned his suit jacket across his plump middle, even though the day was warm. Telling the story had chilled him.

"Had Sarah and Hiram been long-time friends when they married?"

He looked back into the window with a room of mourners and a smile pulled up the sides of his generous mouth, "It's not a romance story worthy of a novel, madam. Hiram immigrated and settled in New York in '43. We have a large and supportive community of Jews, as you know, in the city, yet he told me how alone he'd felt, a shell of a man after all he'd been through. He'd go to Sabbat service and then return to his tiny apartment so filled with grief he couldn't stop crying at the thought of killing the fellow prisoners in the camp.

"Our Sarah was a teacher in the Bronx, having been a nurse assistant during summer vacation, working at a veteran's hospital during the war. She would have been such a good mama if they'd met at another time, as she wildly loved little ones. I see an unspoken sadness in her life, but only God knows why she didn't marry before Hiram came along. A strong, big-boned gal like her would have been a good helpmate. Hiram once told me that he'd learned how Sarah's father refused to consider a mixed marriage, to someone who wasn't a Jew. The story went that she loved a Lutheran or maybe he was a Catholic, totally disagreeable to her orthodox parents, I was told."

He whispered then, "Sarah was long past the age when a woman would marry, and if not for Hiram, she would still be a spinster. She was already teaching while caring for an elderly friend whom she lived with. Now, let me see, she's middle-aged, over fifty." Then in a less serious tone he said, "Hiram had been married as a young man, lost his wife and baby son in childbirth, I heard through a mutual friend."

"They didn't die in a fire?"

"No, in childbirth. A tragedy. It was about then that Hitler's army started rounding up 'troublemakers' and anyone who dared object, including African Germans and intellectuals, gypsies, midwives, you name it. According to what Hiram told me, he was outspoken and was tossed like garbage into prison. Then the prisons sent Jews to workcamps. Yes, to be exterminated, he was forced there. No trial. No means to prove his innocence in the protests, which mattered little as he was Jewish. Such *troyern,* such sadness, and it still haunts our people."

Beatrix heard crying and wailing from inside the rabbi's home and the cadence of prayer and comfort for Sarah. "Yet, this is still a romance story?"

The man shook his head. "Oh, no, not in the traditional way of boy meets girl. This coupling was more of a convenience, I think, as eventually they met through shared friends. It always made me think, when Sarah told the details, how they were like puzzle pieces. They fit together and were stronger. They suited, she liked to say. Sarah is a good woman, conservative in speech and dress. It is not easy being a rabbi's wife, or so my wife tells me. Oy, now what will happen to her?" He unbuttoned the jacket and shoved a tear off his cheek. "I was told there's no close family left. I cannot imagine how she'll afford to stay here in Santa Barbara with the cost of everything so high." He bowed his head as if in silent prayer.

"I'm trying to piece together more about Hiram, sir. Did Hiram ever speak of traveling before he and Sarah moved here?"

"After he and the girl escaped Poland? He still had money. From whom? I dared not ask. One night, we stayed up late without the wives to listen and he told me how he'd bribed passage for the girl and him on a fishing boat bound for Sweden and slowly got to England before, God only knows how, making it to Canada and then New York."

"I meant when Sarah and Hiram left New York. But this other information might be useful, too."

"Yes, yes, I know they drove here from New York, during the war. I only reconnected with Sarah during the High Holy Days in 1944. I vaguely remember her saying they took their time, visited some of the cities and because it was winter, they took the southern route across the country."

"Thank you for talking with me, especially at this complicated and sad time, sir. I hoped to attend the funeral. I know that's not confirmed yet. After the *shiva* I'd like to return and give Mrs. Krause my condolences. I'll telephone next week." Beatrix's mind latched onto how the couple drove across the states. Her vivid recall brought up a map of the US and could see their car driving down the Atlantic coastline and then through the major cities of the South, including New Orleans. She'd bet her best church hat on that.

Was there any way of proving it? She would call John when she returned to the house and find out if he was still in contact with the rabbi who had spoken to Krause that day. It was just too much of a coincidence. "Thank you, again."

"One moment, please?" The man touched her arm and once more in a whisper said, "Hiram was well thought of in the community. As you work with the police as a consultant, should you find that not to be entirely the case, what will happen?"

"Do you suspect there might be something unseeingly about him?"

"No, oh, never, of course not," he sputtered.

The pupils in his chocolate brown eyes dilated. Yes, he did expect some secrets to be revealed. What?

"If I should discover something questionable, only things pertinent to his death will be released to the authorities. Then it's up to the police to choose what they reveal. As for me, I am not here to judge one's character or mistakes, I am here to pursue truth."

The day stayed in the 70s and would for another month; then October and November would cool a bit. She felt the sun on her shoulders and wished for a moment that she was in the garden yanking weeds rather than hunting down a possible killer.

She headed back to the Rosembaum tailor shop thinking, that was a fruitful and highly curious conversation. Beatrix thought, that friend insisted Hiram was a good man, but if I find something sketchy; does everyone have to know? What gives with that? What does he know? What should I have asked?

Beatrix walked to the door of the shop, twisted the handle, only then noticed there was a CLOSED sign hanging inside the window. *It is barely four, too early for dinner*, she thought. *Perhaps he's just out for a coffee or even the evening newspaper?*

She looked both ways on State Street and at the newsstand. The tailor was not in sight. There was a long alley to the side of the shop, and she imagined there was a delivery door and exit from Rosenbaum's personal quarters. With knuckles ready to knock on that side door, she heard voices.

Yiddish, Beatrix thought. While her German was workable and she'd been able to converse when as a teenager she studied abroad and when visiting a prisoner of war camp at the beginning of the war, she could not decipher what was being said.

During one of her countless courses in languages, she knew that Yiddish was a complex language. Yiddish words often had meanings that were different from similar words in German. Quickly she thought back to a textbook on the topic and the words appeared in her mind as they'd been written on the page. It read:

> The primary language of Ashkenazic Jews, Yiddish, is spoken mostly in Russia, the United States, and several European countries. Yiddish

> is more than 1,000 years old, and it started primarily as an oral language. In contrast, Hebrew is a Semitic language, a subgroup of the Afro-Asiatic languages, languages spoken across the Middle East. Yiddish is a German dialect which integrates many languages, including German, Hebrew, Aramaic, and various Slavic, and Romance languages. Yiddish does use some Hebrew words and is written in the Hebrew alphabet. Yiddish is more closely related to German and Slavic languages than it is to Hebrew.

It didn't matter what was being said as it was the anger in the voices that stopped her. There was a crash as if something hard had fallen or been thrown against a wall. Now she banged her palm against the door. The voices were louder, first a woman's and then a man's. *Rosembaum? Could that also be Gerta's voice?*

Beatrix hammered a fist on the door. "Open up? Do you need help? Let me in," she yelled.

Then there was only silence. She waited for a long, soundless minute that felt as if it stretched into an hour.

Then she dashed around to the front door. The closed sign had been flipped and Otto Rosenbaum was behind the counter organizing slips of paper.

"What happened?" she demanded.

"Madam Patterson, how are you today?" Otto was the same color as his drab gray suit and his forehead was sprinkled with sweat.

No, he's more green than gray, she thought and then said, "I heard yelling. I knocked hard on your side door. Is Gerta back? Is that the woman's voice I heard?"

He stared at her, flattening his lips. She watched his face and knew at once that whatever he said would be a lie. But why?

"Oh, you heard me with a neighbor. Nosey creature. She's horrible and loud and crude, like a fishwife. She lives behind me, always arguing over the back fence about something. Doesn't like my lemon tree's branches encroaching on her yard." He looked down at the receipts, stacked them neatly and slipped the bundle into a desk drawer.

"I heard a crash. What was that?" She held the edge of the waist-high counter. He wasn't a good liar as he swallowed and blinked between fabrications.

"The wind, this awful wind from the desert slammed my patio door."

"Where is Gerta, Mr. Rosenbaum? She didn't show up for her shift at the hospital, I checked. Friends are worried about her, and the argument I just heard makes me concerned, too. Tell me the truth, right now." Her voice was quiet but held the threat that if he did not do so, she'd call the authorities.

He plunked down on the chair by the industrial-sized sewing machine and made a choice to talk. "It is of no use. She is gone again."

"That was you and your sister arguing then?"

"She came to steal more money. Took it straight from the till, threw some clothes into a suitcase, and stormed out. I tried to stop her; she's not in her right mind. Always yelling, hot tempered, out of control. She took my bicycle. Maybe if you're fast you can catch her. She told me she's leaving town, getting away from me. I don't know why," he threw his hands into the air. "You must hurry down the street if you are to catch her." He looked up hopefully, but Beatrix didn't budge.

"Where would she go? If she were to leave, how would she travel out of town?"

Seconds ticked by, and he seemed more confused and not ready to come up with a response. Then he said, "The train to Los Angeles comes through at five. Maybe that is where she'll go. I tried to ask, to calm her, but she threw a lamp at me. You could catch her at the depot. You must leave at once if you are to catch her."

Beatrix was still. "Why does she think she must run away, Otto? From whom or what is she running?" Her voice was quiet, and words came out slowly as if she were talking to a frightened animal or a child who was in danger.

"You don't need to know," he snapped, but the snap lost its sharpness and sounded like defeat.

"Someone needs to know, possibly to get her help."

He sighed as if air had been trapped inside and as it was released, there was a long and ragged stream of breath. "I promised I would not tell, but she's crazed. Dangerous to herself and others." He covered his face with his hands and Beatrix expected him to sob, and although his thin shoulders quivered, there was no noise. "You should run after her, bring her back if you find her." Yet, this time his determination to lie to Beatrix was flimsy.

"I know this is not true. Tell me what really happened in her past to make her like this. Maybe I can help." She slipped through the divider and sat on a stool near Otto. She waited.

"I was not there. I came to America in the early 30s. Gerta, my baby sister, was in medical school and thought she was stronger and bigger than the unspeakable horror that was in the wind because of Nazism. She refused to immigrate when I left, and even with our parents. As a girl, she was opinionated and obstinate. I remember how she ran away. She laughed at danger. She managed to travel, alone and without money, to our aunt's house in Bavaria. I didn't know why she left. I was stupid, I was naïve. Eventually I was told that she was pregnant, it had to be kept a secret. So terrible. Gerta refused to keep the baby because it would get in her way of being a doctor.

"Papa said he was proud of her and her determination even though she was living an immoral life. I lacked that approval. He was displeased with me, leaving Poland to become a simple tailor here in America, telling me so countless times. I do not have fight in me. I care only for a quiet life, which it was until she showed up here." He spread his hands. "Even as a child, Gerta loved to argue. Papa thought she should be a barrister or a politician. She had her heart and mind set to be a doctor and Germany needed good ones. She insisted I was wrong, and the

Nazis would never hurt anyone. They loved Germany as much as she loved Poland. Hitler, she said, would pull the country together, all religions and nationalities, and she became an early supporter of him. Now so shameful."

Beatrix remembered how on September 1, 1939, Germany invaded Poland. To justify the action, Nazi propagandists accused Poland of persecuting ethnic Germans living in Poland. They also falsely claimed that Poland was planning, with its allies Great Britain and France, to encircle and dismember Germany.

Otto blinked back tears and continued, "The Third Reich mandated that Jews could not be physicians or even nurses. Gerta never would be told what she could and could not do; she took her medical training and practiced underground, so to speak. She accepted positions in private hospitals, hiding and denying her Jewish heritage when serving in rich people's homes, and then was forced to become part of an SS plan as a nurse in their quest for perfect light-skinned babies. You've heard of the Lebensborn, the fountain or spring of life, and that program began to populate the world with pure, white children."

Beatrix could see his shoulders slump and understood he was unloading the guilt and truths that had bent his body like a twig in a gale. "Yes," she responded. "I am familiar with this concept, the tragic consequences where racially worthy unmarried women could, in secret, deliver their babies, if fathered by racially pure men. SS men and police officers were 'pure' by their own standards and because of the occupation.

"I know that the homes provided good prenatal care, delivery rooms with competent medical personnel, and good postnatal care. The mothers got a nourishing diet even when Germans, Poles, and most of Europe were starving."

Beatrix remembered completely the article that she'd read in the *New York Times* about how once the baby was a month old, instead of a christening, a naming ceremony was held. A civilian government representative, as well as some SS officers, were present. The mothers dressed in their best clothes, and coffee and cakes were served. The ceremony inducted the baby into the society of the SS. The mother was then able to take the baby home, if she wished, and receive payments for the infant's maintenance, or she could leave the baby with the government caregivers, which happened most of the time. The babies then were put up for adoption, to be arranged by the SS with a childless couple approved by the Nazis.

Beatrix grimaced and said, "I recall how if a child was born with visible deformities, the mother was told that the child was born dead. Such babies were also killed. The death certificates were filled out the day the newborn arrived; I wonder if not before."

"Gerta worked in one of those places, places where they killed the malformed babies or even those they suspected were not perfect." This time he was crying.

"Then hell broke loose, and she was sent to a camp."

He began to feverishly straighten the spools of thread in a basket on the sewing machine and then picked it up and threw it against the wall.

"In September 1939, the Nazis created the concentration camp of Stutthof in a wooded area near the port of Gdańsk, east of the city near the Baltic Sea. This is where Gerta was transported when it was discovered she was a Jew."

Beatrix knew that it had been built as a civil prison camp for political enemies of the Nazi regime in the free city of Gdansk and Western Prussia. Only two weeks after it was set up, over 6,000 members of the Polish intelligentsia, Jews, people of color, the disabled, Jehovah's Witnesses, and other persecuted groups like Mennonites had been interned there. In November, 1941, Stutthof was labelled an SS special camp.

In seconds, as if it was a movie playing ultra-fast through her head, Beatrix thought all this through, along with how these formerly prized little ones, the pure children, were ostracized and shamed just a year after the war.

Otto stared blankly at the wall. "Gerta was there."

"That is indescribably horrible for her. I cannot even imagine her deep fear and feelings of guilt. There's more, isn't there?"

He nodded. "I did not know this until one night Gerta got drunk and told me everything. She became the midwife when babies were born to the Jews in the camp. Gerta's role was to take the babies away from their mothers at once and drown them. She did it, time and again. If a toddler was out of line, they too would be drowned."

He held his throat, struggled to breathe, and said, "Gerta. My baby sister. My papa's pride and joy. Executed babies. She killed hundreds and hundreds of infants." Otto slipped to the floor, unable to control his body, and he trembled. Suddenly his body flinched and was deathly still.

CHAPTER 14

BEATRIX FROZE, not from seeing the withered body crumpled on the threadbare carpet or the words that came from the man. She'd seen the dead before, yet what shocked her was that Otto Rosembaum's eyes were wide open. *Like the rabbi,* she thought. Nothing made sense.

She crouched down to the man and lifted his limp hand. There was a pulse. He wasn't dead, and she realized she'd been holding her breath. "Otto, it's okay. Otto, try to breathe." She slowly rolled him over on his back and found a length of cotton. She stuffed that behind his head as if it were a pillow and pulled a bolt of heavy wool fabric from the shelf for a make-shift blanket. His confession had caused a fear that could be fright or, perhaps in some unfathomable way, it was a relief from the burden he'd been carrying. Either way his body shut down. She looked around for water, not wanting to leave him, but knowing the closest would be in the kitchen.

"Stay right where you are, Otto. It's okay, we'll talk as soon as I get you a glass of water." She patted his arm and pulled back a heavy gray curtain to reveal a door to his living quarters. The kitchen, small and dark, was to the right. It had an icebox and a two-burner stove. The curtain on the window was frilly, compared to the surroundings, all sparse and clean. She grabbed a glass from the open shelves and filled it with water.

Then stopped.

In the sink were two chunky, white earthenware mugs, with remnants of milky coffee, two plates with the evidence of eggs along with a slice of half-eaten toast.

He's lying. Gerta was here. Fishwife, my foot, she thought. Was all the withering and trembling an act?

Without a second thought, Beatrix moved toward the living room. A newspaper was neatly folded on the seat of a brown brocade wingback chair, and a large window faced a tidy garden with a lemon tree ripe with fruit. Purple, rust-colored, and golden chrysanthemums edged a postage-stamp sized lawn and brick patio along with a small, black cast-iron bistro table and two chairs to complete the décor located near the back fence. She walked further into the home.

There were two modest bedrooms. In the first there was a double bed covered with a white chenille bedspread. The second bedroom was slightly smaller with a twin bed, a nightstand, small dresser, and a chair. There was a Torah, the Jewish bible, on the nightstand. A compact bathroom separated the two bedrooms. Returning to the first bedroom, she opened the dark walnut wardrobe, a piece of furniture far too massive for the room, its finials nearly scraping the ceiling. The cabinet was filled with quality men's suits, mostly wool, with the addition of three made of linen, as one might see a gentleman wear on his southern plantation. There was a plaid blazer in colors not known in nature and Beatrix nearly chuckled at Otto's untamed side, if he had one.

The closet floor was aligned with finely polished shoes, not expensive as was Thomas's only indulgence, but sensible and well-made. On the shelf above were three hats, a fedora, a cowboy hat, and a Panama, that would have suited the wearer of the egg-shell colored suit well, and two t-shirts with the Smith's hardware store's dancing hammer and nails. "Otto's room," she said. Then she looked at the clothing again and suddenly the storyline made sense.

Moving to the other bedroom, she'd expected to find Gerta's clothing, perhaps dresses, gardening clothes, or hospital uniforms and aprons she'd wear in her work as a cleaner. This wardrobe was narrower, surprisingly narrow, and it was empty.

"The two had breakfast. The siblings fought. The loud voices I heard told the truth. For whatever reason they argued, she's now disappeared and taken her things with her." She quickly scanned the room for anything indicating that a woman slept here. It was void of personal objects. She picked up the Torah, flipped through it. It was so new the pages stuck together as if it had never been opened. She looked inside the front cover; no name of the owner.

Beatrix stood in the living room for a moment, then snapped up the glass of water, returning to the front of the shop. Otto was sitting up, leaning against a cabinet. His face was ashen, breathing was ragged.

"Now you know. The Nazi hunters can come here and pull me out of my shop, take me to Nuremburg to torture me for information as to where my misguided sister is hiding. They will find out all about me, my secrets as well, and ridicule how I live and what I am."

"Where is she, Otto?"

"I do not know. She left. I told you; I've told you everything." Now anger edged his voice. He took a deep breath. "The Nazi criminal hunters will send me to trial now for abetting a war criminal, I will die in prison. I am innocent of anything to do with war crimes, Miss Patterson. I promise I am." He pushed tears off his face. "I will not go to Germany. I will not be held responsible for what she's done. I will kill myself now." He reached into an open box next to where he was lying that contained a hodgepodge of sewing tools. His hand trembled as he pulled out a long, sharp pair of scissors and pointed the tips toward his heart. The shears glistened in the sunlight. He stretched out his right hand and took aim.

Beatrix was quick and strong, stronger, at least, than a man who'd just fainted. "Not so fast, Otto. No one is going to torture you or pull you from the city. No one will put you on trial." She wrestled the shears from his hand and threw them across the room. "The police might want to talk to you, since Gerta has disappeared."

Then she handed him the water. "No one is going to hurt you or anyone you care about. You've been in the States long enough to know that."

He swallowed half the glassful as if it would stop him from saying what had been on his tongue. However, she already knew, and her first assessment of the home and Otto was completely wrong. There was evidence of a personal relationship; she'd just missed it searching for a sign of Gerta's presence.

"You and your partner's relationship will be safe; your secret is protected with me. I really doubt the majority of free spirits in Santa Barbara, as liberal as the city is with all the cults operating up in Sycamore Canyon and the Mountain Drive group of Bohemians, will seek to out you or make an example of you and your partner. That said, Otto, if Gerta was right in her claim that someone she helped while working in the hospital has an allegiance with the former Third Reich, there may be an inquiry of some sort."

"You know about that?"

"Yes, Otto, and I've already spoken to Dr. Schmitt, and that's one of the reasons I need to talk with Gerta. After meeting the doctor and hearing his history, I think your sister is wrong."

He pulled himself up to a sitting position. "You know my secrets?"

"Yes, Otto, and it doesn't matter to me. What matters is why Gerta disappeared.

With a thunk, the glass he was holding fell to the floor. "She is not the person she pretends to be. She is no sweet, war-ravaged woman. She is hard and angry and vengeful. She talks of revenge and blackmail. I am afraid of her, Miss Patterson."

"I know that. You told me before you passed out. Do you know about karma, Otto?"

He shook his head. "Is it what will happen to people like me?"

"Oh, Otto, unless you've done something horrendous other than sharing your life with a man, then no one is going to assume you're evil. No, Hinduism identifies karma as the relationship between a person's mental or physical action and the consequences following that action. It also signifies the consequences of all the actions of a person in their current and previous lives and the chain of cause and effect in morality. I have studied most of the world's religions and knowing this might help you."

"Karma will make Gerta confess to her sins?"

"Not that easy, but it is a possibility that her acts will catch up to her; both your Torah and my New Testament say much the same. Now, if you're able, one more question." She tried to get more comfortable on the floor, decided that was useless, stood up, then helped the tailor to his feet. He sat with a plunk. The chair quivered but held as he steadied himself next to the sewing machine. She took a place on the stool.

"I know that Gerta had a child when she was a teenager. Tell me what you recall about that? Did she kill that baby, too?"

Otto Rosembaum struggled to mouth words. He started and stammered, clearly shaken, and upset. Beatrix knew with all her being that he was about to lie. *I'll come back tomorrow, I will find the truth*, she swore.

It was time she left the tailor to his own nightmares, and she quietly exited the shop. "Now on to visit Sarah Krause," she said to herself, crossing the main thoroughfare in the city.

At the house, Beatrix stepped back to the sidewalk after knocking.

"Mrs. Krause?" Beatrix said as a woman opened the front door. She'd seen her at various fund-raising events and in a photo on the late rabbi's desk. Her open face and square jaw were unmistakable. The kindly eyes were now puffy with grief.

"Miss Patterson, hello. I followed you after you spoke with my dear friend, but you were faster than I was and realized accosting you on the street to talk might not have been my wisest decision so soon after Hiram's passing. I so need to talk with you in private," she pulled a lace-edge hanky from her shapeless dress pocket. "I'm relieved that you've come here to the house."

"Why don't we go for a walk, Mrs. Krause. Do you need a cup of tea? Come with me, there's a little shop right on Garden Street, and we can sit on the patio."

The woman nodded and reached inside to a hall table, grabbed a black leather serviceable but not attractive purse, stepped outside, turned, and locked the front door. Beatrix linked her arm into Sarah's elbow and the woman obediently followed.

Sarah was tall and strong, her face lined with wrinkles, and her hands were meaty, looking more like those of a laborer than a rabbi's wife. While Beatrix was five-foot-eight, Sarah's proportions made her feel petite. Large as she was, her voice was tiny, and Beatrix leaned closer to hear her quiet comments. They made small talk as they walked the few blocks to the tea shop where Beatrix ordered jasmine tea and they took a place on the patio.

The afternoon was warm, and they settled at a table on the east side of the street where the shadows gave comfort from the heat.

Once the tea arrived and the server disappeared, Sarah looked around as if someone could or should be eavesdropping. "I know you find answers to questions, Miss Patterson. Your reputation in New Orleans followed you here, I'm afraid, and people do talk. I want to hire you to find out what happened to Hiram."

"I'm sorry, Mrs. Krause. I'm not a private detective and right now I'm consulting with the police to do just what you've asked."

"Perhaps I wasn't clear," she said, and her Bronx accent making the next statement more intense and voice louder. "I want you to go to New Orleans and find out why Hiram was there and who he killed."

Beatrix sat back thinking, *Now that is a new wrinkle.* "Killed? Why do you suspect that?" She watched the woman's face change, noting that there was resolve in her request, nothing to indicate lies.

"When we moved from New York City in '43 and Hiram took the position here, we traveled slowly. Took us four weeks to drive to California as the old car was not reliable. Getting to New Orleans, we stayed in the city, and we walked a bit to see the sights, buy a trinket or two. Later, I begged my husband to let us attend Sabbat services there. He refused." She folded and unfolded the paper napkin on her lap. "Hiram was opinionated. Controlling.

"On Friday that week, he disappeared from our hotel, a place full of cockroaches and questionable guests that came and went by the hour, if you can imagine," she made a face, either about the bugs or the other guests. Maybe both.

"Did you ask where he was going?"

"He gave me a song and dance about needing to locate a friend. He'd only been in the States for a year and in New York the whole time. A lie. How could he have a friend in New Orleans? He fooled everyone, looking like a wholesome man of God, but if the truth didn't suit him, he'd make up his own version and speak it with such authority, it was unreasonable to doubt him. I'd seen that happen time and again with people asking about his theology."

Beatrix wanted to ask: *However, then, how did he get the position to lead this congregation if he lied?* That had to wait, she didn't want to have Sarah lose her determination. The woman was infuriated and ready to tell all.

"He returned about eleven that night and sat in silence, wouldn't say what happened and drank all the tiny liquor bottles in the room's small refrigerator. I fear whatever happened had to do with the gun he'd placed on the table in our motel room. A gun? When did a rabbi, a leader of his people at the temple, need a gun?"

"Gun? Didn't you question him? Did he normally carry a gun?"

"Yes, I asked. I certainly did. He told me to be quiet and submissive as the Torah says I must be as his wife. He tried a spiel about how there were bandits in the West, and we needed protection. Did he really think we were driving to the wild west, cowboys, and stagecoaches? Ha.

"Beatrix, this frightened me. I'd never seen a gun except on the hip of the military police when I served, during a summer vacation break, as a nursing assistant at Fort Dix, in Trenton. He scared me, and not for the first time. Did I actually know my husband? Who was this man who could take lives or even threatened to?"

Beatrix wondered, as well, who Hiram Krause really was. "When he returned that night to your hotel, how did he seem?" She sipped the quickly cooling tea and felt her heart break for the woman across from her.

"He wouldn't speak. I pleaded to know what happened, and he said, 'Now it's done.' I never knew what that meant. An hour later he told me to pack up, we had to leave, right then. He was drunk and when that transpired, he said terrible things. We headed out of New Orleans before midnight and he could barely keep the rickety old car on the highway, driving recklessly. The alcohol was in charge, and it's only by grace that we made it to California." She sighed and blotted her eyes with the hanky, not touching the tea. "I don't drive, or I would have grabbed the wheel."

"How was it that Hiram got the position of rabbi here in the city?"

"He'd escaped the death camp in Stutthof, did you know? Yes, he never spoke of the atrocities or that journey. I did not ask. I tried to be a loving, Godly wife. He had a paper, which I think is still in his desk, although it's locked, and I cannot find the key. Yes, I tried to open it. The letter said, I overheard him tell someone, that he had been a rabbi in Gdańsk, in Poland, before the Jews were rounded up like cattle to market. He visited friends and leaders, who were active in our temple in New York, becoming acquaintances of sorts. I think they felt they were helping a hero, someone who needed a chance and of course, Hiram was a rabbi from the Old Country who had escaped. This meant the temple leaders, in New York, were even more puffed up.

"A while back, I remember the day Hiram knocked on my friend's door with a recommendation from a rabbi in Gdańsk. I'd been caring for the elderly lady, living with her, although this was the first time I'd met Hiram. They were friends; I never understood how they met. He showed us a letter written in Yiddish and the lady was impressed. He left the apartment after that and just ten days later, a group of elders from the temple came to me, saying that they'd arranged that I marry Hiram. It was best for me, a single woman. Everything happened fast after that and suddenly we were moving to Santa Barbara.

"I'd resigned myself to being single and yet, when I learned that Hiram asked to marry me, I was honored. A Holocaust survivor, a hero, a man of integrity. Then I slowly realized that Hiram often chose to lie, to better himself, like having bogus credentials as a rabbi, which I've come to realize."

"Do you know of other lies?"

"Oh, Beatrix, may I call you that? I never could tell what was the truth and what was baloney about his past, and feared it was all fabrication. Please do not misunderstand, Hiram never touched me. His words were the abuse. Compared to other wives, I had it easy. There was money for clothes, for food, for a bit of fun, and we entertained a lot. I love to cook and bake, and he even encouraged me to enter my rugelach, little jammy cookies, into the county fair's competition. We laughed and I enjoyed his company, but I could never fully accept the feeling of distrust."

"Was he an attorney in Poland? He told our mutual friend John Brockman that he had been."

"I didn't know that." With both hands she twisted the cloth napkin that was covering her lap. "He told me, laughing when the kitchen sink clogged, that he had worked as a plumber like his own father before becoming a rabbi. He once told a friend, in my presence, that he'd been a scholar and taught at the university. Another time, he said he was working as a stable hand and knew lots about horses. To be honest, I never questioned any of it. It wasn't worth it. I tried, instead, to be a compliant wife and a respectable person so he would be gentle and kind to me."

"Sarah, thank you. This has been hard, I know, and you are generous to speak to me. If Hiram were alive, he could explain all this, but we must gather the bits of information to find out what happened to him. Then we can put his history together, much like stitching a garment or baking a cake. The parts separated mean nothing until one combines them in the right way."

"You are kind to listen to me, Beatrix."

"Do you know that the coroner believes that his death was not natural?"

Sarah straightened the prim white collar on her stiff, dark-brown rayon dress. She smiled and then removed the *tichel*, the headscarf worn by married orthodox Jewish women in compliance with the code of modesty known as *tzeniut*. "Yes, I am a widow now, so I do not need this." She twisted the silk scarf in her hands and tied it into a tight knot. "I assumed that was the case or they'd have released his body for burial immediately as is our custom." She fingered the teacup, took a sip, and replaced it on the table.

Beatrix watched as Sarah put the knotted *tichel* on the table, took out the bobby pins from her bun, and let her lush brown hair fall to her shoulders. The scarf had hidden a large streak of white hair, called poliosis, that made the plain woman far more glamorous.

"Do you think he used the gun in New Orleans?"

"That is why I'm here. That is what I need to know," Sarah replied, covering Beatrix's hand with hers. "It is for my own peace of mind, you realize. I have money to pay you. Hiram, I found out today, had more than $100,000 in our savings account. Oy, so much. I cannot imagine how that money came there, but it is mine now. If you agree, can you go to New Orleans and find out what happened there? I know from Mr. Brockman that you lived in that city for years and possibly have contacts in, what do the hoodlums say in movies, the 'underworld'? I must know the man I married. I cannot and will not continue to live his lies."

CHAPTER 15

"SARAH, COMING TO ME FOR HELP TOOK COURAGE." Beatrix and the rabbi's wife stood on the sidewalk in front of the tea shop, still whispering. Workers were streaming out of the city and county offices across the street, and they took little notice of the women. If they did, they'd have seen two friends in a cozy chat.

Sarah opened her purse and withdrew a packet wrapped in brown paper, tied with a yellow silk ribbon. "I need to get back the house and pretend to be the bereaved, devoted widow; visitors are coming at six. Just promise you'll think about it, Beatrix," she said, handing Beatrix a fat parcel. "There is enough money in here to take an airplane to New Orleans and to cover your expenses and your fees. I have more. I must find out what happened that night, as I believe it will tell me who my husband really was. I know it's a longshot, yet you're the only person I can turn to."

"Do you, by chance, know if the gun is in your home or Hiram's office at the synagogue? Could you find that reference letter for me?"

"I'll try. I saw the letter once when dusting and I'll break the lock on his desk if I must," she hesitated and continued, "I want to see what else he hid in the drawers of his desk. I have not trusted him for a long time. May I telephone you in the morning? Suddenly, I feel drained but gratified that you were willing to listen to me. I could not, would not, go to anyone in our congregation with this information. It's a cultural obstacle in our community, even though we're pretty liberal, but women do not speak ill of their husbands. What if I am wrong, and I pray that I am. Hiram's name would be sullied forever."

"I'll try to find the truth, Sarah. Please just continue as you have, and we'll talk in the morning. I'll have my decision by then."

There was no rush to return home, so Beatrix strolled, recalling the events that had happened in the last few hours. There was a confession from Otto Rosenbaum that his sister played a terrible role in the Nazi's war machine, but was it the whole truth? Then there was Sarah Krause doubting her husband's service as a rabbi and the events of that night in New Orleans that needed a gun to be dealt with. Was she withholding something?

She was halfway up the broad front steps to their house when she glanced up. Thomas was sitting on the front porch of their still unfinished home. "I left early. To surprise you. Do you have patients' appointments this afternoon? Might we walk on the beach?"

"Oh, my goodness, that sounds divine." The day was now gently warm, and she sat on the swing next to Thomas. "My head is swimming and there is so much to talk over with you." She slipped her arm beneath his elbow and leaned into his chest, the comfortable solid form she'd memorized. "Let me change and I'll grab a bottle of wine, too. We can watch the sunset and raise a glass."

Beatrix slipped into a strappy cotton dress with a green background dotted with pink flowers the size of dinner plates. She swapped the ballet flats for sandals, grabbed a white cotton cardigan. In the ten minutes it took, Thomas was in the kitchen, slicing a block of cheddar and pulling crackers out of a box to take along. "A picnic? Why not? We are Californians after all," he laughed and then squinted when he studied his wife's face.

"How about I tell you what happened today when we are sitting on the beach?" she said picking up the olive drab woolen blanket they'd always taken to the beach as Thomas toted the picnic basket.

He bundled everything in the back of the Woody and opened the driver's door for his wife. "I see the MGB is still here. Have you changed your mind about trading it in for something more practical, Bea?"

She twisted the key, and the big Ford V-8 engine came to life. "Not at all, I simply put it lower on my priority list." She patted the steering wheel, as if the car was a devoted golden retriever.

They were both quiet during the short drive to the beach and the walk across the broad expanse of cream-colored sand. Thomas wanted to tell Beatrix about the adoption agency working in conjunction to the Chinese consulate, the correspondence to ensure they'd get healthy little war orphans, and the forthcoming Asian trip. Yet with the clouds on her face, he knew she needed to talk first. That was okay, as he wasn't quite sure how to spring the whole "we're going to be a family" thing on his wife.

Beatrix spread the blanket and sat down, curling her knees beneath her as Thomas poured a glass of white wine from a local vineyard. He pulled out a plate, put the cheese and crackers on it, and waited. He mulled over the news. The last phone call with the agency in San Francisco said the five little ones waiting for him in Hong Kong, were siblings, all orphaned. Ages one through eight. All boys, except the oldest. It would just be a matter of going there, paying the money, which was about six months of his salary, and then he could meet the children. He knew that Beatrix couldn't get away because of her clients and of course the mysteries she'd become entangled with. It was perfect when he contracted with the agency to hire a nurse to accompany him back from China. He could hardly contain the news, but Beatrix didn't seem to notice how he started to say something, stopped and waited, and then tried to start once more. He poured more wine and said, "Ready to tell me about what you're thinking?"

She did, slowly and with a detailed account of the wardrobes in Otto Rosenbaum's closet, with dual sets of men's suits. Then meeting with Sarah Krause and wondering if the rabbi was genuinely a religious leader. It took a full glass of wine before she got to the point where she nearly accused their good friend John of murdering Krause. It came out in spurts, but the spurts fit snuggly together.

"Sarah asked me to fly to New Orleans to find the truth. Her husband is dead; can his reputation matter that much?"

"If it were me, Beatrix, and you had to find the answers, wouldn't you go?"

"I'll be gone four or five days, Thomas. If I go." She nibbled a piece of cheese. "I'll ask John to contact the rabbi at the temple where he had seen Krause that day. I'll ask John, too, if there are others in the city who might have known him."

"Couldn't you just telephone these people, Bea? I know it's expensive," he said, thinking about the investment with the orphanage agency. "Yet, it would save your energy. What about your clients? Your practice? Can you manage to get away for that long?"

"Yes, I could just telephone. But it's not the same. I cannot read faces over a telephone wire, tell if people are lying or if they're withholding information." She laced her fingers together and placed her chin on her hands. "I'll contact my regular therapy clients and explain I need to switch appointments.

"My mother might even know some gossip about the goings on of the religious community in New Orleans. I feel the need, as well, to spend a bit of time with her." Beatrix thought of her *maman* and smiled, wondering if she could get their future children to use the French variation of mama for her. "She always was good at collecting stories."

"I don't know, Beatrix." Thomas thought of the dangers they'd faced when they first came together to stop Nazi terrorists in the city, and a chill tingled up his arms, although the wind was warm. "What if you're in jeopardy and I'm here, slaving over those Bunsen burners you're always talking about."

"Thomas Ling, are you going to get all protective on me? How did you think I managed before you barged in on me and turned my life upside down?" She finished the wine and held out her glass. "Let's walk in the water. Slip those fancy shoes off, darling, and come with me to get your toes wet," she yanked his hand.

The sun was dipping into the horizon as they dusted the sand off their feet. "Did you want to tell me about your day? I totally usurped the entire conversation." She put the picnic basket in the back of the Woody and got into the driver's seat, still not fond of Thomas's driving, because he absently swerved into the left lane when he should be in the right.

"It'll wait." Because he didn't have any notion of how he was going to tell her. Maybe the longer he waited, the easier it would become. "There's leftover baked chicken and lots of potato salad. Let's eat on the patio under the stars," he said and smiled.

Returning home, Thomas assembled dinner, all the while congratulating himself on how procrastination to share on his travel plan was working. If Beatrix were flying to New Orleans, then he wouldn't have to tell her he was leaving for Asia.

He put ice in glasses and brought out the pitcher of cold tea from the refrigerator. He smiled as he schemed how he'd take Beatrix to the Los Angeles Municipal airport, walk her to the gate, hug and kiss her and wave goodbye as she walked across the tarmac to climb the stairs to the plane.

Immediately he'd get the next flight to San Francisco and go as requested to the adoption agency connected with the Chinese consulate. If all went as planned, he'd be at the service's office by three and could fly to Asia the next day. A night's stay at the hotel was already booked for whenever he needed it. The plan was seamless. Nothing could go wrong. He'd already forwarded the money, if truth be told a small fortune, but what price could he put on a family.

Thomas felt stronger and better about this decision than about nearly anything else in his life, and he had to contain his smile or Bea would know he was hiding something big. *She'll be over the moon when I return with these tender, precious children who will become the Patterson-Ling family,* he thought taking the tea, dinner, and plates to the patio. He rubbed his hands together, thrilled with anticipation on Bea's face when she returned from New Orleans and he had the little ones run out to greet her. "This is going to be brilliant," he whispered out loud.

"I'll be right out. I've got to call Sarah and tell her yes. Then phone Gordon Blackfoot at the tavern, let him know I'll be out of town and where he can find me, at the Windsor Court Hotel, if he needs me, and then call my clients to change their appointments. Just give me five minutes."

Sometime about midnight, Beatrix sat up in bed and Thomas opened his eyes. "I'm going. I need to pursue the truth." She got out of bed, a list of phone calls to make about the trip swirling in her mind.

"I agree," he muttered and thought of children who waited for their new dad.

Six hours later, Beatrix and Thomas drove to the Los Angeles airport. Her flight was at noon, but the drive on the two-lane Highway 101 could take them three hours, and traffic was always unpredictable.

Reaching the airport, Thomas dropped her and a suitcase at the curb so she could check in and pay the fare, which had to be in cash. Besides he didn't want his wife to know that he was leaving the Woody in long-term parking because he wanted to fly to San Francisco as soon as possible.

They made small talk; she shared her simple plan as they sat close on the wooden bench in the waiting room. "I'll settle at the Windsor Court hotel and call you at the university. If you're in class I'll just leave a message with one of your assistants, so no worries about calling me back."

Oh my, he thought. *I'd forgotten that she'd check in once she'd reached her destination. Shoot.* Then he smiled and reminded himself to call the university so that the staff in his department would not tell his wife he was on the way to Asia.

"Then I'll contact the rabbi for an appointment. I'll see if he remembers the incident with Krause or knows anything more about him. Detective Rodriguez gave me some contacts with the New Orleans Police Department should I need help. John promised to call his organization, um, people, well the folks who work in his gambling hall, so I can use his office if need be. He told one of the bouncers to accompany me, if I felt I needed protection."

"I wish you had not told me that part."

"Teasing, Thomas. There's no danger at all. I'll look up contacts I had in the city, talk with *Maman,* and spend some time with her. I shouldn't be gone for more than four days. A week at most. Will you be okay on your own?"

"Beatrix Patterson, I lived for thirty-four years without you, although it was horrifying from morning to night," he squeezed her hand, always shy about a public demonstration of affection. "I can manage this. Besides, I'm about to undertake a gigantic endeavor that will keep me out of trouble for more than a week, perhaps my entire life."

He squeezed his eyes tight pretending they were alone, pulling her to him after her flight was called. "Don't get into any mischief, now, right?" She chuckled, imagining Thomas would spend most of his time in the lab at the university, eating at the cafeteria, and complaining about the quality of the tea.

"If it were not for this task, I'd accompany you and we'd eat at Antoine's, get gumbo at a dive along the waterfront, have a Hurricane drink and take the paddleboat up the Mississippi. Then an evening cocktail at the Old Absinthe in the French Quarter. Give my love to the city and your mother, of course."

Beatrix turned to wave as she climbed the stairs to the Douglas DC-6. She'd brought a coat knowing it would be cool in the cabin during the flight. She'd change planes in Dallas and if that flight was delayed, she could fold her green wool coat and use it as a pillow while she waited. It would be a long day, but the Windsor Court would welcome her. One of the most posh hotels in the country, the staff would treat Beatrix like royalty, so she thought of that as she settled into her tiny airplane seat. Looking out the window, ready to wave to Thomas, she scanned the crowd. He was gone. *That big project has really grabbed him this time,* she thought. *Good, it'll keep him occupied.*

Thomas dashed to the car for his suitcase, hidden under the beach blanket in the back, and then quickly to the ticket counter. "Next plane to San Francisco, please," he asked the clerk.

"You're in luck, sir. There's one leaving in a half hour and it's not entirely full. Do you want a return ticket as well?"

He counted out the fare. "No, as I'm not sure what day I'll be returning." He smiled and sighed, thinking of his future children, and patted the breast pocket of his suit jacket, confirming that his passport was there.

His own flight was bumpy and uncomfortable. He did not like flying but put the fears aside for the mission he was on. An older man sat next to him, gripping the armrests and moaning with every twist or turn the airplane made. When the man reached for the nausea bag, Thomas closed his eyes and wished he could close his ears.

When they landed, Thomas glanced at his companion, watching sweat drip from the man's forehead. "First flight?"

"My daughter's getting married. Tomorrow. She told me this morning. Didn't think I'd live to see her walk down the aisle."

Thomas patted the man's damp back. "You made it, old chum, and still in one piece. I'm going to be meeting my daughter and four sons, soon as well." He puffed out his chest, so proud to be able to say that to a stranger.

He replayed his plan as he waited for this suitcase to come into the baggage claim area. He'd take a cab to the Chinese adoption agency on Market Street. He'd been to San Francisco, but still marveled at the number of Asians, Hispanics, whites, and a range of others on the hectic street. The fact that he didn't stand out felt nicely agreeable after growing up in Britain and being a transplant to California.

He located the address on the tiny tablet he always kept in his breast pocket. "1455 Market. Here it is," he said to the cab driver; he got out and looked up at the eight-story building. His heart raced. He'd talk with the manager of the adoption agency and verify how to find the orphanage, then get the details on the nurse who could accompany Thomas and the little ones home. He'd decided on five so each would always have a friend and they were already a family, orphaned when war struck their town, then deserted. Various American religious groups started orphanages, he was informed. He'd been told that the children were thin but healthy and had all the necessary papers. He'd confirmed everything and as he was fluent in Cantonese, he couldn't wait to welcome them into his arms. Nothing would be amiss.

Seeing a store next to the skyscraper, he threw caution to the wind and dashed inside for a gift for Beatrix. That settled, he took the elevator to the eighth floor and walked the quiet, marble hallway to the door marked "Children of Love." He straightened his posture and hoped his hands wouldn't sweat. His heart was racing. "The journey begins. We will be parents. I'll be a father."

He twisted the door handle.

It didn't turn.

He used more effort.

Nothing.

Damn sweaty hands, he thought. He wiped them on his trousers as he assumed the sweat made the handle slip.

He twisted it again and pushed.

It wouldn't budge.

He checked the gold-lettered sign on the glass of the door. It said what he expected. 'Maybe they're out to lunch." He checked his watch. It was 2:30. He looked around; the floor was as quiet as midnight. He walked to the end of the hall, looked at the sign on an office. LAW OFFICE, written in cursive gold script. He knocked and walked in.

A woman in her forties, black hair piled high, and with a Dictaphone's wires clasped on her head, glanced at him. She looked up but finished something on the bulky typewriter before she spoke. "Good afternoon, sir. Do you have an appointment?" She smiled, but that didn't make Thomas feel any better.

"No, not at all. I am looking for information and hope you can help me. It's about the staff at the Chinese adoption agency down the hall? Your neighbor?" His right arm shot out indicating a direction.

The woman frowned.

"Um, the door is locked, but I've been expected. Do they usually close in the middle of the day?" Hope was dwindling, but he was a rational man so there had to be an explanation.

She squinted, slipping on glasses that had been dangling around her neck from a fine silver chain. "That's the company a few doors down? Oh, oh, no. You're not another one of them?" She grabbed a frilly hanky from the pocket of her lacy blouse and cleaned her glasses. And waited.

"Whatever do you mean?" His stomach did a hurdling somersault, fearing already what she'd say next.

"I don't know what to tell you, sir. They were busy with people coming and going just last week, couples going in and out. Mostly white folks, not Asian like us. When I got here to work on Monday, there was a crew carrying desks and lamps and chairs. Seemed to be closing the office. I haven't seen anyone who worked there since."

Thomas teetered. He grabbed the edge of her desk more tightly. "They're gone?"

"You might want to sit down, sir. You don't look so good."

He swayed and held the top of the desk.

"I'll get you water." She didn't wait for a reply but scurried to another room, coming back with a tall glass. "Just rest for a moment." She motioned to the black leather sofa and then sat next to him in an adjoining visitor's chair. "There was a couple in here this morning, asking the same questions, looking for the managers of the agency. The wife broke down, fainted dead away in her husband's arms. I couldn't tell them anything either. I'm so sorry. You might check with the manager of the building for a forwarding address. Are you okay?"

Thomas held his head in his hands. This close to weeping. He gulped the water and swallowed hard. "Bloody hell," he whispered and then apologized to the secretary. "Yes, the manager, he'll know where they've moved to. I'm sure they just didn't inform me of the change of address." He lied to himself; it hadn't been the first time either. He headed down the elevator and then to the manager's office.

The report was nearly the same as that which the secretary gave him. "Nope, Mac, left over the weekend. Bilked me. Gone without paying this month's rent. Told the police. Heard they'd done this same scam for a year, moving when they got enough cash from those fools. Hey, sorry pal, not that you're a fool. Why not go to the police and file a claim, like that other couple said they were going to do when they stormed in here this morning. I got cheated too, lost $300 bucks."

Stunned, Thomas walked out of the office building in a daze. If it had only been $300, he would have straightened his spine, told Beatrix it all, and they have made another plan to adopt war orphans. "Scammed? No…no, this cannot be happening. Those agency people were so sympathetic, compassionate and had the answers to all my questions. Blimey, buck up, man. The Chinese consulate will know where they are." The word fool played again and again in his head, louder and louder. If what the manager and the secretary said was true, he was a loser, inept, and stupid, all the things he felt right at that moment.

"Fool," he repeated as he hailed a cab and headed for the office of the Chinese Consul General's offices on Laguna Street. Traffic snarled and horns blared. Thomas heard nothing except the pounding of his heart as he repeated that one word. "Fool."

As the taxi pulled to the curb, he clutched his suitcase and the file folder with the documentation from the agency. His feet didn't seem to want to leave the safety of the taxi, the taxi where there still could be a crumb of hope that this had just been a complicated misunderstanding.

"Here's your address, sir," the driver grunted twice and then added. "That'll be two bucks."

Thomas got out, handed the driver a five, and stood on the crowded sidewalk. He looked at the large cement dragon statutes guarding each side of the imposing entrance. In his mind, he repeated "bloody hell" and "fool" over and over, tried to take deep breaths, but they were ragged.

A brisk wind nearly pulled off his felt hat. It was so much cooler in San Francisco than Santa Barbara. H shoved open the heavy glass door with the symbol of the imperial household. A scowling uniformed officer of the Chinese army stood at attention, blocking the entrance to the office.

"Hello. I need some information." He used English and bowed slightly.

"Your specific reason to be here? This is not a museum, you know," he asked in perfect Mandarin and then repeated it in English.

"I must see speak to someone who is in charge at once." Thomas took a step toward the hall; doors seemed to be marked and he'd navigate the maze for answers.

The guard stuck out a beefy arm and blocked the entrance. Thomas thought of scooting under the powerful appendage and then decided better. Even if he got past the guard, he didn't know with whom to speak.

In Mandarin, Thomas said. "I had a contract with a Chinese business here in San Francisco for the adoption of children from the mainland, those who'd lost parents in the war. The company has disappeared along with my money and the contact to get my children from Hong Kong."

The guard put down the substantial arm and replied in English. "Yes, you are the second man to come in here today. A white couple came screaming at me earlier. I pretended not to speak English."

"With whom did they speak?"

"They screamed racist insults at me. There was a ruckus, and my lieutenant came out and he told the undersecretary about them. They got an appointment and the undersecretary talked with them here in the lobby, but would not let them enter."

Thomas felt his heart drop to his knees. "Would it be possible for me, kind sir, to speak with that undersecretary?"

"Absolutely. Please take a seat. Are you from mainland China? You do not have an American accent and you are fluent."

Thomas spoke in English. "I was born in London to Chinese parents and educated in many languages and dialects during my studies. My family speaks Mandarin at home. I am a scientist and now reside in Santa Barbara with my wife. My name is Dr. Thomas Ling."

The guard bowed lower. Moments passed as the guard spoke in a whisper into a telephone and a petite woman in a smart blue suit and high heels strode to the lobby, her posture was that of a military presence. Her smile was warm.

"Good afternoon, sir." She spoke English without a hint of any accent, but turned to the guard, and in Mandarin, thanked him. Back to Thomas, she said, "I understand there's been a crime committed, not with us, but between you and the bogus adoption agency. You are not the first. Although that doesn't help. Would you like to follow me, or perhaps we could go to the restaurant next door and have coffee."

"Coffee. I've had a problematic day." He followed her outside. The wind had calmed, and they chose a sidewalk café where late afternoon shadows dotted the pavement and people scurried in every direction. Glancing at his watch, he thought of Beatrix and wondered if she were safely ensconced in the lush Windsor Court Hotel on St. Peter Street. He hoped so and then realized he'd have to tell her about what happened, and once more his stomach constricted as acid twisted and churned inside. He carefully sat at the bistro table. Fatigue wrenched away the adrenaline that had kept him focused for the last six hours. Taking yet another deep breath, he pulled out the files from his attaché case and handed them to the undersecretary.

She said, "Ah," reviewing the official-looking paperwork about the adoption and fingered his receipt for the "fee." She blinked at the figure and blinked again. "That much?"

"I'm afraid so. The other couple you saw this morning, what were they charged?" *Yes, I am a fool, a complete idiot.*

"The husband screamed it was $500, but I never saw the correspondence," she responded.

"They tagged me, didn't they, because I studied at Cambridge. I have this British accent that makes some folks think I regularly have afternoon tea with the queen. And for my occupation, of course, I am professor, as I'm doing research and teaching at the university in Santa Barbara."

She picked up the papers and straightened them, not making eye contact. Then she said, "I am troubled, Dr. Ling, yet you are correct. I am sorry to tell you that this company was a charade. They have been working this scheme for the last year, as I've learned recently from the police."

"They gave me a contact here at the consulate, a, wait, here it is, a Junfeng Yu. Does he work out of your office? Or is that a lie too?" He sensed the response before the undersecretary looked at her hands, clasped them and frowned.

"He did until the beginning of the month. He was let go. He was sacked as you British say, for taking bribes on some dealings to bring businesses from China to the United States. I learned recently that he'd returned to mainland China. There's much unrest in our homeland, you know."

"I've been closely following what seems will end up in a revolution." Thomas read the daily reports of the battles, another reason he felt he'd needed to act quickly if the children were to be able to leave. The Summer Offensive of 1947, as it had been called, in Northeast China, was a series of battles initiated by the communists against the nationalists. It became a heated Chinese Civil War, so quickly after the world war had ended.

They finished their coffee, she bid him farewell, and Thomas sat staring into nothingness. *How could I be so damn stupid, so gullible? I should have done more to check references, but I spoke to Mr. Yu on the telephone. He assured me that we'd have a family, the family we wanted, and save these beautiful orphans from a life of poverty and starvation. He'd assured me that the adoption agency was on the up and up and even offered references. He sent me paperwork.*

Thomas wanted to cry and realized he'd never even checked the validity of the agency's claims. He looked down at the empty coffee cup with coffee grinds making an empty circle on the bottom. He felt the same. Empty of hope.

When he looked up there was a young Chinese couple pushing a pram just in front of him. They stopped. Thomas heard a baby whimper. The man bent down to adjusting the baby's blanket.

Then Thomas cried.

CHAPTER 16

IT WAS DUSK WHEN THOMAS STUMBLED BACK to the imposing St. Francis Hotel on Union Square, where he'd made reservations so he could fly to Hong Kong in the morning. He walked through the palatial lobby, got his key from the front desk, found a note from one of his lab assistants that read, "Mrs. Ling arrived in New Orleans safely." He quickly took the stairs to the seventh floor, not willing to even look at another traveler and to punish himself by running for being a fool.

He flopped backward on the bed and cursed. "I've made a mess of our lives again," he said, longing to hold Beatrix and bury his face in her neck. He wanted to explain how he just longed for her to be happy and honestly admitted he longed for the little ones to fill their home. In his heart he knew she'd forgive him for being that fool, which made it worse. She'd manage to make the best of this disaster, as she always did.

He rolled to the right side and slipped his wallet from his back pocket, pulling out a tiny photo. While they'd planned to be married in London, it seemed foolish to wait and instead had the wedding at city hall in Santa Barbara. She'd dressed in a creamy white wool suit with navy trim, and wore a ring of baby's breath around her head, like a halo. He was dressed in blue, and while the photo was black and white, he could see it in colors. They'd exchanged thin gold wedding bands and he twisted his then, remembering every detail of the day. He ran a finger over

Beatrix's face in the photo, kissed the finger, and put it to her lips.

Then he caught his reflection in the mirror. The color of his face matched the gray walls: Gloomy. Matched his suit: Shades of concrete. Didn't match the disappointment, the stupidity, and the embarrassment he felt stamped in his reflection. That was the color of midnight. He went so far as pretending to smile, having heard once that even a fake smile could change one's disposition. He failed miserably at that, as well.

"What would Bea do?" he asked out loud and demanded an answer from the mirror as he pushed himself up to his elbows. "She certainly wouldn't withdraw to this hotel room, wallowing in a self-affected pity party. She'd take action." *But what action? How? Where?* There was no way he could locate the unscrupulous adoption agency in a city the size of San Francisco. Even the Chinese government sacked the bloke who colluded with the fake agency and did a runner back to China.

No way, he realized, would he ever see the money again. "It's gone. It was all a fiddle; they were dishonest from the start and took advantage of my desires to have little ones." *It's not the money, that's just money, although a stinking lot of it. It's my heart. They broke my heart. I wanted to give Beatrix the family I promised her. Some husband, I can't even make a baby and can't even adopt one.* His heart ached, and he collapsed back against the mattress again.

He tortured himself again, thinking of just months back with how he'd left her after a crazy, drug-induced dream, and she forgave him. Then he recalled how at the beginning of their relationship, Beatrix had been kidnapped. He thought she would die. He thought he would, too, if anything happened to her.

He didn't deserve to have a wife like Beatrix Patterson. He didn't deserve to have any happiness at all and when he had it, he just botched it. Royally.

It was dark when he mustered the energy to push himself to a sitting position. He walked to the window and opened it.

There were sounds of the city coming from below yet when he looked up, stars glittered in the blue-black sky. "Same stars Beatrix is seeing, my darling Bea." Then a spark of possibility bubbled up from nowhere.

He picked up his wallet again. There was plenty of money in it, and he was thinking now he'd been a dolt to plan to carry that much to a foreign country, an easy target for thieves. He didn't need a trip to China to be robbed, he could manage that without leaving California.

He rubbed his temples, flexed his shoulders, tried to release the guilt that churned his stomach and clouded his thinking process.

Then he thought of the days when they first met. He had been sorely convinced that Beatrix was a Chinese witch, a *wu,* believing she'd mesmerized him for some evil plan. Then he became her bodyguard and helped stop a potential Nazi invasion into New Orleans. "By golly, I'll do it again."

He picked up the telephone on the nightstand, arranged to be connected to a travel agency located in the lobby, and got a reservation to fly out the next day. "I'm going to New Orleans and will help Bea. It's decided." He stretched, opened the window wider, filling his lungs with the salty air from the bay and decided it was time to quit feeling sorry for himself. "Food. I need food," he said, realizing he hadn't had a meal, a real one, since the evening before. Luckily, he didn't have to even leave the hotel as there was a stylish dining room in the lobby. He wanted shepherd's pie or a pub dinner, but settled for a French creation that looked pretty but didn't fill him.

He paid the bill, settled his account at the hotel, confirmed with the front desk that his tickets for New Orleans would be left at the airline counter. He organized his suitcase, climbed into bed, and missed Beatrix more than he could ever imagine. Thomas fell asleep grasping the wedding photo.

Fog greeted him the next morning. Thomas quickly dressed, hailed a cab, and waited for his flight at the San Francisco airport. If all went well, he'd be in Louisiana by midnight, and he wondered if he should knock on Beatrix's hotel door at that hour. *Will that terrorize her?* He'd never known his wife to be afraid and didn't want to test that concept. He'd call her room from the lobby of the Windsor Court hotel when he got in, giving her a moment to realize he was in that city rather than at home, where she thought he'd be.

Two thousand miles southeast and earlier that evening California time, Beatrix was having a late dinner with long-time friends who worked at the Old Absinthe, the historical bar on Bourbon Street and Bienville Street. Locals flocked there especially during Mardi Gras, but in September it was, by New Orleans standards, sleepy in the French Quarter. Beatrix knew it because her friends, during the war, also supported the French Resistance, sending money to fight the Nazis, and she'd supported that effort with whatever funds she could spare, which was often quite sizeable.

Before entering the bar, she'd stood outside and admired the rich architecture and history. The bar was allegedly the meeting location for General Andrew Jackson and the infamous New Orleans pirate, Jean Lafitte, prior to the Battle of 1815, during the War of 1812. During Prohibition it was a speakeasy, serving bootleg booze and opportunities for mischief. It still thrived because of its sordid reputation.

Now Beatrix sat at a table with friends, all workers at the tavern. She told them her reason for coming to New Orleans. "It feels nearly impossible to track down a visitor from over five years ago, but that's why I'm here. A chump's errand?" She rarely got concerned about the direction of her investigations, but this time coming all the way to the Crescent City seemed like an awful long shot. *Will the elderly rabbi even remember that one day in 1943? Do I even remember, with my crazy and perfect ability to remember things, one particular day?* But of course, her answer was yes.

Her friends refused to believe that Beatrix couldn't find out information, and one even personally knew the rabbi at Touro Synagogue, saying she'd call the rabbi first thing in the morning to introduce Beatrix, although John Brockman had done that early that day.

It was after two in the morning when she returned to the Windsor Court, exhausted but knowing that progress had been made. She'd decided to visit the rabbi before going to the sheltered home, Poydras House, where her biological mother was a permanent resident. She walked to the hotel's front desk, exchanged pleasantries with the night clerk, got her key, and turned to go to the elevator. As usual, even during the worst years of the war, the lobby's center held a gigantic lavish flower arrangement. That day's included lavender and white roses and blue and pink hydrangeas, studded with huge white orchid sprays. She stopped to smell the roses, was tempted to snatch one to put in the room before she looked up.

"Thomas?" *My Thomas?* She blinked.

Across the opulent lobby, he was settled in a wingback green leather chair, head resting on the side, legs stretched out, mouth open, and quietly snoring.

He's adorable, she thought, so at peace. *But why is he here?*

She walked quietly to his side, admiring the splendor of his features and the pale, smooth olive tone of his skin. His jet-black hair, as usual, spiked in all directions and as she bent to kiss him, his eyes fluttered open. "Bea?" He rubbed his eyes as if they were lying.

She sat on the arm of the chair and put her mouth on his, then quietly said, "I don't know what you're doing here but I am ever so glad you are."

He sat forward, looked around the deserted opulent lobby, and pulled her to his lap, breathing in the rose perfume she always wore, nestling his head in the warmth of her neck.

"Darling, let's go upstairs before I start something that could even make titillating New Orleans blush," she whispered in his ear, taking his hand and walking to the elevator.

Thomas slipped his arm around her waist and once the elevator doors closed continued to show her how much she'd been missed.

The next morning, Beatrix ordered room service, coffee with chicory and croissants with butter and strawberry jam, actually two orders as Thomas polished off the first one before Beatrix got out of the shower. "How come we decided to leave from here?" he asked wiping jam off his fingertips.

"We have to come back more often," she replied. "Now for today, my plan is a visit to the synagogue and a talk with the rabbi. John said I could have access to his sources. I'll talk to a few of his employees and find out how to check the pawn shops in town and if anyone remembers Krause, or if he bought a gun. It's a long shot."

"Your *maman*? Please tell me we're going to visit with her. Have you told her we're planning to start a family?" Thomas finished the remaining croissant, adding a dollop of jam off the plate, and dusted crumbs into a little triangle on the crisp white linen tablecloth before scooping them onto an empty saucer.

Beatrix focused more intently on organizing her purse when Thomas mentioned the future of their family. When there was nothing to tell, why mention it, but she did want to talk with her mother, quietly, about the topic. Rather, she said, "I thought, if she'll allow us, we'd take her to Commander's Palace for lunch." Beatrix put on maroon gabardine slacks, a lacy white shirt, and pulled out a black hip-length jacket.

"How about if I make a start on the pawn shops and places that sell dodgy stuff, like guns? You still have that newspaper article with the photo of Krause?" Thomas asked. "Can I take one?"

"In the file on the desk, I brought two. It'd be remarkable if the rabbi remembers Krause, if in fact it was Krause that day. I'll leave a message for you at the front desk to let you know if I get any leads. Can you do the same, darling?"

"Righty-o, then. We'll reconnoiter and meet here at noon, shall we?"

She smiled all the way down to the lobby, feeling better knowing that she and Thomas were a team once more. She turned left on Canal Street, waiting for a trolley to bounce by and then take Decatur to John Brockman's antiquated bookstore, and the gambling hall in the back.

An older woman was at the cash register in John's bookshop, next to where Beatrix once had her fake psychic office. The woman was knitting and barely looked up as the bell over the door jingled. "Good day, madam."

"Good day. I'm Beatrix Patterson," and she was about to explain her mission, but the woman simply waved a hand indicating that Beatrix should go through to the back.

She opened the door to be greeted by Henry, John's all-around assistant and trusted helper. "This is wild. Henry? Whatever are you doing here?"

"I could say the same to you, Miss Beatrix?" he said and surrounded her with a massive hug.

"Is John with you?" He had not mentioned any plans to be in the city when they'd talked a few days prior.

"No, he's still in Santa Barbara. There were a few pieces of sculpture he wanted from his home here and I'm just making sure that the movers package them correctly. Why are you here? Mr. Brockman didn't tell me."

They walked into John's office and closed the door. Books lined the walls and the inner-office window looked out to the gaming parlor. It was early but already crowded with customers. "I'm here to find out if there's a connection with Rabbi Krause and the city. His widow told me he'd bought a gun here and was terrified of something."

"In 1943? I've been with Mr. Brockman since before we met. Hired me as a kid, after the accident that took one of my eyes and got me listed as 4-F by the army, so I couldn't join up."

They both looked through the glass door and out to the crowd in the next room, glancing at each other when the mayor took a seat at one of the poker tables. "Back then, Henry, when I had my office next door, if I needed a gun, where would I go?"

"Magazine Street would be a good start, if you weren't a local. Locals would probably just ask a buddy."

"Thomas is going there this morning."

"Want me to check on Doc? I don't need to be at Mr. Brockman's home until this afternoon when the moving van comes to get the ship's figurehead. She's a big one, and heading to the museum on State Street in Santa Barbara."

Beatrix hated to ask, but she did. "John doesn't have a collection of Indigenous baskets or artifacts here or in Santa Barbara, does he?"

Henry shook his head. "I know the Rabbi gave him a clay jar, short and brown. Looked fragile. It was on a side table for a week or so. Then Mr. Brockman had the curator of the local museum over for drinks and after that I didn't see it again. Think it was Navajo and not Chumash. Why?"

She smiled. Now she could ask John about that. She breathed a little easier, never wanting to doubt her friend, but the niggling fear kept resurfacing.

They were silent as the mayor jumped up, threw his cards on the table. "Duty calls, Miss Beatrix. I'll catch up with Thomas as soon as I can. Don't you worry about him."

Beatrix rebuttoned her jacket, slipped her purse over her shoulder, and headed toward the street, hailing a taxi. "Touro Synagogue, please," she told the cabbie. She handed the driver the fare and a tip of two dollars as they pulled up to the building on St. Charles Street. There were a few people on the street, but the neighborhood was quiet. She'd been by the house of worship before and marveled at the structure.

She'd read that Touro's magnificent sanctuary was a Byzantine Sullivan-esque building designed by the renowned Emile Weil, constructed in 1908 and dedicated in 1909, and she knew the Byzantine and Moorish elements were a nod to Sephardic heritage and a differentiation from Christian buildings. Mr. Weil's design of Touro was influential and fit firmly into the more modern stylistic movement; plans were published in a 1909 American Architect. The exterior was a golden blonde brick with white terra-cotta decorative relief work and polychromed terracotta decorative detailing with a green-tiled dome. The sides and rear reflected a Sullivan-esque flair. The vast arched window bays mimicked the curve of the dome, highlighted by multi-colored geometric art glass.

Beatrix smiled, wondering how many citizens even appreciated the artistry of the grand building. She checked her watch and focused on the mission at hand. She'd called the rabbi's office earlier and had an appointment for ten. She walked around the side of the building, and entered a door marked "office."

Rabbi Emil Leipziger, head of the temple, was waiting for her. "Good day, Miss Patterson," he bowed slightly, and she offered her hand.

"Thanks for seeing me on such short notice, Rabbi. John Brockman speaks highly of you."

His Swedish accent and warm smile made Beatrix feel comfortable at once. "And he says the same of you, madam."

"Can we talk here?"

He motioned to two visitor's chairs. "My secretary is on vacation this week, so I'm manning the fort, so to speak. John said you wanted some information about a man I may have known in the past?"

She took a chair across from him. "The man I've come to you to ask about was called Hiram Krause."

"Hiram Krause? No, I don't think...wait I knew a man named Herman Krause. He'd been a recent immigrant, a miracle escapee from Stutthof. Came here, trying to settle into the community, then moved to New York, then...oy, I know now who you're talking about." He grimaced and shrugged.

"Herman? It must be the same person."

"He was a tragically troubled soul. I tried talking with him, but his fears of being tracked down by the Nazis were too real.

I remember it clearly," he rubbed his hands together, as if he wondered how much he should tell this stranger.

"Rabbi, Hiram or Herman Krause is dead. The coroner in my city, Santa Barbara, believes it might be suspicious. Perhaps even scared to death. There seems to be no other cause, although he wasn't in good health."

"Scared? Yes, oy. When I met Herman, he was terrified. He believed evil was following him, something about past transgressions. He told me he'd seen it, seen the devil make a pact with voodoo forces to murder him. He stayed with me and my wife for about three months; he had no one else. Then one day, he said he was going back to New York where he'd first settled after the trek from the Old Country. He wanted to seek his fortune there. With that decision, he seemed, honestly?"

"Honestly, please."

"More normal. Not whole, but no longer ranting about the devil and curses and the voodoo arts. My wife and I were hopeful."

"He presented himself as a rabbi in my city," Beatrix said.

Rabbi Leipziger's forehead wrinkled. "I am afraid I don't understand. My hearing isn't as good as it once was. A rabbi? Herman was certainly not a rabbi, although he knew the Jewish Bible, or Tanakh, inside and out. He did fill in once helping the children's school when they were on a lesson about the prophets and the law. Never heard he had been a rabbi in Poland or Germany, and he certainly would have mentioned that."

"He knew all the three books that comprise it? The Pentateuch or Torah, the Prophets, called Nevi'im, and the Writings, also known as the Ketuvim?"

"You are well versed in our culture and religion, Miss Patterson. If you ever want to leave California and come and teach in our school, Gentiles are certainly welcome."

"Learning about religions and religious practices is one of my favorite areas of study, although I'm a psychologist."

"Ah, yes, the sciences of the mind and our emotions. People are fascinating. That's why I became a rabbi, because each person has their own stories, their unique truths which often are not, and they like to tell their own lies, when necessary."

"Could Herman or Hiram have been telling you lies?"

"How so? Oh, where are my manners. Would you care for tea or coffee?"

"Another time, I don't want to keep you, but could you sense anything untold or even fishy about Hiram's past or what he told you of it?"

The rabbi sat back and folded his hand, looking down for a few moments before he spoke. 'I am loathe to speak ill of the dead." He squished his lips and said, "I take people as they come to me, accept them, and try to love them, although some are harder to love than others."

She nodded, not wanting to stop his train of thought.

His index finger rubbed a spot between his eyes. Then he said, "I couldn't quite make out how he had escaped from Stutthof. Countless of our congregants are Holocaust survivors or their relatives are. I have heard stories. It's the stuff of nightmares. I've never heard of anyone who attempted to escape from that death camp that managed to survive. When I asked Herman during a quiet time, he told me he couldn't talk about it."

"Did you question him further?"

"He said it was too painful to talk about, when I prodded, and then I didn't want to pry. Well, my dear, I did want to pry, but stepped back. Whatever Herman or your Hiram did to get away, it tortured him."

"Thank you for being open with me. John said, in 1943, he was attending a sabbat service right here and Hiram rushed in afterward, nearly flinging himself at you. Do you recall that?"

"How could I not? I hadn't seen him in such a long time. Then there he was ranting about the enemies, voodoo, again the devil, and how they were going to slaughter him. He screamed about a *shiksa* who was after him."

Beatrix cocked her head waiting for the Yiddish version.

"Ah, yes. A *shiksa* is an often disparaging, although not always, term for a non-Jewish woman or girl. The word has a Yiddish origin and has moved into English usage and some Hebrew usage, especially in the Polish and German languages."

"A girl? He was frightened of a child?"

"That it seems. I guided him to my office, tried to calm him and have him make sense. Kept shouting 'grizzly' or something of the sort. His face was the color of a sheet; I thought he might have a heart attack."

"Could he have said 'gris-gris'?"

"I suppose. What is that?"

She was surprised that the rabbi, a resident of the city, wasn't familiar with the term. Yet, unlike Beatrix, he most likely lived a more sheltered life than the then-fake psychic of the French Quarter. She explained that New Orleans Voodoo was also known as Voodoo-Catholicism. It is a religion connected to nature, spirits, and ancestors. Voodoo was bolstered when followers fleeing Haiti after the 1791 slave revolt moved to New Orleans and grew, as many free people of color made its practice a part of their culture.

"You see, Rabbi, the voodoo doll is an effigy called a gris-gris, but it can be used as a religious object or a superstitious one depending on how the user treats it. The Guide Voodoo Doll is a summoning item for the Wall of Flesh. It is a guaranteed drop from Voodoo Demons, a rare enemy in the underworld."

"I know only a small amount about voodoo in our community, as of yet never have I had to deal with it. Could Herman have believed in the power of this dark magic?"

"Hiram or Herman was a disturbed man, Rabbi. You know it well. He managed to escape the death camp, but those horrors came to haunt him. It may be that someone convicted him of the evil he'd done and, in his heart, he believed he deserved to be threatened. I fear whatever terrorized him caught him in California. What on earth it was, Hiram was found dead in his office with his eyes wide open at the moment he took his last breath."

The rabbi was still, head bowed, "*Gud i Himmel,*" reverting to Swedish in his shock.

"Rabbi, do you know where Hiram, or the man you call Herman, went to when he left here? Was he calm or more determined when he left? Did you see if he was carrying a gun?"

CHAPTER 17

THE ELDERLY RABBI WRANG HIS HANDS. "The poor man." He pushed a tear off his wrinkled cheek.

"He'd bought a gun when he got to the city, Rabbi. A person doesn't do that unless they're terrified and plan to protect themselves. Or kill someone."

"A gun? Brought into our synagogue? Oh, no, if he had one, he never showed it. He was with me for about an hour, never fully stopped shaking. Often incoherent. Before you ask, I smelled no alcohol on his breath. Then he ran out of my office as mysteriously as he came in."

The rabbi told her he'd pray for the departed Hiram and his widow, whom he hadn't met but had heard about. Beatrix learned everything the elderly gentleman had to say and said goodbye.

Back on the street, she glanced at her watch. "Plenty of time," she said and walked the long blocks back toward the Windsor Court, taking a detour to stroll the Mississippi waterfront, still bustling even after the war was over. She watched the barges strut in a flowing parade down the wide river and the crafty little ferry chug between Poydras Street and the small city of Algiers. She stopped to look out over the waterway to where the former POW Nazi camp had been and thought of the three sisters who'd been entrapped into helping terrorists infiltrate New Orleans. It seemed like decades, when she'd been involved in that mystery, yet it had been less than seven years. Her life had changed in so many ways she could never have imagined, and she smiled at the goodness that was part of her life.

Now married, which was something she'd never planned, ever, she and Thomas were renovating the once derelict mansion home in downtown Santa Barbara, and she was a licensed psychologist. She'd made peace with her past, found her biological parents although the relationship with her father, General Charles de Gaulle was knotty at best, and somehow, someway she'd determine just who the fake rabbi Hiram Krause was and how he died. She didn't realize how long she'd stood there but sensed that the cafes that dotted the area were prepping for guests. Delectable smells of onions and spices were being prepared and picked up in the breeze. There was a whiff of freshly baked breads and a hint of shrimp gumbo. She turned her back to the half-mile-wide river and was comforted knowing how the city had recaptured its elegance after being a hub for the ghastly war and a producer of weapons. New restaurants had sprung up and she was tempted but decided to make her way to Café du Monde for a café au lait, like old times.

She walked, and needed to think. Herman/Hiram was not a rabbi. Hence sometime between moving from New Orleans in 1941 and making it to New York City, he'd acquired forged documents and recommendations saying he was actually a church leader. Beatrix knew anything under the sun could be had in both cities, so that wasn't a surprise. But why did he do it?

"Ego," she breathed the word and then settled on a bench across from the iconic St. Louis cathedral. "Yes, the man did whatever he needed to boost his self-worth which seems to have been larger than those massive church spires." She leaned back on the bench, feeling at once as if she were home in the throngs of tourists and artists who lined the street, selling paints and a hodgepodge of crafts, along with the occasional voodoo symbol. Her shoulders relaxed in the humid sunshine. *He had an abnormal appetite to garner higher self-esteem. A man like Hiram, and I need to call him that rather than Herman, needs to have his lofty opinion of himself nourished at all times.* She nearly slapped her forehead. *He was a full-blown narcissist. Textbook, apparently.* In her mind she could "see" the definition she'd once read in a book:

> Narcissism: A disorder in which a person has an inflated sense of self-importance. Narcissistic personality disorder is found more commonly in men. The cause is unknown but likely involves a combination of genetic and environmental factors. Symptoms include an excessive need for admiration, disregard for others' feelings, an inability to handle any criticism, and a sense of entitlement.

From everything I've been told, that was Hiram Krause.

Beatrix was so deep in thought she didn't notice that Thomas and Henry had strolled up and stood before her. When Thomas barely touched her shoulder, she jumped. "If I were a cat, that would be one less life, my dear husband," she exhaled.

"I thought you would have heard us or sensed us, like in the old days, and besides I called out to you, didn't I, mate?" Thomas said, offering yet another apology.

The three headed toward the iconic Café du Monde and settled at an outdoor table. Henry joined them sipping coffee and polishing off a plate of beignets. "We found nearly ten places where any Jill, Donna, or Hiram could buy a gun, with no questions asked. Even introduced the doc to my high school physics teacher, a pawnbroker now that he's retired, who was more than willing to dish the dirt on gun acquisition in his beloved city."

"No one recognized Krause," Thomas added. "Damp squib, all the way."

"Not quite so, old bean," Henry was enjoying mimicking Thomas's accent. "Mr. Booker said that Hiram looked familiar, minus the yarmulke. I wouldn't trust the old guy, however, as he kept calling me by my late brother's name, then asked what

I was doing there at ten in the morning and why I wasn't at school." Henry's robust laugh was contagious.

Beatrix relayed what she'd found out from the visit to Touro Synagogue and the rabbi there. "Speaking of Hiram. Herman was the name he used while in New Orleans before he returned to New York."

"What happens now, Bea? We head home? Shall I purchase tickets? Henry, when are you leaving?"

"Not until those sculptures are on a truck heading to California. The company telephoned today saying they had a mix up and can't get to them until tomorrow." He just shook his head.

"Henry, Thomas and I are meeting my mother, Adelina, for lunch. Will you join us?"

He looked at her with disbelief. "Miss Beatrix, that's kind of you. You do recollect that this is New Orleans and that most of the places in the city won't welcome me."

"I am keenly and acutely aware of that despicable situation, Henry," she replied with a frown. "Let's go to Dooky Chase's, a fine place for a po'boy if I ever wanted one, and I am craving a foot-long po-boy with shrimp. And French fries by the mountain. We'll take a taxi to get *Maman* and she'll be delighted to see you again."

Thomas rubbed his hand in anticipation. "Come on, my good fellow. You've not lived until you've seen my delicate wife ravish a po'boy."

In less than an hour, they arrived at the café. Dooky Chase's had been just a sandwich shop in the Treme district before Emily married Edgar Dooky Chase, Sr., and within a year it became a family restaurant and popular night spot. As the four entered, they were greeted and seated like family.

Adelina brought stares, which Thomas and Beatrix had grown accustomed to because she typically wore a nun's habit, today with red basketball shoes. In the middle of laughter and love, Adelina took Thomas's hand and said in a tiny voice, "You know, I see."

"Yes, Mother," he said in a whisper and the hair on the back of his neck twitched. He never wanted to believe that she had second sight, yet too often her visions were true. He always listened.

She breathed in his ear. "You do not need to go overseas to adopt children. You'll find them close to your home."

Thomas could not respond. As far as he knew, Beatrix hadn't mentioned adoption and definitely not about longing for a family. He looked up from the now-empty plate and whispered back, "I don't have to go to China?"

She tickled his chin and giggled like a teenager. "Oh, my baby girl, your husband's kind, yet he seems to be the silliest of men."

"Add clever to the list and resourceful and he makes me laugh, too, *Maman*," she chuckled, mystified by whatever secrets they were telling.

Adelina patted her daughter's hand. "Your father made me laugh."

Beatrix studied Adelina's face, wondering if there was any resemblance between them. It was hard to tell as her coif, or veil, covered her head, just leaving her face exposed. Her eyes were greener than Beatrix's and that was about all the comparison between mother and daughter that could be matched.

Should I tell her that Thomas and I may travel to France in the fall, to meet Charles' family? Should I tell her that my father has confessed to that family about his affair and about me? Beatrix looked up and Thomas was watching her closely, as if he could read her thoughts. He smiled and there was a tiny "no" as he flicked his eyes shut for a second.

If we go, then I will tell her. It's only fair, she thought.

The group returned Adelina to the sheltered home and as Beatrix walked her mother up the marble steps, the older woman stopped her. "You asked me on the telephone yesterday if I knew of any practitioners of voodoo, any that could be hired to curse someone even across the country."

Beatrix had thought Adelina had come up without any answers. "You found somebody, someone you believe can do this?"

"No. That is my point, darling. Unless the person who the curse is against believes in it, the curse can do nothing. Your rabbi in Santa Barbara had to believe it. Then a priest or priestess here in the city could put a supernatural rumination on that man, and even a messenger could be the conduit to pass the invocation to hurt, harm, or destroy their enemy."

"What you're saying is that the cursed person must believe, and then even a go-between could tell him about it?"

"Yes. I think you may have come all this way for nothing. There are hundreds of people in this city who would gladly stick pins into an effigy or concoct a poison for a few dollars."

"Do you know anyone who, this sounds odd, specializes in 'long-distant curses?"

The older lady laughed. "You make it sound like a party trick."

"No, no, *Maman*, I am taking this dead serious, and this is exactly what I needed to know. I want to find how what happened to the rabbi in Santa Barbara, who could do this, who could make a frightened man so terrified that he would die."

"Then look for the messenger, my darling daughter. Open your eyes, remember, like I taught you to do. You already know the answer, you know who is doing this."

Beatrix watched her birthmother's habit sway in the breeze as the woman scurried into the imposing safehouse. *I know the person who did this?* Beatrix scowled, as she reviewed all the "suspects" in the investigation. The only person could be Gerta, and if she fled to Los Angeles or took the train east, she could disappear forever. Period. Could the recovering physician, Dr. Schmitt, be the evil doer? But why? Then there was Otto

Rosenbaum who had secrets of his own but seemed harmlessly caught in the web of his own romantic doing.

Henry grabbed another cab and headed for John Brockman's large home, waiting for the movers. Beatrix and Thomas walked through the French Quarter, and she talked about how to proceed with the investigation.

"Thomas, it makes no sense. Krause was not truly a rabbi, but apparently, he fooled the congregation and higher-ups enough not to scrutinize his letters of recommendation. Yes, he escaped the death camp, but how many thousands tried? Few records on the topic. Most died in the process. Krause was found with his eyes wide open, but does that make it voodoo that killed him? Heroin was discovered in his system."

"We need a night out, that's the ticket," Thomas said pointing to Preservation Hall. "We'll have dinner at the hotel and then relish an evening with Dixieland Jazz, come on, Bea. I'm chuffed to bits to be back here, and I haven't seen you really relax at all today. We won't get drunk, so we'll be bright and shiny tomorrow if you want to fly home."

"Yes, you're right. My mind keeps circling and coming up without any suspects."

"Smashing."

She turned and grabbed his arm, patting his chest where there was an unusual bulge in his jacket. "Tell me you didn't buy a gun when you were searching out shops that would sell them."

"I did not buy a gun. You've seen me with them, I'm afraid even to hold one." He reached into the inside pocket of his suit jacket and pulled out a tall, slim aqua box tied with a matching ribbon. "Do you want to wait until we get back to the hotel to open this?" He looked around, feeling like a boulder in the middle of a river as people swarmed past them. "Just a little something, don't get too excited." He couldn't help but produce a nervous smile and nearly shook with anticipation. Then thought: *What have I done? This was stupid, once again. Will she understand? Will it upset her? Am I promising something that*

I cannot deliver? Like the futile trip to the crooked San Francisco adoption agency?

"Thomas, it's not my birthday and certainly not a special occasion."

"Darling, you bought that sporty car and told me it was my birthday, when it wasn't. You started this."

She moved out of the middle of the sidewalk and headed to a quiet bench. Then she said, "Now. I'll take it now. I need something else to think about rather than who or if someone sped the rabbi's demise. If in fact the man just had a heart attack, even though the coroner didn't detect it. He was overweight and smoked and those are deadly to the body."

"Beatrix, so you do want to see what's inside?" He pretended to pull it away.

She fingered the tall, trim, pale blue box. "It is perfume? No. Okay, how about a dagger for all of my switchblade needs? No? Okay, let's see. Stalks of asparagus? Stop laughing, Thomas." But she didn't want him to stop. "I've got it, it's a pipe for the utility sink in our garage that you keep saying you're going to fix?"

"A drain pipe? You guessed. No. You are way off, darling. Why not just open it?"

"Celery? You bought me a bunch of celery?"

"How did you guess? Of course, it's celery."

She bent and kissed his forehead and then opened the tall box to reveal yet another box inside; this one was black and had the name of Tiffany & Co., San Francisco, California, printed in gold on the top. Beatrix held her breath. The store had only the finest jewelry and other collectibles.

She gingerly opened the box. Five slim plain gold bracelets nestled on an aqua-colored pillow of silk. The box only looked tall so as not to give away the secret inside. She cocked her head and squinted at Thomas. "Five? There's a significance to that number?"

"It's top-secret for now. Put them on, please. I never give secrets away."

"Oh, yes, the inscrutable and enigmatic Asian." She smiled, leaned in to kiss him, and slipped the five bangles on her left wrist. "How lovely they look with my thin, plain gold wedding band. I like them, Thomas, they're perfect. I don't understand the significance, but they're marvelous. Uncomplicated and wearable and honest jewelry."

He sighed at the botched but simple plan. The bracelets were to be engraved with the name and birthdate of each of their five future children. He really wanted five. Someday he'd tell her that in Chinese lore five was a lucky number linking the five elements, which are wood, earth, water, fire, and metal. This number was usually connected to the Emperor of China as well, and the Tienanmen gate.

They returned to the Windsor Court on St. Peters, changed into dinner clothes, and headed to the opulent dining room. Beatrix had, on impulse, thrown in a long black gown with the V-neck plunging far enough to reveal cleavage, but modest enough for her taste. Thomas's black suit fit well and the crisp white shirt with the gold cufflinks she'd given him for the previous Christmas made him look especially dapper. Other diners stared as the couple were seated in a cozy corner table.

The indulgent meal in the hotel's Grill Room seemed like a celebratory dinner. *But what is there to celebrate?* Beatrix thought. *Am I farther along in knowing anything more about Krause than when I left Santa Barbara?* She didn't pose these troubled questions, not wanting to dampen Thomas's buoyant mood.

Just reading the menu made her hungry. She'd chosen the eggplant and squash cassoulet and Thomas selected the halibut sauteed with herbs and butter. There was wine and an after-dinner glass of fine bourbon. "Remember when we met that night in New Orleans with police swarming the neighborhood?"

"You thought I had to be some supernatural witch?"

"You are still magical and always will be," Thomas said, caressing her arm. "Okay, I cannot keep the secret anymore, the reason I bought you the bracelets is..."

A staff member scurried to their table and bent low to offer Beatrix an envelope in the middle of a silver tray. "Madame Patterson, a telegram has arrived for you. Shall I wait to see you want to send a reply?" he asked.

Beatrix's forehead wrinkled. "No, thank you. If I need to reply, I'll come to the reception desk." She fingered the yellow envelope with its signature logo.

During the war, telegrams always meant the worst news. They told of a son, father, daughter, mother killed in the battles as this was how the armed services notified next of kin. Although Beatrix had never received a condolence telegram, the immediacy of it made her inhale sharply.

"Open it," Thomas said. "I'm here, you're here, your mother is fine as we just saw her today. I'm sure it's nothing."

She picked up a butter knife and slit it open. "It's from Gordon Blackfoot, Thomas. There's been a death on the reservation."

"Someone of importance?"

"It was one of the officials who is trying to take the children to the Indian Schools. The message is brief, but the deceased was found in his car, near the front gate of the reservation with one of the tribe's ceremonial knives in his back."

'Oh, Beatrix. Gordon hasn't been arrested, has he?"

"He wants me to call him. At once. He knows I'm here in Louisiana. I should wait until tomorrow perhaps, although it's not that late in California."

Thomas looked at the telegram, always written in the briefest way as the company, Western Union, charged by the word. "It sounds urgent, Bea. Call. If Blackfoot doesn't answer, then you can try in the morning." She made her way to the lobby and a private telephone booth.

Gordon Blackfoot answered on the second ring. "Thank goodness, Miss Patterson," he said, his voice husky from sleep.

"I've awoken you. I just received your telegram. There's been a death."

There was a pause. "I'm turning on a light, just a moment. Yes, we've been recently plagued by officials coming out to talk with the elders. They were from Riverside, and the Sherman Indian School."

"Just to talk?"

"That's what we thought. These are criminals. They are the men who force our children into the schools, only to harm them physically, sexually and emotionally. They talk a pretty story about how smart and non-Indian the children will be. Why, they lie and say that our kids will be able to succeed in the world of whites."

"You know the truth about the school, Gordon, as if this is personal. I remember as a child how my mother fought and won the tribe's exclusion from them."

"But that didn't last. Now they come with educational books and games. They woo our elders as if they want to marry them."

"Why? It cannot be because they think this is for the good of the children, Gordon?"

"That's a pile of sh--, um, baloney; they do it strictly for the money. They get reimbursed from the US government for every child who is enrolled and lives at the boarding schools." There was silence and Beatrix waited, knowing Gordon would have more to say. "So, they bring books and even show the elders the uniforms, all pristine. Last week there was a member of the Cherokee Nation with them. A young, strong man who told our elders how successful their children will be when they graduate. Even had the guts to tell me about how the schools had changed in the last ten years. That they were good places for children to learn to be real Americans."

She heard him breathing heavily as if recalling atrocious events of the past. "I laughed in his face. I'd been sent to one."

CHAPTER 18

"No." Beatrix wasn't aware Gordon Blackfoot has been forced to live at an Indian boarding school and had intimate knowledge the horrors within those walls.

"I didn't tell you, Beatrix?"

Why had I not asked? she thought. *Gordon is the right age to have been forcibly taken to the schools.* "Your experience, Gordon?"

"The punishment used at the boarding schools was brutal, especially for those, like me, who refused to believe in their dogma or obey the authorities. I was twelve when an official came to my house, handcuffed me when I refused to go calmly, and dragged me to a car. The other children in the tribe saw what happened to me, the young man who would someday be their shaman, and they went peacefully. My time there, just three years before I ran away and returned here, was an education in how to murder a child's hope. Crush their spirits. Their ways of 'guiding' us heathens, as we often were called, and that's actually one of the more polite names, was to use solitary confinement, flogging, withholding food, whipping, and slapping as forms of discipline. Schools would also sometimes make older children punish younger children and when I refused, I got a taste of white justice at the hands of a few cruel teachers."

"The word sorry doesn't even come close, Gordon. Did those who were taken when you were ever return to the reservation? How do they feel about the new group of teachers and administrators there now?"

"After I ran away, telling others how I planned it, about half of the kids left. Just under thirty came back here to the family compound; others lost their desire to be Chumash, believing they were sub-human, despicable and worthless, as we were told daily. And dirty. Dirty Indians."

"Have the elders and you argued with the people from the Indian School?"

"Beatrix, they have. I have. Even Grandmother, who has seen it all. The truth is," he hesitated. "I telegraphed you because I am their chief suspect in the murder of this fat, old white man. His car was parked right by the open gates leading to the compound, to our homes. One of the men found him when he came home for lunch, slumped over the steering wheel as if he were asleep. But when my brother touched the man, he slumped to the side and there was a knife." Silence and then, "One of my hunting knives. In his back."

"Did you kill him, Gordon?"

Gordon didn't respond to the direct question. Instead, he said, "He was the man, young at the time, who handcuffed me and dragged me off the reservation."

"I see," and what she saw was exactly what the police would put together, as well. "A motive. The boy who was appointed to become the next all-powerful medicine man, a shaman, was to be used as an example, humiliated and beaten to prove no one was above the Federal government's laws. That was a reason, for sure."

"He remembered me, and I remembered him, too. He saw me when he and a small group of people drove into the reservation a few weeks back. He spat on the ground when I was introduced. I tell you truthfully, I wanted him dead especially when I was imprisoned in the school and for what the school's leaders did to my Chumash brothers and sisters. I prayed to my spirits and the Christian God whom I now believe in to have him die, but I would never kill a human. I hunt sometimes with a knife for meat to feed our tribe, but taking a human spirit as brutally is against everything I and my Chumash family have confidence in, where we place value."

"Have the police cautioned you not to leave the reservation?"

"Yes, and I will not. It's my word against these white men and my knife it that bastard's, um, sorry, that man's back."

"Thomas and I are returning to Santa Barbara tomorrow. Go willingly, Gordon, if the police arrest you. I will contact my good friend John Brockman and he'll know an attorney to represent you and get you out on bail. One more question: Do you know who might have killed this man?"

"Maybe, but I will only tell you in person. This is a party line and others may be listening."

"Understood."

"Thank you, Beatrix. I didn't know what to do and then Grandmother reminded me of the generosity of your mother, Jennie, and when we talked, I saw the same kindness and trustworthiness in you. If they come for me, no, when they come for me as they have no other suspects as far as I know, I'll go quietly."

"I'll find you when I return, no matter where you are, including the city jail. Have hope, my friend. Wait, Gordon. Is there more to tell me?"

There was silence, but she could hear Gordon breathing. "According to what I can get from the police who kept me in a locked room most of today was that the guy died in his truck, behind the wheel, in the mid-morning. Most of the men and women were working in the bean fields. You know that's the only employment open to most of us. I was at the bar in town, left the reservation at about 9:30, stopped at the grocery store for lemons and olives for the cocktails, and filled the truck with gas. If the police cared, they could easily check it out from the owner of the grocery store on Milpas or the gas station on Cota. You're going to ask, so yeah, I was alone, as it was not even noon, and the bar doesn't open until two."

"Who could have been there, then? On the reservation at that time?"

"The elders. Just the elders and a handful of young kids," he said, hating the sigh in his voice that Beatrix immediately picked up. He sounded defeated.

"Why your knife? Who wants to send you to prison? For murder?"

"I can't figure that out. Mind you, Beatrix, I have a few hunting knives all kept in my home and I never lock the front door. None of us do," he said.

"Just to think about, Gordon, maybe whoever killed this man is ready to kill again. What was the victim's name?"

"Leslie Mottle. Dr. Leslie Mottle," he grunted more than spoke. "I didn't know until I got back here early this morning and Grandmother told me. Everyone is pretty shocked. Technically, he wasn't killed on the reservation, since he was found just outside the gates. But the police already are pointing fingers at us, as usually happens when whites are killed, and our tribe is within a ten-mile radius."

"One last question, for now. Do you think your knife was used because you couldn't have possibly killed Mottle since you were at the bar? You have an alibi, right?" Beatrix looked at her watch, to calculate if Gordon would have had enough time to get to the shops and buy gas and return to the reservation to kill Mottle and still open the bar at two. It didn't seem possible. As soon as she got home, she'd zip to the reservation in the MGB and see how much time a fast car required to make the round trip; however, she'd seen Gordon's old Chevy pickup in the tavern's parking lot. There was more rust than metal left on the body, and she imagined the engine looked about the same. Along the route, she'd see if there might be fruit stands where they'd seen Gordon and his pickup driving by and vouch for him. *Or if Gordon was actually driving his own truck,* she thought.

Then the notion surfaced that troubled her more. Would the elders lie for Gordon, giving him a rock-solid alibi? Of course, they would. He was their leader, the trusted shaman.

"I was at the bar. The night before, a customer had decided it would be funny to throw cherries from her cocktail at the front window. I went in early to try to scrub the mess. I didn't see any customers until I unlocked the door just after lunch, about two, I think. Then a few regulars came in for a chat. No, that's not true. Wait. About noon the beer truck came, and I talked to the driver. He was a new guy, substitute, but the company should have a record of who he is. It was close to eleven."

"Good, that's good, Gordon. I can track that down, but it doesn't help any of the others who may have been in the compound's housing."

"Beatrix, you cannot imagine that any of the elders would do this? You're wrong, it has to be a tramp and an opportunist. Mottle's wallet was gone, too."

Rather than going out on the town, Thomas and Beatrix needed some quiet time in their room.

The next day they were in luck. There was an early morning American Airlines flight from the newly opened airport called Moisant Field, named for aviation pioneer John Bevins Moisant. They got the last two seats to fly to Dallas, where they'd change planes before flying to Phoenix and another change. They'd arrive in Los Angeles after eight, if everything went smoothly and the weather was good.

As they waited in the drafty terminal, Beatrix leaned into Thomas. 'Do you know who Moisant was?"

"The guy whose name is here on the airfield? No, but you'll tell me, right?" He folded the day's *Times Picayune* newspaper.

She fiddled with the five slim gold bracelets and decided to pester Thomas for the truth or top secret-ness about them. She said, "Now, you're making fun of all the useless information I have inside my head." She tried to look serious, but then said, "John Bevins Moisant, known as the 'King of Aviators,' and originally from El Salvador, was an American aviator, aeronautical engineer, flight instructor, businessman, and revolutionary. He was the first pilot to conduct passenger flights over a city, as well as across the English Channel, from Paris to London."

"A useful factoid, my dear. Hence, my learned teachers probably didn't think it was worth mentioning."

She slipped the bracelets off her left wrist and handed them to Thomas.

"You don't like them, Bea?" he asked, his forehead wrinkled, his eyes wide.

"I love them, love you more, but I want the truth, Thomas Ling. What is the reason you bought these? Why were you in San Francisco? Why all the mystery?"

Thomas looked at her green eyes and then glanced at his watch. *If only they'd announce our flight, I wouldn't have to tell her. Now...* "It's complicated. I fear I've blundered and made it more complicated, too."

"The flight doesn't leave for 45 minutes. Is that enough time to explain your mystery?" She took his hand. There was not a doubt in her mind that whatever Thomas was involved in, he meant well. The man couldn't seem to do otherwise even when, in the past, he'd managed to botch a few things up.

"There are five bracelets for five children," he said. "And in Chinese culture, five is supremely lucky."

"When we have children, Thomas. If we don't, then perhaps we're not meant to. I have come to grips with this, we've talked it through, and some couples are happy and childless. If that's the way it's to be, let's make the most of it and go on endless adventures." It all sounds brave and exciting, but she thought, *Can I really believe what I'm saying? Why do I care to spare his feelings? Have I really stopped longing for children?* She had no hope to fully answer those questions.

He exhaled deeply, closed his eyes. Opened them and took a deep breath. "For months now, I have been corresponding with the Chinese Consulate and an agency connected with them that's affiliated with another in Hong Kong."

"For work? Something on which you're researching?"

"No." He looked at his shoes and then back to his wife. "I hired an adoption agency based in Hong Kong with an office in the Bay Area."

"Oh?"

"Yes, oh. The liaison was through the Chinese government in San Francisco and the agency had a stellar reputation."

"Thomas, spit it out, for goodness sakes. Had? You just used the past tense?"

"I paid them a princely sum and when you left the other day for New Orleans, I flew to San Francisco. The agency was to give me all the visas and paperwork to then travel to Hong Kong. There I could go to their sister organization and the orphanage where five children, war orphans and biracial little ones, would accompany me and their nurse back to Los Angeles a day later. It was like a well-oiled plan. Nothing could go wrong."

"Wait, nothing could go wrong, but instead you flew here. From San Francisco?"

"Yes."

"Explain the rest, but the five bracelets are starting to make sense."

"Five. One for each of the little ones who desperately needed a home. I saw their photos. Big almond shaped eyes, the boys had cowlicks right here," he touched the top of head, "Just like me. They're siblings. Just seeing them broke my heart. I wanted to surprise you. I wanted to give you little ones even if I cannot, well, I'm unable to, well, give you them in the old-fashioned way."

She reached over the armrest dividing the airport terminal seats and hugged him. He held her tight.

"The agency wasn't legitimate? Is that what happened?"

"Yes." He pushed his face more deeply into the cotton fabric of her suit jacket. "When I got to their offices, they'd disappeared. I went to the consulate and the liaison had been sacked for taking bribes."

"Oh, Thomas, oh, you poor dear. Your heart must be hurting."

He pulled away. "That's it? You're not going to divorce me or open the airplane window to toss me out?"

"What you tried to do was one of the most altruistic and unselfish acts anyone has ever done for me. You did it because you love me."

"I did, didn't I? The money? I need to tell you we lost a boatload. Poof. Gone."

"We'll figure that out. I was to get one bracelet for each of the little ones?"

"I was going to have their Chinese and American names engraved and then with their birth date, if it was known or their adoption date inside."

"Just so you know, I am almost glad this happened, Thomas, because springing five children on me without notice might not have been a feel-good event."

"What?"

"Darling, I've never even had a dog. Could you and I actually manage five kids? Do we know anything about being parents?"

"When did that stop us?" he tried to laugh. "Um, well, that did make me wonder a bit, especially with your practice and me at the university most days. Rather, I hired our friend Jo's mama Lillian Benson as their nanny. She's thrilled and wants to be their grandmother, too."

"I love Lillian and when we have children, we'll definitely see if she's available. What do you say we get some coffee from the cart over there before they call our flight."

"You're okay with me making a muddle of this?

"If this were done from any perspective except love, I might not be, but your heart is always in the right place."

"Wait? I think they just called our flight."

"Grab the paper, dear. Hope we get coffee onboard."

"Don't forget your book," Thomas added and handed her the just released copy of *Diary of a Young Girl*, by Anne Frank.

It was an all-day-and-into-the-night journey from New Orleans to Los Angeles, and then the hours-long trek to Santa Barbara along the two-lane coastal Highway 101. That time of night, traffic was sparce, but Beatrix felt it was extremely dangerous along the winding road to go more than fifty.

Morning came too soon, but Beatrix had been up since before dawn when Thomas trotted downstairs. 'Give me a strong cuppa and nobody'll get hurt."

"You're channeling your inner Hollywood private detective again? Ever since you saw that movie 'Exposed,' I've been noticing how you get that American accent mingled with your staunch British one." She handed him a large mug of black tea.

"Did you sleep at all? I woke at five and your pillow was cold. I don't remember the gray pleated skirt or the cream-colored flared jacket you're wearing. New?"

"You are perceptive even when you're a sleepyhead. I got it at Bon Mache in New Orleans. Too dressy for Santa Barbara?"

"Not on you, but maybe for the reservation?"

The trip to the reservation had to wait, although her thoughts were circling about the killing of the supposed educator. "I cannot get my mind around the death of Mottle. Why kill him? He couldn't grab children away from their parents by himself. And why was he parked outside the reservation's gates rather than driving in?"

"Suppose his body is at the morgue by now? Could you drop in on the new coroner for a chat? See if she has any information? Gordon said the guy's wallet was missing so maybe a stranger happened along, saw Mottle asleep, and stabbed him for his money. Sounds outlandish to me, but could work in a Hollywood gangster film."

She wrapped her arms around him as he yawned. "Visiting the coroner is definitely my plan for today. I also have a difficult chat with Sarah Rosenbaum, and this isn't a visit I am looking forward to."

Thomas knew she'd have to tell the rabbi's wife of how hysterical he'd been in New Orleans, as well as that he'd lived there before. She'd tell the widow how he probably bought the gun there and how she still had no answers as to why he died, or if it had been murder. That there seemed to be no record of

Krause ever having been a rabbi. Had his degree in real estate law been a sham as well? Would Beatrix ask Krause's widow if she knew any of his background and exactly how he escaped from the death camp?

Beatrix kissed the top of Thomas's head, and similar thoughts were in her mind. Her golden bangles jingled, and she smiled. Then she came to an abrupt stop. "Oh, Thomas, I've been blind."

"You've just realized a dull scientist couldn't be your knight in shining armor even if you got me a horse and the armor to go with it?"

'It's the box...the box that the bracelets came it. It was really tall. Now it all makes sense. I've been seeing only what others wanted me to see. Not the truth."

CHAPTER 19

"THE BOX THE BANGLES CAME IN was skinny and tall. It was to fool you," he said refilling the tea from the pot on the counter.

"I'm lost, but that's not unusual, right? Whatever are you talking about?"

She opened a kitchen cupboard and stared inside. Cups and saucers on the bottom shelf and then two stacked serving bowls on the second one. On the top were six cut glass vases she'd found months back when rummaging through the cluttered attic with the debris that came when they'd bought the crumbling house. She opened the pantry and looked inside. Then she walked in, stood in the middle of the small room, once a closet, and now housing canned goods, staples like flour and sugar and a bag of russet potatoes. She walked back to the middle of the kitchen.

Thomas just stared. He'd seen his wife processing information and memories and knew that was what she was doing.

Beatrix eventually said, "It's just as I thought. I saw this in the tailor's home." Details of the visit flashed through her mind so vividly it was if she was once again in Rosembaum's guest bedroom with the enormous walnut wardrobe. "It was narrow inside, too narrow compared to the dimensions of the cabinet. Thomas, you are brilliant. It's just like the box. How could I have not noticed?"

He plunked down with the tea steaming in the mug at the kitchen table. "You realize I have no clue what you're talking about, right?"

"The wardrobe in Otto Rosenbaum's guest bedroom? I didn't mention anything about it?"

"Still lost, Bea."

"It must have a false back. It's too narrow for a clothes hanger to be used, even though the rod was there. I'm certain as anything that it leads to a hideaway, much like people did to secret away Jews from the Nazis, just like this heart-wrenching book I'm reading about the Jewish family and the girl named Anne Frank and her family and the people who bravely concealed them in their attic." She walked around and opened and shut more kitchen cabinets. "How did I miss that?"

"Is that a rhetorical question?"

"I must get to Rosenbaum's house at once."

"You cannot leave the house without me. It's too dangerous. Let me get dressed. You cannot barge in on the tailor alone; if he's hiding his lunatic sister, there must be a reason. If it's worse and he's got her imprisoned, again, you should not do that alone." He dashed out and then darted back into the kitchen. "Why, Rosenbaum could even be Krause's killer. What if the sister is imprisoned and he lied about her leaving town? He's probably killed her by now. Tortured her. He could be a madman, a psychotic murderer."

He charged out of the kitchen and a second later he was back, his forehead etched with fear and his lips tight as he said, "We must tell the police, Beatrix."

"I only have Otto's word that she left town." She stood now at the bottom of the ornate staircase to the second story and called after Thomas. "If he's been hiding her in a secret room, perhaps that's where I'll find her and get the truth of why she's here. Every blasted person I talk to concerning Krause seems to have a possible motive, and I wouldn't be at all shocked if Gerta knew Krause in the old country."

"Call the police," he shouted, flying across the landing and then returning to their bedroom to retrieve a suit jacket.

"Police? Not yet. If you're with me, it'll be fine. What about work? Do you have classes to teach today?"

"Can you telephone the university and say that something personal has come up and I need to cancel the afternoon classes?"

She headed to the telephone and then stopped as he ambled down the stairs. "Thomas. Shoes. You forgot them."

"Wait, do not leave without me."

She shouted again. "I also need to revisit Dr. Schmitt, as something I've realized doesn't add up. That, too, was a plain and simple misdirection and yet I don't understand why he wasn't straightforward. Why did he have to conceal the truth?"

He was slipping into the suit jacket when he got to Beatrix. "I'm at sixes and sevens, now, Bea. What is this about Schmitt? I thought you said he was on the up and up and not a Nazi war criminal."

"It's another concealed truth, Thomas. Let's go. I'll tell you everything, Thomas, as soon as I figure it out. I must get to the Rosenbaum house."

"Want me to drive? That way you can think."

"No way. I mean that in the sweetest way possible, but your driving scares me silly."

He grabbed her hand and kissed her. "A kiss for luck and as for my driving, it scares the bejesus out of me as well."

She grabbed keys from a hook by the back door. "We'll take the MGB as it's faster than the station wagon. We're headed downtown and I'm going to open that wardrobe whether Rosenbaum wants me to or not. The man's lying and I'm certain he knew where his sister was, knows where she is."

Ten minutes later, they pulled in front of the tailor's shop. The front blinds were still drawn, and State Street was nearly deserted at that early hour. Beatrix pulled the key from the ignition, got out, looked both ways down the silent street. There were cars parked a few blocks away at the synagogue, and

Smith's hardware store just down the road had delivery trucks blocking one lane of traffic in front of the shop.

She closed the door of the sports car as quietly as possible, and Thomas did the same. Then the two walked noiselessly down the alley and toward the door leading into Rosenbaum's house.

Beatrix put an ear to the door. Voices? The radio? There were no windows facing the alley, she couldn't see in, nor could whoever was in the house see out. She didn't dare sneak through the open side gate to peer into the living room windows. Instead, as Thomas stood behind her, she pounded a fist on the door.

Thomas thought back to another time when Beatrix faced eminent danger and he let her go first into it. This was different because then he imagined she was an evil spirit. *She faced down a crazed, bent copper while I stood in back of her and quaked with fright,* he thought back to that day in New Orleans six years before. He'd wondered then, and again as he watched Beatrix bang on a potential killer's door, how far his life had come when they collided and became a couple. Years before they met, he'd assumed the future would be in a laboratory in Cambridge and his only excitement would be going to Saturday matinees where he'd watch Hollywood's version of gangsters clashing with the good guys.

Now he was one of those good people, or hoped he was, yet still let his wife take the lead. Unlike the memory, now he was but a foot away and ready to disable the maniac inside with his practiced black belt in Ju Jitsu if that monster even lifted a finger against Beatrix. It unexpectedly hit him, like a knife in the heart. He loved Beatrix more than he loved life and would do anything in his power to protect her. He felt his stance move into a position that would incapacitate the lunatic behind the door.

"Who's there?" Then in Yiddish came a shout, and Beatrix and Thomas knew that it had to be Otto Rosenbaum's voice. "Who is it?" the voice demanded again.

"Mr. Rosenbaum? Otto? Open the door. It's Beatrix Patterson. My husband Thomas is with me. We need to talk. Do not be afraid."

Thomas heard the last sentence, and it took his thoughts straight back to a similar encounter in New Orleans where Beatrix rushed in to a crazed potential killer's home. "Turn the handle, Bea," he whispered. "Or shall I?"

Beatrix didn't need Thomas to tell her what to do, as by the time he encouraged her, she had stepped into the tailor's small home. "I'm coming in, Otto."

There was silence and Beatrix and Thomas walked through the small, tidy galley kitchen and followed the hall to the living room. Otto Rosenbaum was sitting on the compact sofa and staring toward the garden.

"Otto, may Thomas and I sit down? We need to talk with you." Beatrix didn't wait for a response. She took the chair across from the sofa and Thomas followed suit. "We've come to talk with you about Gerta. We know what has happened. Do you want to tell me?"

Thomas was stunned. We do? She knows what happened to Gerta? That he's killed her and hid her body in a cupboard or secret room? Or chopped her into inch squares and buried her beneath the lemon tree in the garden?

Beatrix's voice was level. No need to threaten him. She spoke slowly so as not to agitate him further. "Why have you imprisoned your sister?"

"That's *schmegegge*," he shouted now, and red blotches peppered his wrinkled face.

"No, it's not baloney or nonsense," she replied, translating the Yiddish term he'd used. "I know about the secret hideaway only accessed through the wardrobe in the spare bedroom. Thomas is going to stay here with you while I look into it. Is it locked, Otto? Give me the key."

Otto didn't move. Long seconds lapsed and he dug into the pocket of his moth-eaten brown sweater and handed her a large, old-fashioned brass key.

Thomas did not want his wife to go to the secreted hideout where a potential Nazi war criminal was holed up. However, he had to stay and monitor Otto. His voice cracked as he yelled, "Holler if you need me, Bea."

She nodded and walked to the smaller bedroom. The wardrobe was the same as she remembered, empty of clothing. She looked for a lock in the back of the closet and found it near the top, hidden in the shadows. Would Gerta be dead, crumpled and damaged on the floor? Would she be livid, crazed with anger because her brother kept her a prisoner? Beatrix worked the lock, and it gave way. She pulled the concealed back off the cabinet open.

The room was dark except for a tiny high window, and it took Beatrix's eyes a moment to adjust. "Gerta?"

"Who wants to know?" came the hoarse whisper.

As Beatrix's eyes grew accustomed to the limited light, she saw the room contained but a cot, a bucket for personal needs, a table and a straight-backed wood chair on which Gerta Rosenbaum was sitting.

"I'm Beatrix Patterson. Lillian, your friend from the hospital, asked me to find you. Can you walk?" Beatrix couldn't tell if the woman was hurt or chained to the table as Gerta didn't move.

"I don't want to go with you. I don't want to face a firing squad or the gas chamber like Otto told me would happen," she looked the size of a child. Even in the stuffy, hot room, she quivered and tightened her arms around her body.

"Gerta? Please listen. Otto will not hurt you anymore, and I will protect you." Beatrix crossed the room and Gerta's eyes widened.

Gerta waved a handful of papers. "Otto wants this. He said if I made this list then he would let me go."

Beatrix saw the tablet, sheets and sheets of paper with a listing of what seemed to be entries of some kind, just one word and then the next. "What is it?"

There was silence. "It's my death certificate, I have written out everything I've done." She gathered the tablet and the loose papers on the table and clutched them more tightly to her chest.

"I saw it. I saw what you've written and the list, Gerta." Beatrix realized it was a full confession and then a list of names. Just names. "Come on, please. Let's get you out of here. You don't have to be with Otto if you don't want to. We'll sit in the bedroom." She reached out a hand, and as if in slow motion, Gerta took it. It felt like a toddler's hand in hers. Beatrix helped the woman through the secret door and into the spare bedroom. She closed the bedroom door and flicked the lock. "Otto is in the other room with my husband guarding him. You are safe."

Gerta seemed even more fragile in the sunlight of the bedroom. She was dressed in ill-fitting men's trousers with a rope for a belt, socks but no shoes, and an oversized tan woolen sweater. She quaked, and Beatrix longed to open the window as Gerta stank of her confinement. Her face was the sallow gray of someone who'd given up hope, her hair greasy and lank, sticking to her cheeks and forehead. "I do not deserve to be out of that prison," she said, her Polish accent heavy, tears welled and cascaded down her soiled cheeks.

They sat on the end of the twin bed. Beatrix waited. She held Gerta's hand. She'd studied the effects of released captives and prisoners of war, but a textbook never told the whole story. The words couldn't truly describe the pain, fear, panic, and horror in Gerta's micro facial expressions that Beatrix knew at once.

"You cannot understand. Otto is right. I am a butcher. I slaughtered and executed. I need to be punished." She seemed to shrink with each word.

Beatrix knew it would be dangerous to try to comfort the woman in that mental state. "Can you tell me who you killed, Gerta?" Beatrix tried to take the papers the older woman clenched with filthy fingers. Gerta flinched and pulled away.

She'd been locked in there for days, Beatrix realized. *She couldn't have killed or frightened the rabbi to death*, Beatrix thought and waited, listening to Gerta's ragged breathing.

Minutes ticked by. Beatrix was patient and thought of Thomas in the other room, guarding the tailor, but from what? His sister? His guilt?

Gerta's brown eyes were ringed with tears as she ultimately looked at Beatrix. "My friend Lillian sent you?"

"Lillian and I are also friends. She's worried about you. We need to talk for a few minutes, and then would you like to go to Lillian's house? Will you feel safe there from your brother?"

"You need to keep him from me. At first, I asked him to lock me inside there as punishment for what I did and so I couldn't kill again. He agreed, yet then he turned around and became my jailor."

Beatrix understood. She gently pried a few pieces of the weathered paper from the woman. They was a list of names, some just an initial, not in any order but with the letter M or F after each one. It was a list of the babies Gerta had delivered while she was in the death camp and a notation of the gender of the child, before she put the infant to death.

There had been scores of tragedies and dangerous moments in Beatrix life, but as she sat next to Gerta, she thought, *This is the saddest.* The list of mother's names went on and on, and each was written in ink and on the letterhead of the Third Reich.

Gerta whispered the facts of the entire horrible chronicle. "I had to keep this, they forced me to, but after the war and when I was taken to the displaced person's camp, then transported to New York with a hundred other damaged men and women, I brought it with me, too. I kept this so I would never forget, never fail to recall my crimes." Her body and face were brittle.

"Gerta? What would have happened to you if you refused the Nazi doctors' orders?" Beatrix knew the answer.

"They would have killed me." A sob started softly and then wracked her bony body. "What would that have mattered? I am dead. My heart is dead. Otto is right. I am a murderer and deserve to be locked away."

"That's not true. It's not up to you, to me, or to Otto to make that decision. You'll need to talk with people from our American government. That won't be today, nor will it be easy. Right now, I'll drive you to Lillian's house. She'll look after you while I make some phone calls and try to figure out the best way to help you." Beatrix put an arm around Gerta's back and helped her to stand, as it seemed her muscles weakened with her confession.

They walked to the living room and there was Thomas with a knee in Otto's back. The older man was face down on the carpet. "He was trying to stop you from talking to Gerta. I asked politely, Bea." Thomas got up and pulled Otto to his feet, still grasping the man's shoulder.

"Evil, evil woman. Baby killer," Otto growled. But didn't try to wiggle free from the white-knuckled grip Thomas had on his shoulder.

"Otto," Beatrix said. "I'm taking your sister to a safe place. I know she asked you to punish her. That was wrong and I will not let this continue. If she's committed a crime in the eyes of the American government, then she'll be tried or sent back to Germany. Right now, we need to protect her from herself. You shouldn't have put her in that prison."

Gerta stopped and turned to Beatrix? "Put *me* in the room?"

"He locked you inside," she replied, and Beatrix then knew. Gerta's mental ability was creating delusional thinking, most likely caused by the ghastly experiences she suffered during the war.

Gerta stamped a foot and screamed, "I begged him to put me in there, and then after much thinking I knew that Otto was right. I am a murderer and I do not deserve to see the sun or feel the wind or touch the rain again. I helped the mothers deliver their babies and then grabbed the infants away, wrapped them in a rough, ugly blanket and took them outside to a—." Her knees wobbled and Beatrix guided her to a chair or she would have collapsed to the floor. "I am evil. I am an assassin. I deserve to be tortured and destroyed. I need to be locked away so I do not hurt more babies."

CHAPTER 20

GERTA'S EYES CIRCLED THE ROOM, Beatrix and Thomas and her brother, pushing his fists into his eyes, doubled in grief. "I tried to get help, I tried to find a way to ease my sister's pain," he gulped the words. "No one would listen, not even those who are supposed to care, whose job it is to care. *Gott im Himmel,* I didn't know what to do."

"Otto," Beatrix spoke his name and that seemed to break the spell of anguish. "I care and I'll try to find the right help for your sister and for you. Right now, I'm going to take her to a friend's home so she can get some food and perhaps even rest. I promise."

Beatrix grabbed a green and blue granny-square crocheted blanket from the back of the sofa and cautiously put it around Gerta's quaking shoulders. She took the woman's limp arms and whispering comfort, she started to help her up. Thomas moved quickly and lifted the woman in his arms, carrying her wilted body, which seemed as light as a child's. He followed Beatrix out the back door of the tailor's home and toward State Street.

He waited as Beatrix opened the passenger door to the sports car. "I'll take her to Lillian's house. She'll watch Gerta and give her some broth. It looks like Gerta's been starving herself."

"What if Lillian's not home, Bea? What will you do? Take her to the police? The hospital? Not our house?"

"I spoke with Lillian when you were getting ready. She's off work at the hospital until one. Would you mind staying with

Otto for a short time? Then I'll be back. I don't know what he'd do to himself if he were left alone. There's more to this, Thomas, but I don't have time to explain."

She got behind the wheel of the car and headed to Lillian's cottage near the beach. "Your friend Lillian will help you, Gerta. Close your eyes and please stay calm." The last thing Beatrix would need was to have the fragile, distraught woman decide to jump out of the convertible as it moved through the city streets. Beatrix drove with one hand on the wheel and the other on Gerta's arm, *just in case,* she thought, *in case she tries to end her misery.*

Beatrix headed south on State Street and turned right on Highway 101, then began to weave into a neighborhood with small homes, bicycles dotting lawns, and planter boxes overflowing with fuchsias, Shasta daisies, and scarlet geraniums. Within sight was a towering trestle of the Southern Pacific Railroad that stretched across Gaviota Creek, just a trickle in September. Lillian Benson's home was not in the most stylish neighborhood of the city; however, there was love sprinkled into every yard and garden. Beatrix caught sight of a woman pushing a carriage down the street, and she returned the wave. In another yard, a teenage boy was hanging towels on the line and smiled back at Beatrix. He yelled, "Swell car, lady."

Beatrix wondered if her best friend's husband, Sam, looked out from his engineer job and saw his mother-in-law's trim cottage as he maneuvered the behemoth freight trains between San Luis Obispo and Santa Barbara's train terminal. She could, in her mind, see always-smiling Sam, wave out the window to children along his route and even toward the house where Jo grew up.

In the distance she saw another mother pushing an extra-wide baby stroller with what looked like two tucked inside as a little girl ran ahead. As she got closer, she realized it was Jo with three of the four Conrad children in tow.

She pulled to the curb and thought, *How am I going to get Gerta's limp body out of the bucket seats of the car?* She stood for a moment and wished Thomas was there. In the next second help arrived.

Lillian called out from the house, "Honey, you just leave that lady right there. You'll hurt yourself and then I'll have two patients to worry about." Lillian was large, not fat; tall, sturdy, and a bit imposing if one didn't know her. Smart people never crossed Lillian Benson.

Beatrix smiled and exhaled, "I cannot thank you enough, Lillian. Tell me what to do."

"Let me put her feet on the driveway and then you wrap an arm around her back and I'll do the lifting. Wait, Gerta, blink your eyes if you can hear me?"

Gerta reacted.

"Okay, that's good. Now, Gerta, this little lady Beatrix and I are going to walk you into my house. You have to help us by moving your feet. Can you do that, honey child?"

Gerta barely nodded, but Lillian and Beatrix saw it as they hoisted the frail woman to her feet.

"Now move those feet. That's a sweetheart," Lillian ordered. "Just one step up, good for you. Now pick up your left foot." They entered the living room as Lillian said, "You're going to sit right there on the recliner and catch your breath." Lillian wasn't even breathing hard has she picked up Gerta and placed her squarely in the well-worn easy chair.

"Mama, I'll put the kettle on and heat the chicken broth," Jo called out, having followed them inside. "Mitzi, could you kindly grab a child?" she asked the young journalist who seemed to have found companionship with Jo and Lillian and appeared from the kitchen. The two rounded up the kids.

Seeing Mitzie again made Beatrix smile. Whatever drew her out of New Orleans, she'd found a home here, Beatrix thought.

As Mitzie and Jo talked, Beatrix was intensely focused on the young woman's accent. Not Southern, but French with a hint of guttural Germanic language; Beatrix thought it absolutely charming. Mitzie was trim, short, and when she smiled, she glowed. Beatrix had seen more, as there was sadness in those luscious brown eyes.

Mitzie picked up a baby and placed him lovingly against her chest, kissing the coffee-colored cheek.

"Let's go, Mitzie. You don't know Mama that well yet, but when the woman's in her nursing mode, we all better follow her orders or else," Jo said with a shake of her head. She gave Beatrix a quick hug and from the stroller grabbed the other twin under her right arm. "Now, Gracie, honey," she bent to talk with the toddler, "You stay with Aunt Beatrix. Good girl, take ahold of her sweater. Do not let go." Then she whispered to Beatrix, "The girl's running wild today, she'd be in Ventura galloping along the beach if I didn't keep watch on her. Please do not let go of that hand or I'll never see her again, I fear."

Beatrix took Gracie to the rear of the house where there was a sturdy swing set and a sandbox sprinkled with trucks and toys. Gracie said something in the unintelligible language of a two-year-old, let go of Beatrix's hand, and threw her body into the sand, screaming with delight.

Beatrix was mystified even watching the child. Then she felt the presence of the newcomer.

"Mademoiselle?" It was Mitzie. "May I come to visit you later today? There's a story I'm working on for the newspaper and you lived in Santa Barbara as a child, Josephine has told me."

"That would be lovely. Do you have the address?" If Beatrix were still pretending to be psychic, as she did during her stay in New Orleans, she would have known, as she did then, that Mitzie had a bigger issue on her mind. "Say about four? I'll be home by then."

"*Merci,*" and she scooted toward the back door of Lillian's trim bungalow. "Come now, Miss Gracie, your mama wants you to have a snack. Would you like a banana?"

Gracie screamed, "Banana," and dashed toward the house, leaving both women laughing.

Mitzie followed the little girl inside, as Beatrix thought, *Whatever she has to tell me really has nothing to do with the newspaper where she works. It's personal,* Beatrix thought. She said goodbye to the women, patted Gerta's hand although the Polish lady didn't look up, and headed back to the tailor shop on State Street.

Thomas sat across from Otto in the cottage's living room. He would have made tea or offered the stunned man some water, but he was fearful if he took his eyes off the tailor, the man would make a mad dash out of the cottage. Who knows what he'd do or to whom in his crazed and grief-stricken state of mind.

There had been times in Thomas's past when he'd had to comfort those in desperate situations, during the Blitzkrieg and shelling of London when people were maimed or stunned from the massive bombing. He never dwelled on that, but at that second, he thought of the victims and bodies he'd once pulled from the rubble. One horrible night he had told Beatrix the details of the constant shelling. An apartment had collapsed, and he could hear screams as the bombs continued. He pulled a family to safety, but learned later that another family hadn't been that fortunate. Those memories were forever engraved in Thomas's mind.

He'd also had to confront stupidity in his past as well, knowing that a mistake he'd made as a first-year student, attending a party when a chum was sick with mumps, would forever haunt him. He'd told Beatrix about the folly and its repercussions when they became intimate.

A few weeks before, he had to reassure his colleague at the university, Dr. Walter Schmitt, that the administration would find funding to continue his work in cancer studies, the scourge that killed Walt's mother. *I'm blasted bad at it,* he told himself. *Words fail me*. He sat with his hands clasped in his lap, looking out to the postage-stamp-sized garden as the sun dappled through the sycamore trees.

Every so often, Otto would moan and beat his head against the back of the sofa. His breathing was regular, and as Thomas started to get up, his eyes flipped wide. "Don't leave me, sir," Otto's voice squeaked.

"Of course not. I will stay with you for a while," he replied, willing the hands to move more quickly as he checked his watch. It had been an hour since Beatrix drove away, one of the longest hours in his life.

Then there was a twist of the doorknob and Thomas steeled his muscles, expecting an attack. He nearly heard frightening music like Hollywood would add if an ax murderer were about to strike.

Instead came the shout: "Thomas? It's me, Beatrix. Where are you?"

"Living room." Thomas wanted to grab his wife and throw his arms around her. Instead, he worked to regain his composure and smiled, trying not to show his fear about being alone with a possible Nazi sympathizer and torturer who may have chained his sister in a secret room. "Everything okay?"

"Yes, brilliant actually. Lillian and Jo, and their new friend Mitzi, are certainly spooning chicken soup or tea into Gerta. With Lillian's nursing training, the older lady will get stronger by tomorrow." Then she took Thomas's hand and walked into the garden, in full midday sun. "A quiet word? I'll talk with Gerta tomorrow. Mitzie, who writes for the newspaper, asked to visit this afternoon. There's sadness in that girl. I don't know her agenda, but perhaps I can help. I have a feeling it has to do with the war. Her accent is French, but I caught a hint of German."

"I thought she was from New Orleans," Thomas said leaning in to breathe the perfume of a lemon flower. He felt his muscles relax now that his wife was by his side, away from the fixated man still in the living room and the frail woman who insisted that Thomas's university colleague, Walter Schmitt, had a father who was a war criminal and disciple of Hitler and the Third Reich.

"Lived in New Orleans, I was told." In a quiet voice she said, "Has Otto said anything valuable and insightful about why he kept his sister locked in a room? Anything at all?"

"He kept try to tell me how he wanted to support her through her trauma, wanted to find qualified medical and spiritual assistance for the horrendous pain."

"I know she is as troubled as he is."

"He insisted that whatever help there was had been inadequate. As if he were in a trance, Bea, he went on and on about being a simple tailor. Such frustration. He sobbed about how others should have been here for him after all he's done for the community and for the men and women he'd previously depended on for advice and even thought were his friends. I could see his resentment and yes, anger."

"He's angry?" That wasn't an emotion she considered. Guilt? Fear? Anxiety? Apprehension for the future? Embarrassment? Maybe even joy, if it was psychotic. But not anger.

"Yes, but not violent, although honestly? The man makes me uncomfortable. Do you think he was, here in the city, a Nazi sympathizer?"

"No, I doubt that, but I know he has other secrets, Thomas."

"Like what? He's kidnapped other women, thrown them into rooms the size of a closet, starved them as he possibly was doing with his own sister?"

"No, the fear is personal. He is in a relationship."

Thomas blinked and tucked his chin down. "My mother always said that there's a lid for every pot, someone for every person out there."

"He's found his mate, and he's a man, Thomas. That's Otto's big secret, I believe. Homosexuals are not welcome in many places in our society, and I hope that will change in the future."

"Oh." Thomas nodded. "That is a surprise. Wait, you said he was a good tailor? I would hate not to have some new suits made."

"This is why I love you."

"Because I care more about my wardrobe then who is romancing whom?"

"Actually, I wouldn't have put it quite like that, darling, but yes. You're willing to accept people for who they are. You don't try to change them. You've never tried to change me, even when you thought I might be an evil spirited *wu.*"

"I have experienced being an outcast, even living in England. Asians were second-class citizens and doubly so during the war. Still are in many places."

"Women, you see, traditionally have not been afforded respect, recognition or fair wages. Females, since the beginning of time, have been openly and subtly discriminated against."

He smiled, "What? Are you telling me the world is not fair? Blimey, Bea. I'm shocked. You'd tell me quick should I ever do that, right?"

"That's why I keep a rolling pin handy."

"Now, I'm gutted. I thought you were going to eventually make a steak and kidney pie, like my mother always bought from the local butcher. You didn't buy a rolling pin for that?"

"You'll have to make that meaty dinner yourself if you actually want one." She nudged his shoulder with hers as they headed back into the cottage. "Would you mind seeing if you can make some tea or coffee for us, Thomas? And I'll try find out what his plan was for Gerta. Or if, in fact, there's something else, which is what I believe."

Beatrix sat next to Otto. "Mr. Rosembaum? Could you please open your eyes. We need to talk."

He did as he was asked. "Gerta? Is she in jail or a mental hospital?"

"She's being cared for by friends."

Thomas returned with three mugs of tea, no sugar, no cream, but at least he thought it would be strong as he'd added two tea bags into each steaming cup of hot water. He placed them on the coffee table and returned to his chair and guarding position.

"Otto, tell me how long Gerta has been in seclusion."

The frail German looked at his hand and tore at his thumb nail. "She came suddenly here in the summer. I didn't know what to do. I was afraid. My life," he gestured and spread his arms, "My life with my lover was quiet. We had secrets. I built the room, accessible through the closet, to keep our clothing and the photos of us. People," he huffed, "People I know would not understand. They would convict us of perversion."

"But then your sister arrived." Beatrix handed the tailor a mug and watched as he sipped the tea.

"Yes, she, oh, must I say?"

"No, Otto. I understand. She walked into your home, through to your bedroom when you and your lover were together. She did not understand."

He placed the mug on the table and withdrew a handkerchief from his pocket, blew his nose.

"She yelled at you, insulted you, called you a deviant or worse. What happened then?"

"My friend, I cannot tell you his name, my friend and I tried to tell her about our love. She changed in an instant. Got quiet. Told me she'd been in love once, a forbidden love."

"Is that because she'd been abused by a man of power and became pregnant when she was barely older than a child? You told me about the pregnancy. Did you know what happened to the baby?"

"Yes, because..." He stopped talking.

"The doctor who delivered Gerta's baby now lives here in Santa Barbara. She'd somehow tracked him down because she had access to medical records when she was in the Stutthof death camp."

He nodded, and Thomas leaned forward. If he hadn't been convinced that his brilliant wife was not clairvoyant, then he would have been guaranteed of it. "The person who adopted Gerta's child is here?" he asked.

"Otto? How did you find out that Dr. Noah Schmitt was Gerta's benefactor and adopted her baby?"

"What? Beatrix, you mean my friend at the university, Walter Schmitt, is Gerta's child?"

She turned to Thomas. "Yes, you see, it was obvious. Walter's father lived as a country doctor in the same region as Gerta was sent to have the baby. Noah Schmitt and his wife, as I've seen from photos on their home's mantel, were both very fair skinned and with blond hair so light it shined in the sunny photograph. Yet, Walter has chocolate-brown curly hair as does his child. Dark hair is a dominant gene."

"She demanded that, unless I helped her kidnap Walter's little boy so she could raise the child as her own and escape to Mexico with him, she would tell the newspaper about my relationship. I could not let that happen."

"You hid her after she realized, from working as a cleaner in the hospital, that Dr. Schmitt was the same physician that delivered her then-unwanted baby."

"She had to leave her job, so I could pretend to take the little boy, Hans. What if the doctor remembered her? Then, when she showed me the list of the women whose babies she murdered during the war, I locked her inside."

"What did you plan to do with her, Otto?"

"Oh, God in heaven, I do not know. It happened so fast. I'm a *schmuck* to even dream of stopping her. Gerta has always been a powerful force, getting what she wanted," he took a breath and continued, "getting what she wanted and not caring, a *fonferer,* a double talker, and I am a *dumkof.*"

"Otto, I know many languages but Yiddish is not one," Thomas injected.

"He means he was a stupid person, a dunce," she responded. Then turned back to Otto. "Then when you learned Gerta had smuggled the list out of the extermination camp, you knew you had the upper hand."

"*Ja,*" Otto said reverting between English, Yiddish and German, as many immigrants did for years. "When she tried to call me an *alter noyef,* a dirty old man, I had to stop it. What she threatened was *schmegegge."*

Beatrix interpreted for Thomas, "He means nonsense."

"You see, madam, I had proof that she killed babies. She wouldn't let me have the lists, of course, but I am not dumb. One day, when she was bathing, I went into the room, and with the Brownie camera I had, I took pictures of the lists. I didn't have the film developed but I keep it as collateral. I told her I'd give it to the American government if she dared reveal my secret."

"She backed down?" Beatrix asked.

"Yes, and that's when she stopped going to work and I locked her in the room, except for a few times a day to care for personal needs." He looked away, but his jaw was set. "I am not cruel. I brought food, Miss Patterson. She didn't eat. I tried treats like ice cream and even *dobostorta*, the fancy Hungarian chocolate cake she once loved. No, she would not eat."

"Did she tell you why?"

He pushed a tear off his face and then used the back of his hand to wipe his nose, smearing both on his trousers. "*Ja, ja.* She wanted to die and then I would be blamed. She is not a nice person. I wanted her dead for hurting me, but I would never have harmed her. Nevertheless, how could I let her out? She would have destroyed everything I hold dear."

"What did you do then, Otto?" Thomas asked, marvelous again how cruel humans could be to another.

"After Sabbat service one Friday, I confided about Gerta's being unstable and needing help. I talked to some people at temple, but I didn't reveal that she was here, in my house, locked way for *my* safety and secret."

"Was Rabbi Krause one of those you opened your heart to?" Beatrix already sensed that he had, and was shunned by Krause.

"Krause was not a man of God. He'd learned, probably from Gerta, about my partner. She likes to blab things to increase her reputation as someone who has all the answers. Rather than assisting me to find comfort for my sister, he got on his high horse and condemned me. I knew more about him than he thought. I had written a letter to the Chief Rabbi in New York City. I never trusted Krause, but *oy*, who could I turn to to assist Gerta?"

"Beatrix," Thomas cocked his head, "What in the world is a chief rabbi, like a pope or president?"

"Sort of." Beatrix explained the guidelines of the religion.

Then Thomas turned his attention to Otto. "What happened after you wrote to the Chief Rabbi in New York City?"

"Miss Patterson probably knows," he mumbled.

"Yes, Thomas. Otto found out as I did when inquiring about Krause in New Orleans that Hiram Krause had never served as a rabbi and from what records they'd obtained after the war from Europe, there was no mention of his, or his father's, serving in Gdańsk, Poland."

"Krause was a phony rabbi? How does someone even do that?" Thomas asked.

"He was obviously well versed with the texts and rules of Judaism and the reformed practices, as well as a good salesman," she said.

"I talked to Mitzie, that new reporter from the newspaper, when she interviewed me about my tailor shop for a feature story she was writing," Otto said. "I decided the day before Krause passed on that I was going to call that lady and tell her what a fake he was. When she came to the shop, I mentioned she might want to talk with Krause, too. By not helping me, he could have killed my sister, my only relative."

Beatrix looked at her hands and then said, "Did Mitzie seem interested in talking with Krause?"

"*Ja,* she made some notes, quickly writing in a language I couldn't read in a note pad."

"Was the language like scribbles? Could it have been shorthand, used by secretaries when taking dictation?"

"Maybe, I wouldn't know," Otto replied.

“Otto, Thomas and I need to visit with Sarah Krause now. Will you be okay here by yourself? Should I go into Smith’s Hardware store and ask your partner to stay with you?”

“Wait? Gerta, the blabber mouth, spreading my secrets. I should have killed her when I had the chance.”

CHAPTER 21

THOMAS AND BEATRIX STOOD on the sidewalk in front of the tailor's shop. State Street was busy, traffic slowing in front of Woolworth's Five and Dime store and the art museum on the corner of Anapamu Street.

He slid his hand in to Beatrix's and said, "I'm confused. Otto says he didn't keep Gerta as a prisoner, and then said he did. She wanted to be locked up, and then she is angry that he did it. What is it?"

"They've both suffered beyond imagination and their cognitive health is fragile. Now it seems they both seem incapable of telling the truth, but rather tell their own truths. Gerta accepted her imprisonment as punishment, yet may even have been tricking Otto into letting her go in order to smear his reputation all over town. And kidnapping Walt and Elsa's little boy was retaliation for the loss of Walter as an infant. He kept her locked up. She wanted that, but also wanted to harm her brother. They seem to hate each other; their hurt is so deep, perhaps they really don't know what they were doing. Who was in jail and who was the jailor?"

"How did you know about Otto's partner, Beatrix? He never said who his 'friend' was."

"The first time I walked into the shop, a large man, in a Smith's Hardware t-shirt was exiting. Then when I investigated, snooped that is, into his wardrobe, I saw two of the same, extra-large shirts hanging in Otto's closet. It didn't take much to see the connection."

"Would have for me, Bea. Now if we're talking shoes, I can spot spiffy ones a mile away."

"Come along, my darling husband. We need to talk with Sarah Krause and tell her what happened in New Orleans."

Thomas stopped and Beatrix did as well. "Would you mind terribly if I bowed out of meeting with Mrs. Krause and reporting about your trip to New Orleans? I have an errand to run and a meeting at three and the dean gets cheesed off if I'm late."

"You go." She held out the keys to the MGB. "No?"

Thomas laughed. "I'm a danger to all of humanity in that sporty car, Bea. I'll trot right home and drive the station wagon back to the campus. You're meeting the reporter, Misty, at what time?"

"Mitzie. She's coming to the house around four."

"Brilliant. I'll see you around five, and," he grabbed Beatrix's hand. "Be careful. I know few things frighten you, but if someone had the power to scare Krause, maybe they could do that to others."

"Nonsense, Thomas, but you are a dear to be concerned. Now off you go."

Beatrix walked toward the synagogue, tried the doors, but everything was locked.

She then walked to the Krause home, stopping at the flower shop across from city hall. Sarah answered the door at once. Today she was dressed in black, even black stockings. A tall woman, her chiseled cheekbones seemed even more gaunt, but her hair was smoothly tucked into a bun at the back of her neck. "Miss Patterson. Good of you to come for a visit."

She handed the white carnations to the widow. "Again, Sarah, I am so sorry for the passing of your husband and coming unannounced."

"Yes, yes, thank you. Please, come in. Shall we sit in the garden? Friends have delivered far too many sweets. Shall I bring out cookies and lemonade?"

"Lemonade would be lovely, thank you. May I help?" Beatrix followed Sarah into the kitchen, counters laden with covered dishes, plates of sweets, baskets of fruit. "Your husband will be missed."

"Ah, perhaps. Would it be alright to speak without reservation, Miss Patterson?" She poured two glasses of lemonade and added ice from the icebox.

Beatrix reached out for the glass. "I hope you will and, again, please call me Beatrix."

"Hiram was a complicated man. He had strong opinions and a strict code of conduct that applied to others. He never hit me, but his terrible words cut me like a saber."

They walked to a shady patio table and chairs. "I have heard that, Sarah."

"Much like in the days of old, Hiram had favorites in our following."

"I imagine that happens in all faiths," Beatrix said. "Now about the details of what I found out in New Orleans."

"Please," Sarah closed her eyes, as if steeling herself for the news.

Beatrix told her about how frightened Hiram had been, how he could not be consoled by the rabbi there and the gun. "He must have met someone in the city he'd known from the old country or perhaps Stutthof, but that's a guess on my part. I wonder if he could have seen a prison guard or some Nazi official he'd bribed to escape? Whatever, he was terrified."

"That makes sense. We left so suddenly and when I tried to ask Hiram about our hasty exit, he told me to mind my own business. Our marriage, Beatrix, was comfortable and convenient for both of us, but love never was part of it. I knew when I married him that he could only ever care for his wife who had died in childbirth."

"Were you devoted to each other?"

"No." The word came out flat.

"Why stay?"

"Well, you see, there's more to it."

"You never shared a marriage bed."

"Exactly." Sarah looked into the distance, twisted the frosty glass, and said, "Hiram never wanted me for anything except appearances. He believed that an unmarried rabbi wouldn't be trusted, couldn't be. He married me, I have come to realize, as an example of how to keep his not-so-little wifey under his thumb. I cooked, cleaned, and spoke when spoken to. I was a maid. I got the things I wanted, Beatrix, material things, security, and a ranking in the community. There was no affection."

"What will you do now, Sarah? Stay in Santa Barbara?"

"I had been planning, even before Hiram's passing, to leave. I have friends in Hollywood, one you met when you visited during the shiva. I am strong and not that old and cannot imagine a life as the poor rabbi's widow. I'll go after the funeral, and that'll be whenever the coroner releases his body. Your visit today is timely."

"The house and all you have here?"

"It belongs to the congregation, not me. I have a few personal objects and my clothing. That's all. There is nothing here for me, and in Los Angeles I can reinvent myself, be whomever I want. I can do whatever I want. Hiram is dead and I'm alive. I'm quite wealthy, as I've told you."

"Thank you for trusting me, Sarah. Would be appropriate if I attended the funeral?"

"It would be a kindness. Hiram had friends and others in the city, and they'll be shocked knowing the truth about him. Word travels fast in our small religious group. I could not let it happen that he would go to the grave pretending to be holy, when he was not, and I'm relieved to tell you. The funeral will take place at the mortuary where his body lies."

"I understand."

"Thank you, for listening. I feel comfortable confiding in you."

"By the way, have you met a young woman, a journalist from the local paper, whose name is Mitzi? She interviewed Otto Rosenbaum about his business, and I thought she'd met your late husband."

"I do not know; however, I have his desk diary in the kitchen. Had to cancel some future appointments and tell others of his death and the truth. Shall we look?"

They returned to the kitchen and Sarah flipped back a few pages of the diary. "Ah, yes, here's an entry for 'reporter' just ten days ago. No name, but it could be the woman you're talking about." Sarah showed the book and pointed to the big X over the appointment time.

Later, walking back to State Street and getting into the car, Beatrix recounted the conversations and Sarah's desire to quickly leave a city where she and Hiram had been pillars of the community for five years. *Why such a speedy departure?* she wondered. *But why not? There's nothing to keep Sarah here.*

It was after two when Beatrix returned home. She'd changed her clothes and put on a sundress as the weather had warmed, warmer than summertime at the coast. She made iced tea for her guest and puttered in the garden, going over all that had transpired in the day.

When she got back in the kitchen with a bouquet of tiny, pink, and perfumy Cecile Brunner roses, the telephone was ringing, and Beatrix smiled when she heard Lillian's greeting.

"How's our patient?" Beatrix asked.

"Sleeping. She had a slice of toast and some broth. That child is troubled, honey. You're a psychologist. What should I do?"

"Just be there for her, Lillian. She wanted to kill herself. Did she tell you why?"

"The list, that horrible, horrible list of women in the camp who gave birth and how it was Gerta's task to murder the babies? Oh, Lordy, I'd be thinking of suicide, too, but she's not to blame."

"That's what to tell her. If she didn't do as she was ordered, the Nazi's would have killed her."

Lillian sighed deeply. "With the guilt that Gerta is weighted with, maybe that would have been an escape. The damage is done. Will you have to turn her over to the authorities? Will she be sent back to Germany for a war crimes trial?"

"I think right now she needs you to watch her and feed her and give her a hug. Is Mitzie living with you?"

"Sure enough is, and that girl is a gem. I have a night shift today and Mitzie is going to watch Gerta. I don't want to leave Gerta alone for nothing."

"Mitzie asked to meet with me this afternoon. Can you spare her?"

"My shift doesn't start until seven."

"I'm certain she'll be at your house by then. Thank you, Lillian, for being a friend."

"You know the Good Book tells us all about treating our neighbors, and I live by that."

Beatrix had just replaced the receiver on the big black Bakelite telephone when there was a knock at the front door.

"Mitzie, come in. I was just on the telephone with Lillian for an update about Gerta."

"Thanks for seeing me."

"Let's sit in the kitchen. We're renovating the house still and I do not have furniture in what will become my home office yet." She waved her hand around. "The place is a work in progress. I made ice tea, come this way."

They settled at the table that faced the back garden. The breeze ruffled the kitchen curtains and the sun dappled the patio, shaded by eucalyptus trees. Peace seemed to settle over Mitzie as she looked outdoors.

"Miss Lillian speaks highly of you and said you are a psychologist."

"Lillian is a compassionate, kindhearted, and knowledgeable woman, Mitzie. Are you in need of someone to confide in or help with problems?"

"Yes, madam. I have money." She pulled her red leather clutch purse closer to her and started to open it. "I can pay you."

"Why don't you tell me the reason you're here and then if I can help with therapy, we can talk about payment."

Mitzie fiddled with the glass, looked at her fingers dotted with condensation. She started to wipe them on the skirt of her navy cotton dress with a crisp white collar and big white buttons down the front.

Odd choice, with those long sleeves for a warm day like this, Beatrix thought, and offered Mitzie a napkin.

"I do not know where to start," she whispered.

"Mitzie, why not tell me when you first met Hiram Krause in Poland."

Her eyes blinked widely. "You know, madam? I've not mentioned it to a soul. How could you realize that? Please do not tell anyone. I beg you."

"You can rely on the oath I've taken as a psychologist. Whatever you tell me, Mitzie, I will not divulge unless there could be harm to you or another."

Mitzie heaved a sigh and began as she pulled back the sleeve of her dress to reveal tattooed numbers on her left forearm. "Hiram and my brother were friends, they met at an anti-Nazi rally in Poland. They were arrested that day. Then the Nazis came for me. I'd been living in Warsaw trying to get help from the American and French governments to release another brother. We were dual citizens. Our mother was French from North Africa and Papa was from Alabama. He was an artist, Papa, studying at the École des Beaux-Arts, the most prestigious school on the continent. They met there. He and my mama were both outspoken and for the people. The family moved to Poland when I was a child and my parents disappeared one day coming home from an anti-Nazi rally. We never heard what happened, but this was not that unusual."

Beatrix sipped her tea. "You went into hiding with your brother?"

"Just my older brother. The other," she gulped back a sob. "The other was killed by bullies on the street for being bi-racial."

"What a tragedy."

"*Oui,* and my oldest brother was like a moth to a light. He could not stay away from the protests. I was ten when the soldiers came to get me, as I'd been living with friends when my brother was arrested. We were all in a ghetto, starving at times. I cannot even put in plain words the dire living conditions, and we all knew that it would only get worse. Oh, the squalor."

"Mitzie, did you find your brother in Stutthof when you were imprisoned?"

"Yes, but, I do not know if I can tell you. It is too horrible."

"May I?" Beatrix waited for the young journalist to nod her head.

"Both you, your brother, and others who were racially diverse were forcefully sterilized. Is that right? Beginning in 1933, the Nazi regime harassed and persecuted people of color because the Nazis viewed Black people as ethnically inferior. Random people were arrested for no reason, imprisoned, forcibly sterilized, and murdered by the Nazis. You were in that group."

"It was performed by a butcher, and I can never have children now." Her face froze in the memory. "My brother had resources I never knew, and I believe, although have no evidence, that he was blackmailing some of the prison guards at the workhouse in the camp. He and I would sneak minutes together, and he told me how we would be escaping, who he'd coerced. He always saved the one piece of bread the guards threw at him and gave it to me.

"The plan? He said he'd told Hiram, his confidant, about the escape, but this friend was too frightened to try to leave, believing, like an idiot, that because he wasn't a practicing Jew, that the Nazi would let him go."

Mitzie fingered the tattoo, got up and paced the kitchen.

Beatrix asked, "When the day of escape came, your brother was shot by the soldiers by someone's orders or for a supposed mistake he'd made. Or do you believe—"

"Yes, Doctor. I knew that Hiram, the cruel self-centered man who forced himself on women prisoners who had no voice, informed the guards about the plan to flee in trade for his freedom. Why he took me? I have no idea. Perhaps there was a *petite* measure of morality in him for turning in my brother to face certain death."

She continued, halting often to breathe or grip the tabletop as she talked. "As we left one night, it seemed, truly, that the guards turned their backs so they wouldn't see us. We walked for days, weeks, stealing food from gardens, surviving on raw cabbage and carrots. It was summer, thank goodness. We foraged, traveling by night, hiding in bushes in the day. Once I took laundry hanging on a line, as my only dress was filthy, in tatters. My biggest fear was that Hiram would kill me or turn me in for his freedom as he did with my precious brother."

"You made it to New York?"

"As far as I can calculate, it took us four months. By fall we were in Sweden. We took a tiny boat, in rough seas. Eventually we made it to England. There Hiram, who was telling everyone he was a rabbi, although that was the first I'd heard of his religious conviction, got us into safe quarters. There was nothing in England for me, so when there was an opportunity for Hiram to leave for Canada and then New York, the Jewish leaders in London forced Hiram to become my guardian. We traveled again. It was a dangerous journey by boat as the seas were patrolled by the Third Reich."

"In New York, Mitzie, did he desert you?"

"*Mais oui.* This time, however, I saw people of my skin color there. Papa had always told me stories of singing hymns in the Baptist church in Tuscaloosa. I didn't speak English well, but managed to ask strangers for a Baptist church. I found it."

"I've worship there. What a magnificent building, at the intersection of Broadway and West 79th Street in the Upper West Side of Manhattan, New York City."

"The kind people took me in without questions. I told the minister my story. I was sixteen and uneducated. They gave me a place to stay and people who fed and clothed me. When that family moved to New Orleans in 1943, I went with them, studied hard, and caught up on my education."

"Was it in New Orleans that you saw Hiram? Again?"

"*Merde,* oh, excuse me. *Oui,* the story gets more bizarre. I was working in the French quarter in a tourist shop. A woman came in to buy a voodoo doll. Because of my color, I'm sure, she asked me what to do if I wanted to hurt someone with it. I do not abide by such blasphemy, but the owner was there, and pushed me to tell a crazy story. I was selling junk, not anything close to magic. However, by then, I heard all the stories of voodoo. I just repeated what I'd been told, and the owner filled in far more graphic details."

"That person was Sarah Krause. Is that correct?"

"Yes, Doctor. She didn't know me and that's probably why she told me who her husband was and why she needed to hurt him as he'd been abusing her."

"Is that when Hiram walked into the shop?"

"No, thank God. Instead, I saw him, pacing on the sidewalk on Royal Street by the shop's door, waiting for his wife. When Sarah paid me for the doll, I left the shop and followed the couple back to their hotel. I waited. I was going to kill Hiram for how he'd murdered my brother and the suffering he'd put me through.

"It was evening when Hiram left the hotel. I walked up to him. He recognized me although I was better fed, clean, and had on clothes that were not in shreds. I pulled a gun that I'd taken from the shop where I worked, as the owner was afraid of street gangs and kept it beneath the cash register. I told him how I was going to pull the trigger unless we went to the police and he confessed."

"He didn't budge. He laughed in my face. I am a coward, Doctor. With all of me I wanted to kill him. I stood and watched him laugh at me. Then I shot the gun into the air, and he ran."

"You had connections in New Orleans because of your adopted family and, let me guess, found that Hiram and Sarah were on their way to Santa Barbara?"

"Yes, but it took years for me to get here. I finished my education to become a journalist. I came to the city knowing no one, but the church kindly put me in touch with our friends Lillian and her daughter Jo. I still had that gun, no, not here but in a safe place, and made an appointment to see the fake rabbi. My plan was to shoot him and watch him die."

"Did you get to the appointment?"

"Yes, and I failed for the second time. I saw him cower, to fall on his knees and beg me to let him live. He was so disgusting."

"Where does Sarah come into this? Because she does, right?"

"I was leaving Hiram's office as she walked by me. In her hand was that voodoo doll, a fake trinket from New Orleans and a large plate of sugary cookies."

"Do you believe she could have scared him to death with it?"

"*Non,* not at all."

Beatrix agreed, but Hiram had died.

"Mitzie, you have committed no crimes, and you are now free to start your life. Let's meet next week and talk more."

"You will not take me to the police?"

"Do you want to go to the police?"

"No, but I do want to talk again. May I come at the same time?"

"Yes, and now if you'll excuse me, I need to make some phone calls."

Beatrix showed the young journalist out and sat on shaded bench on the spacious front porch of their Victorian-style home. *Sarah killed Hiram. But how?*

For the second time that day, she changed clothing, now into jeans and a blue chambray work shirt, feeling the softness of the fabrics relaxing her. She tied her hair into a ponytail and walked to the front room, dialing the coroner's office. "Dr. Rayne, Beatrix Patterson here. A few questions, please?"

"Sure, Detective Rodriguez said to give you or tell you whatever you need. Shoot."

"Just confirming that Hiram Krause was a diabetic."

"Spot on. Gave himself insulin injections daily."

"You found needle marks?"

"I would have been suspicious if there weren't any. Have a moment to talk about another death? This one not as suspicious as there was a knife in the victim's back?"

'Oh, my goodness. Tell me everything."

Beatrix listened. While doing so, she reviewed the death of Krause. Cookies, diabetes, heroin, voodoo effigy, insulin, nursing assistant during the war, leaving right after the funeral.

"I need to act at once," Beatrix said out loud.

CHAPTER 22

Sarah killed Hiram. Beatrix was certain. Proving it was another matter.

Thomas walked through the kitchen door, smiled, and pulled Beatrix in for a kiss. "It's been a long day, Bea. Ah, but now I feel better," he sighed.

"I have so much to tell you, Thomas, but it's got to wait. I need to drive out to the Chumash reservation right now. Come with me?"

"I'm knackered, Bea. The dean thinks I need to go on a tour of universities, mingle with corporate bigwigs, and write a book. I misspell the word misspell. How in the blooming world could I write a book?" He opened the icebox and pulled out the pitcher of tea. "I need a stunt double, like in the movies. I could then be one thing and another for others to see." He took a tall tumbler from the cupboard, added some ice, and poured a great glass, drinking it in two swallows.

"I'll be back before dark," she said, grabbing the keys to the station wagon and her purse. "Scrounge for dinner. There's aways peanut butter and jelly."

"That pretty much sums up my ability in the kitchen," he said and stood at the open back door and watched her drive away. "Reservation? Well, tickey-boo and blinking hell, there was a killing on the reservation. How could I have forgotten the plea for help from Gordon. Blasted, it's the thought of writing that bloody book. Geeze, I've botched it again. Some bodyguard." He pulled the keys to the MGB off the hook, took a deep breath, and dashed out to follow Beatrix.

Thomas concentrated on driving on the right, obeying the speed limits, and never being so close to Beatrix in the old Woody that she'd see him. He was determined to guard her against whatever, but not give away his presence. His heart hammered in his chest for fear of what could happen.

At the reservation's compound, Beatrix pulled to the side of the road and parked under an oak tree that afforded a bit of shade, realizing when she turned off the engine that spot was most likely where the federal agent had been killed, the one supposedly determined to take children to the dreadful Indian boarding schools. It might have been a crime scene, but nothing at that moment looked dangerous or even suspect. She drove the rest of the way onto the property and parked next to Gordon's rusty truck.

The shaman walked out to greet her, and they stood next to the Woody.

Thomas slowed the car and parked behind the first house on the parcel. He peered around the corner. Beatrix's back was to him, and she was in deep conversation with Gordon Blackfoot. The shaman waved his arms and spoke with hostility, not noticing that Thomas had entered the reservation.

Thomas couldn't hear them, so he crept closer until he could catch what was being said, yet still not be noticed.

"Gordon, do you know who might have killed Leslie Mottle, the agent from the school?"

"No," he replied, but nodded yes.

"You don't know who it might have been?"

"No," again he said, but once more his head went up and down.

"Do I want to know what happened?"

"No." Again, his head agreed.

"Is Grandmother home today?"

"Grandmother has gone."

"Where? Gordon, where is she?"

"Beatrix. I do not have proof that Grandmother killed that hideous agent. I fear if she did, she would not have told me. You cannot expect me to turn my own flesh and blood, my grandparent, over to the police."

"Nevertheless, it was your knife in his back, right?"

"Like I told the police. I own many knives and Grandmother always gives me more each Christmas. I do not believe she could kill anyone, Beatrix, but then my grandmother would protect every person on the reservation, every child she'd ever known, with her life."

Beatrix's memory flashed back to the day, years before, when the grandmother had done just that for her. "Is she in the cave, Gordon? The one with the relics?"

"If so, she's decided to die. We need to find her before something happens." Gordon dashed toward the coastline and with Beatrix right behind, they followed the trail to the caves they'd visited before.

Crouching behind the scrubby sage bushes, Thomas was not even remotely bothered about getting his fancy loafers dusty. He continued to follow at a distance until Gordon and Beatrix disappeared into a small, dark opening in the rock formation. He watched as they crawled on their knees through it.

"Grandmother?" Beatrix called out and as the final syllable echoed in the cave, she heard the sounds of soft drumming.

"She's here," Gordon headed into the darkness, shining a flashlight to guide Beatrix. "She is connecting with our long-dead ancestors to join them."

Moments later they found her, tinier than Beatrix remembered, chanting and playing a small, decorative gourd that had been artistically turned into a ceremonial drum.

Beatrix knelt down next to the elderly woman. The lady's hands stilled on the stretched deer skin across the top of the drum.

"I am asking to go on to heaven, child. My time is short, and I want to be with my family, those who have gone before," she smiled and then reached up a hand to smooth a wayward lock of hair from Beatrix's face.

"Grandmother," Gordon sat next to her. "Please do not go. I need you. Our brothers and sisters still need you. Do not be alarmed. Everything is going to be okay. The police agreed that I couldn't have killed that federal agent, the man named Mottle."

Grandmother smiled. "I did not, either." She looked into Beatrix's eyes and nodded. "I wanted to. I was walking back from the little grocery store in Solvang and saw that monster's car parked by the oak tree near our front gates. I took a knife from my bandolier bag, slung over my shoulder, and crept close. I shouted at him, angry words. He didn't move. His body slumped to the side. I thought he was asleep. I plunged the knife into his back, but he was not breathing when I did it. I checked, but it wouldn't have mattered."

"You were planning to kill him?" Gordon asked.

She nodded. "Oh, yes. I could not let him steal our children again. I've never forgiven myself for what happened, Gordon, when you and others were young."

"Please, Grandmother," Gordon said, "Come out of the cave. It is not your time to die. We believe you, please come back home."

"Forgive me, Gordon," Grandmother whispered. "I have done the unthinkable."

"The man was dead before you attempted to kill him, right? You've done nothing wrong."

"I am guilty of more. I must tell you the truth," said the lady.

Beatrix took the drum from Grandmother's hands and helped her stand. "Gordon," Beatrix interrupted. "It was Grandmother who was stealing the artifacts and selling them."

The grandmother turned her head away in shame. "We needed money to fix our homes, feed the families, buy things. There is never enough of anything, the bare essentials, sometimes no milk for the children. I had no choice. I sold our heritage."

Much later that week, Beatrix sat on the front porch overlooking Anapamu Street and held a mug. The English breakfast tea had long chilled, and she still remained. All that had happened in the last few days replayed in her mind, never missing a detail or a fact.

Once Gordon, Grandmother, and Beatrix returned to the compound, Beatrix called Detective Rodriguez and found the woman still at the station and at her desk.

"Stella, so glad to catch you. I'm here on the reservation with Gordon Blackfoot and his grandmother."

"Coincidence, Beatrix. I was just re-reading the coroner's report. That Dr. Rayne is a genius. The previous one would have strung the older Chumash lady up and sent her to prison."

"Could you explain that?"

"Yeah, well you see, the autopsy showed that Mottle died of a heart attack about six hours before he was found, well before the Chumash grandmother stuck a knife in his back. Yeah, I know about that. There was a guy from Pacific Gas and Electric fixing something who called in the supposed murder. You see, Dr. Rayne reported that there was no bruising or bleeding around the knife. The guy was dead when the grandmother knifed him."

"Oh, Stella, thank you. No charges?"

"He was dead. She couldn't kill a guy who was dead, right?" Beatrix thanked the detective and cried along with Gordon and Grandmother as she relayed the coroner's report.

The evening was balmy later as she sat on the porch and smiled at the memory. *Grandmother knew he was dead, but still plunged the knife into him for all the merciless things he'd done and been part of.* That would be a remembrance the woman would have to wrestle with, but Beatrix trusted the tribal council would understand. Gordon certainly did.

Then Beatrix's mind moved on to the other events, grateful for being alone with her thoughts. John Brockman and Thomas had accompanied her to the mortuary for the funeral. Hiram's supposed friends and devotees had deserted him after discovering his lies, including the treatment of Sarah and Mitzie. The three were alone in the hall except for one man, who sat in back. At the end of the brief memorial speech, the man had walked up to Beatrix and shook Beatrix's hand. Then turned and quickly walked outside.

As soon as they left the mortuary, Thomas had asked about the tall, strong-looking stranger with an unusual white strip of hair contrasting to the rest that was jet black and neatly trimmed.

She had whispered. "That, Thomas, was a person known as Sarah."

"A bloke?" He kept shaking his head. "The fake rabbi was married to a fake woman. Well Bob's my uncle."

"I suspected it for a while. Sarah, or whatever he calls himself now, told me they'd been married as a convenience to both of them. They'd never been intimate."

"Well, I'll be gob smacked. Did whoever he or she or they are actually kill Hiram?"

"It's not conclusive, as far as the police and coroner are concerned. Hiram was diabetic and couldn't turn down sweets. His wife, let's just call the person Sarah, baked a lot. She could have easily administered an overdose of insulin, but there's no way that would turn up on the autopsy. He was also addicted to heroin, and my hunch is that he was getting from their friend who works in Hollywood's movie industry."

"From what you've told me, Hiram, was a despicable human being. If Sarah killed him with sugar or too much insulin, perhaps that's justice and justice has been served."

Beatrix remembered the details, and it still troubled her that Sarah and Mitzie and her brother had all suffered at the hands of the fake rabbi. How many others, she wondered? She looked out onto the street and put her mug on the floor just as the telephone rang.

Beatrix caught it on the fifth ring. It was Lillian. "Is everything all right? Gerta's okay, Lillian?"

"Oh, just fine. We've talked a lot and she'd going to turn herself in to the German government's office in Los Angeles. I want her to stay here for a week or so before that happens and get her strength back. She wants to meet and apologize to her brother. She's feeling remorseful about how she hurt Otto and his partner. She has willingly decided not to confront Dr. Schmitt or acknowledge Walter as her son. This is best."

"Thank you for that but it's late, must be after midnight. Is there a reason for the call?"

"It's that after seeing Thomas at the hospital the other day, I wondered if everything was okay. Just got off my shift now and had to call."

"Thomas? At the hospital?"

"Oh, Lordy, you don't know. Oh, Beatrix, honey, I didn't think it was a secret. I've got to go." The line went dead.

Beatrix dashed through the house, up the stairs to their bedroom. She sat on the edge of the bed. *If anything is wrong, I cannot imagine life without this irrational, funny, looney man,* she thought, touching him and rubbing his bare forearm.

"Couldn't sleep?" he asked.

"What secret are you keeping from me? Why were you at the hospital? Why were you talking with Lillian?" she demanded.

Thomas sat up and tried to hug Beatrix, but she pulled away. "I've been attempting to tell you but with all that's been going on, we didn't have a private moment." He flicked on the lamp on the table next to their bed.

"Are you ill? Does it have something to do with why we're not able to conceive?" She bit her lip.

"The afternoon I met with the dean, and you were meeting privately with a patient, Mitzie, I got a call at work from Lillian. Just breathe, Bea, everything is okay, better than okay, if you'll agree."

"Stop rambling, Thomas Ling, what are you saying?"

"The other day a young woman came into the hospital during one of Lillian's shifts. She was Asian. Lillian did know who from where, perhaps she was Japanese. The girl, she was not more than 16, held a bundle in her arms, wrapped in an army surplus blanket. She just handed it off to Lillian. Then the girl ran out."

"A baby?"

"Yes, hours old. Lillian immediately took the tiny girl to the maternity wing. The foundling was examined and yes, she'd been born that day. The police were called, but there was no way to trace the mother. Lillian called the foster care authorities and because the baby is small, she's still in the hospital. Want all the details?"

"Make it fast, mister."

He chuckled, 'Backing this truck up, I had, a few days ago, started proceedings for us to become foster parents, eventually if God is willing, to adopt any child that would come to us for care. Jo's husband Sam knew because we'd talked about it, but I never thought that there would a baby. Sam told Lillian, she told the foster agency."

"Are you saying that we're going to have a baby?" Beatrix put her head deeply into Thomas's bare chest, and he thought that's what she said.

"We still have to be approved, with background checks and interviews, and a social worker will visit us a lot and inspect the house and under our fingernails, probably."

"We're going to have a baby," she cried, and Thomas felt the hot tears on his skin.

He cried, too.

When he could talk again, he said, "I thought we might name her after our mothers, all of them. She could be called Jennie along with your birth mother's name, Adelina, and my mother's, which is Ya," he pushed tears off his face. "Are you okay with a baby of unknown race?"

"Thomas, when we have our natural children along with the precious chosen ones, they'll be bi- or even tri-racial. I am an American melting pot of Mulatto and Cajun, then there's the fact that my biological father is the now-president of France, and who knows what else might be found in me. And you are a non-US citizen and British, but Chinese. Any child will fit in our family."

"Cracking." He punched the air like a winning boxer. "It's decided. Let's call her Jennie Adelina Ya Patterson Ling!"

"She's tiny. That name is bigger than she is. How about we call her Jay?" Beatrix asked.

"Deal." They shook hands and then held each other tight as Thomas whispered in her ear. "Jay's going to be a good start on filling these bedrooms."

"One more question. When shall we tell her?"

Thomas pushed Beatrix away, just slightly and squinted his eyes, his forehead wrinkled. "That we chose her, fostered her, and adopted her as a baby?"

"No, silly, when should we tell her that her father has a chronic affection for corny dad jokes?"

ACKNOWLEDGMENTS

DO YOU ALWAYS READ THE ACKNOWLEDGMENTS in books? I do. They're often like getting the writer's insider scoop about how the book came about, who helped them, and what inspired the process, which takes far longer than Hollywood ever portrays in movies and on TV.

A huge round of applause for my publishers, Betty and Wally Turnbull, of Torchflame Books Publishing, along with their gifted book designers, editors, and key players. Special thanks to Meghan Bowker and Jori Hanna, who know every inch of the publishing world and gladly share it.

Thank you to Suzy Leopold, Suzy's Approved Book Tours, for not only connecting my mysteries with book influencers and book bloggers but supporting my goals and writing. Thanks to Sarah Jarganan who helped me with navigating the social media. These women are funny, smart and make working with them a joy.

I'm beyond grateful that my chosen family continues to step up and support the mysteries and my writing. They are so generous listening to my ideas, asking questions about my latest who-done-it, and going along with me as I discuss my characters, or as I prefer to call them my imaginary friends.

Special thanks to the Bestie of the Best, Ellen Hobart, who not only pays attention to plot lines and asks who and why did what to whom, she knows the details of the three mysteries in the Beatrix Patterson series and the backstories that never make it into print.

Dr. Devora Lockton, friend and neighbor, was my go-to source for all things Yiddish. She assisted and encouraged me, teased me, too. Dev was especially helpful as I was naming my characters in this book. Any mistakes made in language, locations or facts concerning Judaism and Holocaust are mine alone.

Big thank you to my creative friend and colleague Nico Garofolo, who encourages me to write better. We've spent countless afternoons with Coco Rose (my little Welsh terrier) on his lap, sharing writing fears, hopes, and dreams.

In no particular order, I must thank the following friends and chosen family for letting me share my visions, for their support of my dreams, and for not cringing when I expose the nutty inside workings of my writing brain: Danielle Light Corwin, Steve Huntley, Sue Huntley, Summer Allison Johnson, Susan Meibaum, Andy Meibaum, Chris Walton, Lisa Patterson Walton, Celeste Mergens, Melody Johnson, Macon Lane, and Lisa Puzo. Thank you, as well, to all of my online writing students. Teaching and mentoring constantly sharpens my skills and I'm so blessed to share how to live, learn and make it as a writer.

As with the two previous books, fifty percent of my royalties will go directly to Days for Girls International, www.daysforgirls.org. Please partner with me and buy a book to help women and girls throughout the world live a healthier life as we strive to close the great chasm of gender inequality.

ABOUT THE AUTHOR

Eva Shaw is one of the country's premier ghostwriters and the author of more than 100 award-winning books including *Doubts of the Heart, Games of the Heart, Ghostwriting: The Complete Guide, Writeriffic II: Creativity Training for Writers, Write Your Book in 20 Minutes, Garden Therapy: Nature's Health Plan,* and *What to Do When a Loved One Dies.* She teaches university-level writing courses available online at 4000 colleges and universities.

A breast cancer survivor, Eva is an active volunteer with causes affecting women and children and with her church. She loves to travel, read, shop, garden, play the banjolele and paint, focusing on folk art and California landscapes.

When not at her desk, you can find Eva walking around the village of Carlsbad, California with Coco Rose, a rambunctious Welsh terrier.

Connect with Eva at:
evashaw.com
facebook.com/eva.shaw.96
instagram.com/shaw.eva

ALSO BY EVA SHAW

The Seer
Eva Shaw

The Finder
Eva Shaw

Printed in the USA
CPSIA information can be obtained
at www.ICGtesting.com
JSHW081613040823
45811JS00003B/153

9 781611 535723